I'LL BE Seeing YOU

THE MULLIGAN SISTERS
BOOK 1

I'LL BE *Seeing* YOU

MELODY CARLSON

WhiteFire
—Publishing—

This is a work of fiction. All characters and events portrayed in this novel are either fictitious or used fictitiously.

I'LL BE SEEING YOU

WhiteFire Publishing
13607 Bedford Rd NE
Cumberland, MD 21502

ISBN: 978-1-939023-65-0 (print)
           978-1-939023-66-7 (digital)

One

Sunday, December 7, 1941

Molly Mulligan loved Sundays. It was the only day the family grocery store was closed and everyone could sit down to breakfast together. As she set a platter of steaming hotcakes in the center of the big oak dining table, Molly glanced at the vacant seat next to her dad. The only one absent today was Peter. Her older brother had been gone for nearly two months now, but Molly missed him as much as the day he'd donned his sailor uniform and told his family good-bye.

She wondered if Peter missed them this morning. Or maybe he was glad to escape his four younger sisters. Especially since he used to complain about how the girls always hogged the bathroom or never stopped talking. Molly imagined her brother—enjoying his newfound freedom from females as much as the tropical Hawaiian Islands.

"Do you think Peter eats bananas and pineapples for breakfast?" Molly set a pitcher of warmed maple syrup next to her dad. "Or maybe papayas?"

Her dad chuckled as he stirred sugar into his coffee. "More'n likely your brother is dining on lumpy porridge and runny eggs this morning. From what I hear, ship food's not such a grand treat,

5

Molly Girl. Not when you're in the navy."

"I'd happily eat cold mush three times a day if I could be in Hawaii right now," Bridget declared. "It sounds so exotic and exciting." She was the oldest of the four girls and, in Molly's opinion, the smartest. Bridget sighed wistfully and turned her attention back to the nursing school textbook nestled in her lap.

"Peter's last postcard to me said it was eighty degrees on Thanksgiving Day," Molly reminded them. "Can you imagine—eighty degrees in November?"

"I don't know that I'd care for it myself." Her mother carried a platter of bacon from the kitchen. "I'd miss the seasons. Imagine having Christmas in hot summer weather. Very strange indeed."

"Sunshine sounds better than this Frisco fog." Margaret patted her auburn hair which, thanks to dozens of bobby pins and the pink hairnet she'd worn to bed last night, now resembled Maureen O'Hara's. "The damp air always ruins my hairdo."

"That's why you should wear a prayer scarf to Mass," their practical mother advised as she sat down.

Margaret held her head high. "You expect me to go out in public wearing a prayer scarf? Like an old woman? *Really*, Mam."

"A prayer scarf is more sensible than those silly hats you girls fancy. And a scarf can keep your hairdo smooth enough." Mam pushed a loose strand of her own graying hair back into her usual bun. "Not only that, a scarf is helpful when you've had no time to primp."

"But they're so unstylish," Colleen declared. Of the four sisters, Colleen was by far the most fashionable and, in Molly's opinion, resembled Lana Turner. Colleen winked at Margaret. "Especially when you just got that sweet little number with the adorable fascinator that I can't wait to borrow for—"

"All right now," Dad interrupted with forceful volume. "If none of you gabby girls minds too much, I'd like to eat my breakfast while it's still hot. And in peace, if it's not too much to ask. Bridget, dear, I believe it's your turn to say grace."

In the same instant, all six of the Mulligans bowed their heads, and Bridget murmured a brief prayer. Finished with her hasty blessing, Bridget's head remained bowed, but her eyes were on the textbook in her lap.

"We forgot something!" As the others reached for food, Molly closed her eyes. "And God bless Peter and give him a good day!" Of course, everyone heartily echoed her "amen," re-crossing themselves.

"Thank you for that, Molly." Mam patted her hand.

"I pray for Peter every day," Molly quietly told her. "I taped the picture-postcards he's sent me on my dresser mirror as a reminder."

The boisterous family commenced to eating—and talking all at once. As usual, everyone seemed to have something important to say, and the volume increased with the enthusiasm. The Mulligans knew how to talk, that was for sure and for certain, but the topics sometimes came and went so quickly that Molly felt slightly lost. Even so, she loved her gregarious family—and she felt surprisingly grateful for each of them today. If Peter were here, it would be perfect.

"Bridget, put your book away," Dad scolded. "Tell us what you've been learning in nursing school of late."

As Molly chewed on a crispy strip of bacon, she listened to her sisters chattering like magpies. Sometimes amongst themselves, sometimes with the parents. Molly tried to inject a word here and there, just to remind them of her presence, but as usual the three older girls dominated the conversation. And why not—they were grown-ups with exciting lives to lead. Bridget was twenty-one and in her last year of nursing school. Margaret, just a year younger, managed the family grocery store. And Colleen, the social butterfly, was eighteen-and-a-half and looked like a film star.

Molly's three older sisters always had interesting topics to discuss and strong opinions to back them. Far more appealing than anything fifteen-year-old Molly could bring to the table. Her sisters could even make a boring subject sound colorful and fun.

"The missing produce delivery finally arrived just before closing last night," Margaret was telling their father. "The truck driver had a breakdown just outside of Sacramento and had to hire a different truck." Margaret was still getting used to her new role at the store. Peter had started training her as manager after he'd made up his mind to join the navy. But it was no secret that Margaret didn't particularly like her new responsibilities. She would rather be a wife than a storekeeper. But Dad's poor health had made it necessary for the rest of the family to take over the store.

"So the produce was in good shape when it arrived—not damaged?" Dad asked in a distressed tone. "And it got unloaded all right?" Molly knew how much it bothered Dad to be stuck at home and unable to help—especially when something went awry at the store. But his physician had insisted rest was necessary, and they were all trying to be supportive.

"Of course," Margaret assured him. "Young Jimmy stayed late to help me. It was almost ten by the time we finished. But it's all taken care of, Dad. No problems."

His smile looked relieved as he turned to his wife. "You see, Mary, I told you the store would be in good hands with Margaret at the helm."

"But for how long?" Colleen asked with a twinkle in her eye. "I'm guessing our Maggie may have other fish to fry. Or should I say, *wedding bells to ring?*"

"What have you heard?" Dad looked worried again.

"Just that someone's been talking to Brian's brother." Colleen nudged Bridget with her elbow, fluttering her thick dark eyelashes in a mockingly flirty way. "Haven't you, Bridgie?" Colleen might've been the closest to Molly's age, but she was so sophisticated and worldly that the gap between them felt bigger than three years.

"I happened to bump into Patrick Hammond on the street car on Friday," Bridget answered in a nonchalant tone, fixing her eyes back down on her textbook again.

"I'm sure it was a complete *coincidence*," Colleen teased.

Molly wanted to defend Bridget and point out that, of all the sisters, Bridget was the least likely to flirt with anyone. Even if it was Patrick Hammond. But, as usual, her tongue felt tied.

"I was simply on my way home from school," Bridget said crisply. "Like I keep telling you and everyone—Patrick and I are only *friends.* That is all. I wish you'd all quit making a mountain out of a molehill."

"Methinks thou protesteth too much." Colleen's fine brows arched.

"And methinks you'd like to go after Patrick yourself," Bridget shot back at her. "No one is stopping you, Colleen."

"I guess I could do worse." Colleen laughed lightly. "But rest assured, although Patrick is very handsome—in a Dick Powell sort of way—he is not my type."

"But what did Patrick say?" Molly asked Colleen. "Is Brian going to propose to Margaret soon?"

"Don't you think that's between Brian and Margaret?" Bridget said without looking up.

Margaret cleared her throat in a dramatic sort of way. "Well, I didn't mention it to anyone yet, but I did get a letter from Brian yesterday...."

"*And?*" Colleen nudged Bridget again, as if she felt they were harboring a secret about Margaret's future. "Any mention of marriage?"

"A proposal in a letter? *Really?*" Margaret looked aggravated as she wiped her mouth with her napkin. "Besides, it's none of your business, little sister." They all knew that Brian Hammond wouldn't graduate from college until June—and that Margaret was impatiently waiting for that day...and for a wedding. But it seemed like Margaret had been waiting for Brian for as long as Molly could remember.

"Then why is Colleen talking about wedding bells for you?" Molly looked from one sister to the next.

"I'm sure I don't know." Margaret rolled her eyes. "Brian simply wrote to remind me of his Christmas vacation schedule. I assume it's so we can spend some time together during the holidays."

"Christmastime is the perfect time to become engaged," Colleen said slyly.

"Speaking of Christmas vacation, mine's about to begin too." Bridget directed this to Margaret. "I'll be able to help out in the store after my final exams next Monday and Tuesday. So I'll be available to work by Wednesday." She tapped her book. "That's why I'm cramming."

Now Dad grilled Bridget about her upcoming registered nursing exam, and she reassured him that it was scheduled for January. Then Colleen told everyone about the USO dance she'd gone to last night. And finally Margaret described the Christmas display she wanted to put in the store's front window—and Molly begged to help. It wasn't long until breakfast was finished.

As usual after a family meal, the Mulligan sisters flocked into the kitchen to wash up. Today they worked to the Hit Parade on the radio and, thanks to the fast tempo, they all moved quickly, singing along with the likes of Bing Crosby, Billie Holiday and Duke Ellington. With Bridget washing, Margaret rinsing, Colleen drying, and Molly putting dishes away, they finished up in record time. With some extra minutes of pre-church primping, sharing the bathroom sink and mirror, the girls were finally clustered by the front door as they pulled on coats, hats, and gloves, filing at last out into the cool foggy morning.

"There goes my hair," Margaret declared as they traipsed down the stairs.

Mam and Dad had left a few minutes earlier, allowing themselves plenty of time to stroll slowly to Old Saint Mary's, since Dad was not supposed to overdo it. It wasn't long before the four girls caught up with their parents, trailing behind them so that they resembled a small, talkative parade. As they headed down Kearny Street, Molly thought that the only thing missing today was Peter. And as her older sisters continued to chatter amongst themselves, leaving her out, Molly missed Peter more than ever.

More specifically, Molly missed all the times that Peter had accompanied her to Mass. He was the only sibling who never treated her like a baby, and she had loved walking with him to Old Saint Mary's. The two of them would remain behind the rest, talking uninterrupted. Peter would inquire about school and friends...and most recently he'd begun to ask her about boys. She giggled to remember the brotherly speech he'd given her right before joining the navy. He'd warned her that teenage boys were not to be trusted. "Not until they're at least eighteen," he'd said in a no-nonsense tone. "Maybe not until twenty."

Naturally, she had just laughed. And then she reminded him that he'd been a teenager once. Of course, he simply pointed out that was the reason he understood this issue so well. "And that is precisely why I want you to stay just as you are," he'd told her. "Pigtails and all."

She knew Peter loved her braids, and she'd already kept them longer than she'd planned. But it was simply because she loved her big brother and wanted to make him happy. Still, she wasn't a child anymore. "It will be rather hard to avoid *all* teenage boys," she told him. "I am in high school, after all."

"That's true. And I want you to remember that you're a very attractive girl," he said in a somber tone. "Those blonde curls and blue eyes could be your downfall, Molly."

"My downfall?"

"Some high school boys will only see you as a pretty face," he explained. "Some may go after you for their own amusement. And I won't be around to fight them off for you. And you know that Dad's not been so well lately. So you'll have to stand up to those boys yourself. Promise me you won't let them take advantage. You hear?"

She had agreed to be on guard about boys in general, assuring him that she'd store his advice in her heart. But now that Peter was gone and she had been privy to some of her older sisters' chatterbox conversations—particularly on their way to Mass—she'd come to realize their favorite topic, besides fashion and film stars, seemed to be young men. So much so that she wondered if Peter had ever warned them about the "dangers" of boys.

They were nearly at the church when Molly, who was dawdling in the rear of the Mulligan parade, heard her sisters letting out some high-pitched squeals, as if someone had just shared a good joke—

probably about a boy. But the shrieks were loud enough that their mother turned around to shake a finger at them.

"Girls—*girls!*" She pointed up at the statuesque brick building just ahead. "Show some respect, please!"

Her sisters' voices softened some as they got closer to the church. Old Saint Mary's wasn't a highly ornate building, but it was substantial and sturdy...and nearly a hundred years old. The big clock above the Madonna statue gave the structure a sense of dependability. Molly's older sisters grew much quieter as they passed through the tall Gothic arches and into the vestibule, politely exchanging greetings with friends, minding their manners around their elders, and going through the usual pre-Mass paces.

Before long the four sisters, still wearing coats, hats, and gloves, filed into their usual pew and took their seats. With their parents on the aisle, the Mulligan family could nearly fill the wooden pew. But without Peter, they could make room for Mr. and Mrs. Nelson on the other end. Because it was the first week of Advent, the church was fuller than usual today.

Molly glanced around with satisfaction. Taking in the familiar faces of friends and neighbors, she felt such stability and security being in Old Saint Mary's. Like a home of sorts. From the carved majestic arches and beautiful windows to the pipe organ's worshipful music...even the slightly musty smell of old wood surfaces and furniture polish...it all filled Molly with the sense that God was on his throne and all was well with the world. And this Sunday was no different. Very comforting.

Did that mean Molly listened attentively and reverently to the readings and recitations? Did she absorb all of Father McMurphey's words? Not as much as she should've...and not nearly as much as she pretended to. But at least she was beyond the age of doodling and note-passing and secretly sucking on lemon drops. Perhaps she was growing up after all. There was hope.

Just as Molly started to feel restless and tempted to check her watch—a habit her parents frowned upon in church—she observed something that made her sit up and take notice. Officer Stone, dressed in his dark police uniform, was striding up the center aisle—even though Father McMurphey was still speaking. With a sense of purpose and urgency, and a flushed face, Officer Stone waved his hands in the air to get the priest's attention. Father McMurphey stopped speaking in mid-sentence.

The whole congregation came to attention as Officer Stone rushed to the pulpit, looking so agitated that Molly wondered if he had come to arrest someone. Now that would be an exciting way to end Mass. She glanced around, wondering if they were in danger. Perhaps there was fire somewhere in the building. The interior of the church had burnt down once before. But Molly didn't smell smoke. Maybe an earthquake like the one in 1906 was eminent. Old Saint Mary's had survived that. But since nothing was trembling or shaking, she knew that wasn't it.

With wide eyes, Molly watched as Officer Stone held his emergency conference with Father McMurphey. The priest's face grew paler and more serious as he listened, his furrowed brow mirroring Officer Stone's. Something was definitely wrong.

The church became so silent that Molly was surprised they couldn't hear the two men whispering for what seemed like several minutes. Waiting impatiently, Molly felt a twisting sensation deep in the pit of her stomach—something was really wrong. *What was it?*

Officer Stone stepped back, and Father McMurphey returned to the pulpit. Laying his palms flat on the podium, he sadly shook his head, gazing out over the congregation. "I have some very difficult news to share," he said solemnly. "News that will severely shake our community—some right here in our congregation. Indeed, this news will shake the entire country...the world at large." He paused to take a deep breath. "It is reported that Japanese forces launched a massive air strike this morning. They attacked the Hawaiian Islands by air. The devastation to our military there has been brutal."

Two

Father McMurphey paused while some in the congregation let out shocked gasps and exclamations, and then he continued. "To be more specific, the Japanese air forces have dropped bombs on Pearl Harbor Naval Base—the very place where many of our US Navy ships are stationed. I am sorry to report that the casualties are severe. That is all I know for now, but as we go home and tune into our radios for further news, I know we will begin to hear more."

Murmurings broke out amidst the congregation, but the Mulligans remained silent, exchanging worried looks with each other. Molly reached for her mother's hand and Bridget's, clasping them both tightly without speaking. *What did this mean for Peter?*

"Now let us all bow our heads," Father McMurphey declared. "Let each of us silently pray for the US servicemen serving in the Hawaiian Islands. And then I will close."

As she bowed her head, Molly could hear her pulse thumping in her ears. Staring down at her white pigskin gloves, recently handed down from Colleen, she was unable to form any sort of sensible prayer. All she could think was—*what about Peter?* Was her brother involved in this dreadful bombing situation? She knew he was in Hawaii, but did that mean he had been bombed too? Perhaps he was all right...perhaps he was not.

Suddenly, experiencing a desperate fear-driven sort of urgency, she began to silently pray. With fervent sincerity, she begged God to watch over her beloved brother—to keep him safe...to bring him home. *Be with Peter,* she repeated silently. *Be with Peter, God. Please, help him.*

"Holy Lord of Heaven," Father McMurphey's voice boomed out through the silent cathedral. "I beseech Thee for Thy protection and Thy safe deliverance for our young men stationed in Pearl Harbor in Honolulu, Hawaii. I ask Thy mercy and Thy comfort for the family members in this congregation and throughout the country. I pray for Thy guidance for President Roosevelt and for our nation's leaders. Thy kingdom come, Thy will be done...on earth as it is in heaven." And then, as usual, he led them in the final doxology, but the voices joining his were much quieter than usual...much more somber.

"And now," Father McMurphey continued, "Officer Stone informed me that all servicemen's leaves are cancelled. You are instructed to report for active duty immediately." He paused as several uniformed men rose to stand and, making the sign of the cross, said, "God go with you."

As the uniformed men exited, the shaken congregation began to cluster in small groups, murmuring amongst themselves. Likewise, the Mulligans huddled, all wearing the same worried expression and experiencing the same unspeakable fear, yet no one spoke.

"What about Peter?" Margaret finally voiced everyone's greatest concern.

Mam let out a choked sob.

"Peter is fine," their father firmly declared.

"How can you possibly know that?" Colleen challenged him.

"Because your brother is on a mighty big ship." Dad paused to cough, wiping his mouth with his ever present handkerchief. "The

USS *Arizona* is said to be the best battleship of its kind. In the last war, it proved itself to be the most powerful ship to ever sail the sea. She's big and stalwart and dependable, and those wee little Japanese bombs—they should not be able to harm a sturdy ship like that." He nodded with confidence, but Molly thought she spied a thin trace of fear in his clear blue eyes. And, as they all hurried out of the church, with her father moving faster than normal, she knew he was as worried as the rest of them. He just didn't want to show it.

Despite her high heels, Colleen began to run as soon as she was outside of Old Saint Mary's. She knew her family would follow at their own pace, but she wasn't willing to wait a moment longer than necessary to hear this frightening news for herself. Was it really as bad as Father McMurphey had made it seem? She felt both aggravated and scared as she hurried up the hill to their house. *Why had Peter been so doggone stubborn?* She remembered when she'd tried to talk him out of his silly idea to enlist in the navy. But would he listen? Of course not. And now this! *Oh, Peter!*

"Let me past!" Molly yelled as she caught up with Colleen just a block from the house. Surprised that Molly was that fast, Colleen stepped aside. But then not wanting to be outrun by her baby sister, Colleen started to run again. To her surprise, Molly beat her to the front door. Gasping for breath, they both burst into the house, racing for the big radio set in the front room.

"Let me," Colleen insisted. And scooting the ottoman next to the radio, she sat down and immediately tuned it to NBC.

Molly, still panting, knelt beside her on the braided rug. "Do you think Peter's—"

"Hush!" Colleen said sharply. "Listen."

"The attack was made on all naval and military activities on the principle island of Oahu—"

"Turn up the volume!" Margaret yelled as she and Bridget rushed into the front room, moving chairs closer to the radio.

"This will naturally mean war..." the radio announcer continued in an even, yet urgent tone. *"The president would ask Congress for a declaration of war—"*

"War?" Margaret cried out. "This means we're going to war?"

"*Quiet!*" Bridget told her. "I want to hear this."

"Japan has now cast the die," he continued. *"Japanese forces were already streaming into the gulf of Thailand. Yet, even this morning, Japanese diplomats were meeting with our Secretary of State in Washington. Within hours of this morning's air raid, President Roosevelt sent a message to Hirohito of Japan, appealing to the Mikado for restraint and peace. But—"*

"What is the news?" Dad demanded as he and their mother burst into the front room. His face was pale and he was puffing, out of breath.

"Sit down," Mam insisted, practically shoving him into his chair.

"It's like Father McMurphey said," Bridget said glumly.

"War," Margaret declared.

"Be quiet so we can hear!" Colleen turned the volume even louder.

"Bombs began falling around eight o'clock this morning Hawaiian time. There were reports of machine-gunning at Ford Island shortly before that. The air attack then moved to Hickam Field. At Pearl Harbor, three ships were attacked. The USS Oklahoma was set afire. No statement has been made by the navy."

"They didn't mention the USS *Arizona*?" Dad asked.

"Not yet." Colleen put a forefinger in front of her lips.

"Everyone was taken by surprise. Torpedoes did their damage on

the ships in Pearl Harbor—"

"Oh, no!" Mam cried out. "He said *ships*. How will we know if Peter was involved?"

Suddenly everyone was talking at once. Some grasping for hope, others predicting tragedy, but no one could hear the actual news broadcast anymore.

"*Hush!*" Colleen yelled above the voices. "We're missing it."

"*Hard to believe an air attack happened on these beautiful islands and that life has been lost. Planes came from the south, dropping incendiary bombs over the city. Fifty to one hundred planes with markings of the rising sun. The main targets were Hickam Field and the great naval base at Pearl Harbor."*

For the next hour, the whole family remained in the front room, hovering around the radio set—occasionally interrupting or emotionally erupting before someone would insist they get quiet again. The news was starting to sound repetitive enough that Colleen felt she could recite it herself. She knew by heart when and where the attack happened and many other details, including that Japanese forces had launched a similar air attack on the army and navy bases in the Philippines. It sounded as if Manila had been hit hard. Although no official announcement had been made yet, it seemed fairly certain that America was going to war.

Everyone jumped when the telephone jangled loudly, but it was Dad, seated next to the telephone table, who answered. "Hello?" he said gruffly. "Who is this?"

Everyone went silent, waiting to hear the identity of the caller.

"Colleen?" he said in an aggravated tone. "Yes, she *is* here. But she cannot speak to you right now. We must keep this line free, thank you very much." He hung up the receiver with a clang. "You heard me, ladies, we will not be using the telephone today. We will keep the line open...in case Peter tries to call us."

Although Mam was still clearly distressed, she stood up and announced she was going to see about dinner. "I have a ham that needs to go in the oven," she said quietly. "And potatoes to peel." Both Molly and Margaret stood as well, offering to help. And before long, the kitchen radio set was running as well. Colleen, who usually enjoyed the radio and was often accused of turning the volume too loud, wondered how much more of this she could take.

The radio station would start into its regularly scheduled program and then, after about ten minutes, interrupt it with another news flash similar to the last one. Standing up to pace back and forth across the front room, she grew curious as to which one of her friends had called for her. But she did not want to ask her dad. Especially when he looked so thoroughly disturbed.

She paused from pacing long enough to study him more closely. Although he was leaning back in his chair, he did not look the least bit relaxed. In fact, it almost seemed he was in pain. Colleen nudged Bridget with the toe of her pump, tipping her head toward their father with concern.

"Dad." Bridget went over to his chair. "You don't look too well."

"I'm fine," he growled.

Bridget returned to Colleen's side. "We need to get him to bed," she whispered. "Turn on your Irish charm."

"Come on, Dad." Colleen smiled as she took one of his hands in both of hers. "Nurse Bridget is right. You do need some rest. You've worn yourself out with church and all this excitement." She tugged gently. "Let's get you to bed for a while."

"But I need to hear the news," he protested as she helped him to his feet.

"We'll listen to it for you," Bridget promised, slipping her arm around his waist.

"And if anything really big comes up, we'll come and get you straightaway," Colleen assured him.

"I can even take notes if you like," Bridget offered as they walked him across the room. "I'm a good note taker."

"Anyway, it sounds as if the broadcaster is repeating the same information now." Flanking him on either side, the two sisters got him to the bedroom and sat him down on the bed, where Bridget took over. Colleen watched as her sister knelt to remove his shoes, gently lifting his feet onto the bed and helping him to lie back before she loosened and removed his tie. She really would make a good nurse someday.

"You have a good little rest now." Colleen bent down to kiss his cheek.

He muttered a complaint about being treated like a baby, but as Bridget adjusted his pillow and pulled up the coverlet, she mouthed *thank you* to Colleen. Knowing her dad was in good hands, Colleen went back to the front room, where the radio was still droning on about this morning's tragedy.

She paced back and forth a bit, but still feeling antsy, she grabbed up her coat and shot out to the front stoop, digging into her coat pocket for the enameled cigarette case she'd bought in China Town last week. She knew her family didn't approve of this recently acquired habit, but it really did calm her nerves. And she felt it made her look older, more sophisticated.

"Colleen!"

She looked up from lighting her cigarette in time to see Barbara Hanley hurrying up the sidewalk toward her, waving urgently. Barbara had been a class ahead of Colleen, but the two had been casual friends since junior high school.

"Have you heard anything from Peter?" Barbara asked breath-lessly as she clomped up the stoop steps. "Do you know if he's all right?" She peered at Colleen with a worried expression.

"No, it's probably too soon to hear anything yet." Colleen tried to sound calmer than she felt as she pulled in a long drag from the cigarette.

"It all sounds so horrible. I can hardly believe it."

"Well, I told Peter it was a mistake to join the navy." Colleen blew out a slow puff of blue smoke.

"Do you have another one of those?" Barbara asked.

Colleen removed the cigarette case from her coat pocket, waiting as Barbara took one. "I just wish he'd never gone to Hawaii," she said sadly. "I wish he'd never enlisted."

"I know." Barbara lit the cigarette. "Me too."

Colleen knew that Barbara really liked Peter. For that matter, who didn't? But at one time Barbara had fancied herself as Peter's girlfriend. Maybe she did again, now that he was overseas. But, although Peter had dated Barbara a couple of times, Colleen didn't think he was seriously interested. As she watched Barbara lighting another cigarette, Colleen knew her brother would not approve. He had been adamantly opposed to Colleen's smoking. Even when she'd teased him, insisting that most sailors smoked and that he'd probably come home a smoker too, he'd assured her that would never happen. But then, he'd assured her that he'd be safe too. Had he been able to keep that promise?

"I feel so frightened for Peter..." Barbara said quietly. "For all those servicemen. The more I listen to the radio, the worse it sounds."

Colleen nodded grimly. "Yeah, I had to get away from it."

"My brother was on leave. It was supposed to last until after the New Year. But he was downtown this morning, with his buddy—both of them in uniform, you know—and he was stopped by a policeman and told to report to his ship. He didn't even know why until he got home. But he got his stuff and took off right away. He's aboard his ship now. Sounds like they'll be leaving soon." She frowned. "It scares me."

"You mean John? He's enlisted?"

"Yeah. Not long after Peter."

"I didn't even know that." Colleen looked out to the street where other young people were starting to mill about. Not anyone she recognized, but she suspected that, like her, they were uneasy. They were probably trying to distract themselves by socializing with their peers. Snippets of excited conversation floated on the air, and suddenly they all looked at the sky, almost as if they expected to see something up there.

"Do you think the Japanese will bomb us too?" Barbara asked her.

"I don't know." Colleen frowned. "Isn't that an awful long way to fly? All the way from Japan?"

"John said they might have an aircraft carrier out there. That wouldn't be too far to fly. And my dad thinks we'll be hit next," Barbara told her. "He said that's why John got called back. The military is getting ready to protect us from an invasion."

"Really?" A shiver ran through her. And it wasn't from the chilly fog, either. "Do you honestly think it's possible that Japanese forces could invade US soil?"

Barbara nodded, taking another long pull of the cigarette.

"Look." Colleen pointed to where the group on the street had split up. Most of them appeared to be heading back toward town. But two of the guys turned the opposite direction, toward the waterfront. "What do you think they're doing?"

"Let's find out," Barbara said anxiously.

"Hold on." Colleen stuck her head in the house, announcing that she was going for a walk. Then, snuffing out her cigarette, she and Barbara hurried down the street, running to catch up with the young men. Even though they were strangers, Colleen wasn't concerned. For one thing, she was used to making new friends. But with the eminency of war, there seemed no reason to be overly cautious about anything.

"Where are you guys going in such a hurry?" Barbara asked, fluffing her brown curls in a slightly flirty way.

"Down to the waterfront," the shorter man said flippantly. "Wanna come along?"

"Why?" Colleen asked.

"To keep an eye on the bay," the taller one told her.

"Why?" Colleen asked again. She directed her question to the taller guy. It had not escaped her that he was quite attractive—in a tall, lanky, boyish Gary Cooper sort of way.

"Maybe we'll spot a Japanese submarine." His dark eyes twinkled.

"Or we might see bomber planes," his friend added with enthusiasm. "My dad said the Nips might try to knock out the Golden Gate Bridge."

"We may need to report what we see down there," the tall one said. "This means war. Everybody's got to do his part."

Colleen tried to absorb those three words. *This means war?* What did that really mean? Would the United States really be invaded by the Japanese? And what about the Germans? What was the world coming to anyway?

Three

Colleen knew that, amongst other things, she was considered the "flibbertigibbet" of the family. But it wasn't because she was stupid. At least she didn't think so. It was more because she didn't give heavy thoughts—like war and death—too much of her attention. Really, what was the point? It wasn't like you could do anything about it. But as she walked with Barbara and the two fellows, it was hard not to wonder what the future might hold.

But on the other hand, did she really want to know?

"How about some introductions," the short guy said suddenly. "If the world is about to come to an end, we may as well be friends. I'm Rick Olson, and this tall drink of water is Geoff Conrad."

Barbara took the initiative to introduce herself and Colleen, and just like that it seemed they were all fast friends. Maybe that was how it was with a war just starting. Colleen wasn't sure. But as they walked and talked, she felt sure of one thing. Geoff Conrad wasn't just tall, dark, and handsome—and he was—this guy had depth. And he was fun to talk to as well. Even if he hadn't resembled Gary Cooper—*which he did*—Geoff Conrad seemed interesting. And he seemed interested in her too.

By the time the bay came into view, Colleen felt surprised that nothing seemed the least bit amiss. There'd been very little automobile traffic on the streets. And no air traffic that they could see. But with all the ships still in port and nothing out in the bay, even the water appeared unusually calm. She felt almost disappointed to see that nothing much seemed to be going on. Had all that talk of the attack on Hawaii been imagined?

"Not much to see down here." Barbara shrugged as she looked around.

"The bay is quiet because all maritime operations were instructed to halt," Geoff explained to them. "I heard that on the radio just before I left the house. It sounded as if there's concern about Japanese submarines out there. Armed with torpedoes."

"Really?" Colleen peered out over the calm surface of the water, wondering what evils might possibly lurk beneath its peaceful surface.

"You never know." Rick pulled a set of binoculars out of his jacket and, adjusting the lenses, peered out over the bay.

"See any periscopes?" Geoff asked.

"I don't think so. But it's hard to see very far with this fog."

Colleen gazed at the other bystanders around the Embarcadero. "Everything feels so strange today," she said quietly. And it did feel strange to see these other people, just loitering about, talking quietly amongst themselves and staring at the calm bay with curiosity. "Like the world is standing still."

"It won't be standing still for long," Geoff said in a serious tone. "President Roosevelt will soon proclaim war. And then it will get very busy—very quickly."

She looked back out over the water, thinking about Peter on the other side of the ocean. Hoping he was all right. She wished just now she was better at praying—like her faithful little sister Molly. But as the black sheep of the family, church and spiritual things had never held much interest for Colleen. Although she could surely remember how to pray the rosary—if she thought about it hard enough. If she could even find her beads.

"Did you listen to all the broadcasts this morning?" Geoff asked as they strolled around the perimeters of the Embarcadero.

"I did," Barbara said proudly.

"I didn't." Colleen wasn't about to admit that she'd missed the first part because she'd been in church. They could assume she'd slept in if they wanted. "I didn't tune in for about an hour or more."

"Did you hear that NBC journalist? The guy broadcasting during the attack?" he asked eagerly. "Reporting live from Honolulu?"

"No." Colleen shook her head. "I missed that."

"You could hear the explosions and air raid sirens and all that chaos around him. And then—just like that—he was cut off. Right in the middle of a sentence. It was eerie."

"He's probably dead." Rick's tone sounded shockingly blasé. "Blown up by a Japanese bomb."

"Don't say that," Colleen sharply chided him.

"Yeah, Rick." Geoff scowled. "That's pretty heartless...considering."

"Well, that's probably what happened," Rick retorted. "I heard it too. I heard gunfire and bombs. If the reporter was killed, why not just say so? Lots of people were killed today."

"That's enough," Barbara said hotly. "Colleen's brother is over there."

"*Your* brother?" Geoff stared at Colleen.

Colleen didn't know what to say. The idea of Peter being over there...where a reporter might've been killed while reporting on the attack...well, it was too much.

"Yes," Barbara said more quietly. "And he's my friend too. His name is Peter Mulligan, and he's stationed in Hawaii."

"In Hono—lulu." Colleen practically choked on the word. "Pearl Harbor."

"Pearl Harbor? *Really?*" Geoff grimaced.

Colleen nodded grimly, trying to explain it without losing control. "He's in the navy. On the USS *Arizona.*"

Geoff exchanged glances with his friend. "Wow, Colleen. That's too bad. I'm really sorry."

"Me too." Rick was now contrite.

"Have you heard anything more?" Colleen suddenly asked Geoff. "I mean, any more news about the ships that were hit? Did you hear anything specific about the USS *Arizona?*"

"No. I did hear the *Oklahoma* mentioned. But that's the only specific one I heard about. Although it did sound as if the Pearl Harbor naval yards were hit pretty hard."

"One reporter described the battleships as sitting ducks," Rick said. "Torpedoed and—"

"*Shut up, Rick!*" Geoff slugged him in the forearm.

"Ouch." Rick rubbed his arm then frowned. "Sorry."

"Your brother is probably okay," Geoff told Colleen. She could tell he was trying to comfort her. "People are always quick to think the worst. Assuming that something is terribly wrong and then, if they wait long enough, it all turns out to be okay. Their worries were for nothing."

Colleen considered this. It sounded like the sort of thing she would normally tell others. She liked to think she was the one who kept her head when others didn't. But this business about Peter... well, she wasn't sure.

"Geoff's right." Barbara patted Colleen on the back. "I'm sure Peter's okay. Think about it. Nothing could happen to Peter Mulligan. I'm just certain of it."

"You're probably right." Colleen smiled bravely.

"It's never good to jump to conclusions," Rick reassured her.

As she reached for her cigarette case, Colleen wished she felt as confident as she was attempting to sound. And it was odd since, of the four Mulligan sisters, Colleen always acted like the confident one. But right now she felt like anything but.

"I'm going down there," Rick pointed toward the Embarcadero. "To get a closer look with my binoculars."

"Can I come too?" Barbara asked eagerly.

He grinned. "Sure."

Colleen and Geoff remained on the sidewalk, standing next to the streetlamp in silence, both of them looking out over the water. Colleen wasn't used to feeling this somber. But the idea that, across that ocean, there could be such suffering—and even death—was more chilling than the damp December fog.

"I haven't told anyone besides Rick, but I'm enlisting in the navy," Geoff quietly told her. "First thing tomorrow."

"Really?" She stared at him in disbelief. "*Why?* I mean, after hearing what happened today? Why would you want to go and enlist? Why not just wait for Uncle Sam to come calling for you? Why rush things?"

He frowned. "Because of what happened in Honolulu today. Because it's my duty as an American."

"You sound like Peter."

He nodded. "Thanks."

She scowled. "I didn't mean it as a compliment."

"I'm sure that I'd like your brother, Colleen."

She shrugged. "Yeah."

"And if I don't enlist, I'll just get drafted. Everyone is predicting the draft will be reinstalled soon. Maybe even this month. But if I enlist, I can pick where I go."

"But why the navy?" Colleen wondered if Geoff was simply declaring this because of hearing about Peter. That seemed a reckless way to plan one's military future.

"Because I want to be a pilot," he said firmly. "I've heard navy pilots get the best training. And that's what I want."

Despite her concerns about the war, Colleen couldn't help but feel impressed by this. She'd always admired movies about airplane pilots. "So you really want to be a flyer?"

He grinned, nodding eagerly. "Yep. I've been interested in flying since I was a kid." He was telling her about building airplane models when Rick and Barbara returned. "And I got to fly with a crop duster when I was twelve. I got totally hooked then."

"Yeah, old Geoff's been a flyboy since for as long as I can remember." Rick laughed. "Did he tell you about breaking his arm when he jumped off his grandpa's barn—using a homemade kite for wings?"

"I figured out that flying in an airplane is much safer. I took lessons during college. Just got my pilot's license last year. But I still need to log in hours."

"Yeah, the navy will probably snag him right up," Rick said a bit dismally. "Especially after today." He frowned. "I won't be so lucky."

"Why wouldn't the navy want you?" Barbara asked.

"I'm sure they'll take me as a sailor," Rick said without much enthusiasm. "But not as a pilot."

"Why?" she asked again.

"Not smart enough," Rick confessed. "I mean, in math. But Geoff's a math whiz. Plus he already can fly. The navy will be all over him."

"Well, not everyone can be a pilot," Barbara said consolingly. "Nothing wrong with being a sailor." She glanced at Colleen. "Peter was proud to be a sailor. Although he went in as an officer. That probably helps."

Colleen suddenly felt guilty for being away from her family for so long. Not that they'd miss her—not with all their focus on Peter and the radio broadcasters. But she realized that her place should be with them right now. "I need to go home," she told them, wrapping her collar more warmly around her neck.

"Don't you want to stay and see if someone blows up the bridge?" Rick asked.

"No thanks. My family's hurting right now. I need to be with them."

"How about if I walk you home," Geoff offered.

Colleen shrugged, trying to act indifferent even though she would enjoy his company.

"Well, I think I'll stick around the Embarcadero for a while...see if anything exciting happens." Barbara winked at Colleen.

"You can come with me if you want," Colleen told Geoff in a slightly cool tone. "But I need to go home right now."

Geoff easily kept pace with her as she hurried back toward town. As they walked, he told her more about himself, explaining about how he was an only child with a widowed mother, and how he grew up on his grandparents' farm north of San Francisco. He told her that he had three years of college under his belt and quite a few flying lessons. "I like the academics okay, but it's flying that really gets me going. There's nothing like being up there." As he described how it felt to sail through the clouds or do air acrobatics, his enthusiasm was contagious.

"I've never been up in a plane before, but I think it sounds exciting. I've even wondered about learning to fly myself. I'm kind of adventuresome too."

"You should learn," he said. "Although I doubt they let women fly in the navy."

"I'm sure you're right about that."

"Anyway, I think I've got a decent chance of getting into navy flight school. Probably even more so now that the war is about to start."

"Well, I'm sure you'll enjoy being a pilot, Geoff. Although flying can be dangerous." She gave him a sideways glance.

"Not if you're a good flyer." He chuckled. "Anyway, that's what they say in the movies. Right?"

"Right." She turned to look more closely at him. Besides being even better looking than Gary Cooper, Geoff seemed like a very decent guy. Much nicer than most of the ones she'd met at dances lately. And yet he wasn't stodgy either. He was a nice mix of fun and seriousness. He was, in fact, just the kind of guy that Peter would approve of. But it was too bad he was so insistent on enlisting. "So you really plan to join the navy *tomorrow?*" She slowed down her pace when her tall narrow house came into view.

"You bet I do." He nodded with a firm chin.

She stopped in front of her house, sticking out her hand. "Well, it's been nice knowing you, Geoff Conrad. I wish you the best of luck."

He just laughed, grasping her hand firmly in both of his hands. "You're not getting rid of me so easily, Colleen Mulligan. Even if the navy enlists me tomorrow, I doubt they'll ship me off on the same day."

"You never know."

"That's true." He nodded to the house behind her. "This where you live?"

"That's right. With my mother and my father and my three sisters and until a few months ago..." She sighed. "My big brother."

"Well, then. If it's okay with you, I'd like to call on you after I enlist tomorrow. Do you want to give me your phone number or should I just come over here and knock on your door?"

She giggled nervously and then rattled off her phone number. "I hope you can remember that."

"Count on it." Tipping his hat, he said good-bye and continued on his way.

But as Colleen went into the house, she knew it was time to put thoughts of Geoff Conrad and his navy pilot dreams out of her mind. Her family was hurting—and until they knew Peter was safe, it would be hard to focus on anyone or anything else.

Four

Margaret tried to hide her irritation as Colleen burst into the kitchen. Flush-faced and smelling of cigarette smoke, she seemed oblivious to the fact she'd missed Sunday dinner with her family. Instead of apologizing, she peeled off her coat and tossed it onto a kitchen chair. Then plucking a small piece of ham from the leftovers plate, she popped it into her mouth, acting as if she hadn't a care in the world.

Margaret exhaled loudly and, turning away from her selfish sister, gave the dirty dishes her full attention. She was determined not to start a row. Not today of all days. And really, why should she be surprised that her irresponsible younger sister would run off with her wild friends at a time like this? Wasn't that just typical Colleen?

"Where've you been?" Molly asked Colleen with innocent interest.

"Just down to the Embarcadero." Colleen grabbed a dishtowel. "I'll dry now."

"Did you see anything unusual down there?" Bridget asked curiously.

"Not really." Colleen described how quiet the bay had looked and how lots of bystanders were standing around, just blankly staring. "It was kind of strange to see."

"We just heard a new report." Bridget handed Colleen a freshly rinsed plate. "There was an army cargo vessel about seven hundred miles from San Francisco. They radioed a distress signal. They may've been torpedoed—"

"Really?" Colleen stopped drying. "By the Japanese?"

"No one knows yet." Bridget handed her a glass.

"We also heard that they're posting military guards on the Golden Gate Bridge," Molly informed her. "And we're not supposed to be driving around the city or running around or anything."

"Dad did not appreciate you being gone, Colleen." Margaret heard the stiffness in her voice but didn't care. "He wants us to all stay close to home until we know what's going on."

"How will we know what's going on if we can't even go outside?" Colleen challenged. "Are we supposed to just cower in fear, acting like a bunch of—"

"Do you not *understand?*" Margaret spun around to face her full on. "We are essentially at war here, Colleen! San Francisco is very likely the next target for a Japanese air attack. Have you not noticed the US naval ships right here in our docks?"

"Of course I have. I'm not daft, Margaret. But shouldn't that make us safer? After all, they're armed," Colleen argued.

"Just like our ships in Pearl Harbor were armed?" Margaret threw her dishrag into the soapy water, making it splash across her gingham apron. "Do you not understand that our battleships are a target for our enemies? If you're out there lollygagging by the waterfront, you are in very real danger, Colleen."

"But if the Japanese were about to attack us, don't you think we would've heard their engines—or seen their planes in the sky?" Colleen pointed out. "We were out there watching."

"Just like our armed forces were watching the sky in Honolulu this morning? A lot of good that did!" Margaret grabbed up the dishrag, wringing it angrily. "From what I've heard on the radio, they were caught completely unaware—and it was their job to keep watch." She shook a soapy finger at Colleen. "Isn't it bad enough we may have lost Peter? Do you think it would help matters if something happened to you too?" And now, despite her resolve to play the brave and responsible older sister, she started to cry.

For an uncomfortable moment, the four of them just stood in the kitchen without speaking, and Margaret, trying to regain some composure, turned away. Why had she gone off like that? What good did it do? Hopefully her parents hadn't heard her.

"I'm sorry." Colleen came over to wrap her arms around Margaret's shoulders from behind. "I wasn't thinking. You're right, it was wrong for me to leave like that. I'm sorry. I really am. But you know me, Maggie, I never think these things through. I'm just basically selfish."

Margaret grabbed the dishtowel from Colleen, using it to blot her tears, which flowed even more freely thanks to Colleen's apology. "I understand...and I appreciate that. But if we're going to be at war, we're all going to have to become less selfish. We're all going to have to grow up and take on more responsibilities."

"I know," Colleen mumbled. "I'll try. I promise."

Colleen hugged Margaret again, leaning her head onto her shoulder like she used to do when she was a little girl. "I really will try to grow up, Maggie. And I'll help more at the store too. Without complaining."

"That would be nice." Margaret sniffed.

"And Margaret is right," Bridget said in a no-nonsense tone. "We *do* need to grow up and take on more responsibilities. So I might as well tell my sisters what I've decided to do. You'll be the first ones to hear about this."

They all turned to stare at Bridget, waiting for her to explain this mysterious prelude to an announcement. But instead of continuing, she simply looked at them and then, running her fingers through her short, curly brown hair, she smiled sadly.

"Come on," Molly urged her. "What is it? What were you about to tell us?"

"Well, I've been considering this for a while now. But I made up my mind today." Bridget nodded firmly. "I've decided to enlist in the ANC."

"What's the ANC?" Colleen asked.

"The Army Nurse Corp," Bridget declared. "I'm going to be an army nurse. My friend Virginia Lewis is taking her board exam in January too. She's been researching the ANC and telling me all about it. It's a great way to get experience. And if we're at war, which seems inevitable, our armed forces will need a lot more nurses."

"Does that mean *you'll* go to war?" Molly asked with concern. "Like Peter?"

"I could be positioned close to the battlefield. But thanks to the Geneva Conventions, medical personnel should be fairly safe from enemy fire," Bridget explained. "So you shouldn't be worried." She smiled bravely. "And, please, do not mention this to Mam and Dad. They won't be ready to hear it yet."

Everyone was quiet for a long moment, the only voice to be heard that of the radio broadcaster, who continued to describe the current political climate in Indochina, including Japan's positioning to invade Thailand.

"It just makes me so mad!" Colleen exploded. "I want to throw something, or kick something, or just scream bloody murder and have a complete fit!"

"What on earth are you saying?" Molly asked Colleen. "Are you angry at Bridget for wanting to be an army nurse?"

"No, no, of course not. I'm angry at the stupid Japanese! And the stupid Germans! All of those blasted Axis who want to destroy the world as we know it." She snatched the dishtowel back from Margaret, snapping it in the air like a bullwhip as she paced back and forth in the kitchen. "Why are they doing this? Why do they want to ruin everything for everyone? We get into a new decade and people are finally starting to enjoy life. Money was starting to flow freely again. People were going back to their jobs. They could afford to shop at our store, which meant we could afford to buy new shoes. Pretty shoes." She wrinkled her nose as she glanced down at her new gray platform pumps. "And I am not completely shallow—I know the state of the world is more important than wearing nice shoes. But I still hate what Germany and Japan and the rest of the Axis are doing. The whole thing just stinks!"

"I agree wholeheartedly." Margaret turned back to the dishwater, which was losing its bubbles. "I hate that Peter is over there in that mess. I hate that Bridget is going to leave us to become an army nurse. I hate that we feel threatened right here in San Francisco. Frightened in our own home. I agree with you, Colleen, it *does* stink!"

After all four of them heartily agreed on that, they returned to washing and drying the dishes, listening to the radio, and occasionally commenting. Finally, the kitchen was cleaned with everything put away, and although Margaret regretted that she'd been unable to hold her tongue, she felt relieved to have spoken her mind. It seemed to have cleared the air. And she liked the sense of comradely comfort with her sisters. This wasn't easy on any of them.

For the rest of the afternoon, the Mulligans stayed near the radios. Either in the front room, where Dad returned to his post in his easy chair next to the telephone, or in the kitchen where Mam broke her own rule by baking on a Sunday. Naturally, no one even questioned her on this.

Later on, Mam broke another one of her rules by allowing her family to eat a very casual supper with their plates in their laps as they gathered around the radio set in the front room. But before they commenced to eating, she did make sure they said a blessing, as well as a prayer for Peter and everyone else in Hawaii.

The girls had just finished cleaning up after supper when the sound of the doorbell made everyone jump. Margaret moved to answer it, but her heart thumped hard as she reached for the doorknob. She knew it was ridiculous—and that they would probably not use the doorbell—but she suddenly imagined armed Japanese soldiers on the other side. Bracing herself, she cracked the door open and peeked outside.

"Patrick!" she exclaimed in relief, calling out to her family that it was only Patrick Hammond. "What're you doing out and about this time of night?"

"I've been thinking about Peter all day," he confessed as he came into the foyer. "At first I didn't want to bother you folks. But I finally couldn't take it anymore. I needed to see how everyone is doing. But it looked so dark in your house. I thought maybe you'd all gone to bed."

"We're attempting to black out our windows like they do in England." She pointed to where they'd draped a couple of quilts over the front bay window.

"I noticed quite a few dark houses on my way here," he said. "I guess a lot of folks are doing that."

"We need to do a better job at it." She hung his coat and hat on the hall tree. "But as you can see, we're keeping the lights low too."

She tipped her head toward the front room. "The family's in there. Well, not everyone. Not Peter."

He nodded solemnly. "I still can't believe the news. Can't believe it happened in Pearl Harbor."

She sighed deeply. "Yes, we're all still shocked."

"And you probably haven't heard anything about—I mean *from* Peter yet?"

She shook her head.

"I never told Peter this, but I really wanted to enlist with him," Patrick said solemnly. "But I decided to wait...."

"Lucky you." Margaret didn't mean to sound like that. Patrick was almost like a brother. And if she married Brian Hammond like she expected, Patrick would be a brother-in-law. Not to mention he'd been Peter's best friend since they were toddlers. She knew that Patrick was hurting the same as the Mulligans right now. "I know you don't *feel* lucky," she added. "But I'm glad for your sake that you weren't there today."

"Brian called from college a bit ago," Patrick quietly told her. "We talked for a while."

"Oh?" Margaret wished that Brian had called her instead. Of course, her dad might've hung up on him if he had. "How is he?" she asked eagerly. "I mean, I did get a letter from him yesterday. But for some reason that seems long ago...now."

"Brian was pretty shocked. Just like the rest of us." Patrick frowned as he ran his hand through his thick dark hair. "I probably shouldn't tell you this, Margaret, but you might as well know the truth. Sounds like he might enlist too."

"Brian? Enlist? Seriously?" A shockwave coursed through Margaret at Patrick's statement. For some reason she'd felt certain Brian would be exempt from this madness—that being a college student would be his excuse to remain on the home front. "What about his education?"

"He'll have to put it on hold...until the war ends."

"Oh." Margaret didn't like the sound of this. Not at all. What about getting married? Would that be on hold too? She had waited so long already...now she would have to wait even longer. Colleen was absolutely right—this war stank!

"I'm sorry. I probably shouldn't have said anything, Margaret. Don't tell him."

"No...I won't." An onslaught of conflicting emotions bombarded Margaret so quickly, she wasn't even sure how to respond. Disappointment, anger, sadness, outrage...but most pressing was a deep-down fear. She'd spent most of the day being afraid for Peter. But now her fears extended to Bridget and Brian and Patrick too. In fact, she felt fearful for all of them. It was as if the world had gone stark raving mad and there was nothing any of them could do to stop it. As if they were all helpless.

"Patrick!" Molly exclaimed when she emerged from the kitchen to see him standing in the foyer. "What're you doing here?"

"Just checking in on my other family." Patrick looked down at the plate of sugar cookies in her hands and smiled. "Looks like I came to the right place too!"

"Mam's baking up a storm." She held the plate out for him. "I think it keeps her mind off other things. Help yourself."

"Thanks." He took a cookie. "I haven't had much appetite today, but these are tempting." He tweaked one of Molly's braids. "I'm glad you haven't given up pigtails yet. Don't ever grow up, Molly."

She rolled her eyes and smiled. "I was simply imitating Sonja Henie in *Sun Valley Serenade.*"

He chuckled. "Well, I think you're much prettier than Miss Henie."

She tucked her arm into his, tugging him toward the front room. "Come say hello to Dad," she urged. "I know he'll want to see you."

"Yes." Margaret lowered her voice. "Our father could use some cheering up."

Margaret followed Patrick and Molly into the front room, watching as Patrick politely exchange greetings with everyone before sitting down next to Dad. The two men spoke briefly of Peter and the news about Pearl Harbor. Margaret appreciated how Patrick tried to put a positive spin on the whole thing, but eventually everyone in the room got quiet, with only the sound of the radio broadcast breaking the silence. When it was announced that First Lady Eleanor Roosevelt was about to speak, Colleen turned it up.

With lights down low and patchwork quilts hanging over the bay window, they all remained in the front room, circled around the radio set, listening to Mrs. Roosevelt's address with intense interest.

"I am speaking to you tonight at a very serious moment in our history. The Cabinet is convening, and the leaders in Congress are meeting with the president. The State Department and Army and Navy officials have been with the president all afternoon." She went on to tell them how the Japanese ambassador had been talking to the president at the very moment bombs were dropped on Hawaii, and she promised that Congress would have a full report and be ready for action by tomorrow morning.

"In the meantime, we the people are already prepared for action." She described how war had been hanging over their heads for some time. "That is all over now, and there is no more uncertainty. We know what we have to face, and we know that we are ready to face it."

As the first lady paused, the room grew so quiet that Margaret could hear the clock ticking above the radio static.

"I should like to say just a word to the women in the country tonight. I have a boy at sea on a destroyer; for all I know he may be on his way to the Pacific. Two of my children are in coast cities on the Pacific. Many of you all over the country have boys in the services who will now be called upon to go into action. You have friends and families in what has suddenly become a danger zone. You cannot escape anxiety. You cannot escape a clutch of fear at your heart, and I hope that certainty of what we have to meet will make you rise above these fears."

They all listened as she encouraged them to go about their daily business with more determination than ever—to do ordinary things and find ways to help in the community, to build morale and ensure security. "We are the free and unconquerable people of the United States of America," she boldly declared.

Finally, the first lady addressed the "young people of the nation."

"You are going to have a great opportunity. There will be high moments in which your strength and ability will be tested. I have faith in you. I feel as though I was standing upon a rock and that rock is my faith in my fellow citizens."

After another pause, Mrs. Roosevelt announced the programming would return to a previously recorded interview she'd done with a young soldier.

Although they all listened attentively, Margaret was distracted. All she could think of was Mrs. Roosevelt's words about being frightened. *You cannot escape fear...but you can rise above these fears.*

Margaret knew she needed to take those words to heart. Somehow she needed to rise above her numerous and prevalent fears. She just wasn't quite sure how.

Five

True to her word, Colleen got up early and went to work with Margaret the next morning. And, despite the early hour and her doubts that the store would get many customers today, she didn't complain. The traffic in the city was unusually light for Monday, but Colleen figured people would be staying close to home, close to their radios.

Margaret drove Peter's Buick slowly and cautiously—almost irritatingly so—but Colleen knew better than to question her. Peter had left his beloved car in Margaret's care—partly because she was taking over his job, but also because, out of his sisters, Margaret was the safest driver. Bridget, after attending to several bad automobile accidents in her practicum at the hospital, was no longer comfortable behind the wheel. And Colleen hated to admit it, but she was a bit reckless. And even though Peter had been teaching Molly how to drive, she couldn't get her license until she turned sixteen in March.

Margaret went down the alley and parked the Buick in back and then, looking cautiously around, she got out of the car. "Are you worried that the Japanese may have invaded the city during the night?" Colleen teased as Margaret unlocked the backdoor.

"I think everyone needs to be extra aware," Margaret said crisply as they went inside.

Colleen hurried ahead, turning on the lights in the backroom and even glancing around—just in case. Despite her teasing, she was glad she'd come with Margaret today. She could tell her older sister was uneasy, perhaps even frightened. Having companionship would be helpful. "I'm going to turn on the radio," she announced as she turned on the lights in the main part of the store.

"Yes. Good idea." Margaret set her handbag on the counter. "Even though it's a little early, I think I'll unlock the front door."

"Maybe we'll have some early birds." Colleen turned on the radio, tuning it to NBC, which was currently playing classical music. "You know, I like what Mrs. Roosevelt said last night," she called out to Margaret. "About how we need to go about our daily tasks and regular responsibilities."

"Yes." Margaret carried the morning paper up to the counter. They'd already gone over the headlines at home, but the news didn't seem to contain many more details than it had last night. "I think being busy is a good way to keep us from worrying too much."

"And maybe it sends a message to the enemy." Colleen removed her jacket, reaching for one of the store aprons. Normally she hated these boring pale green aprons that obliterated a perfectly stylish outfit, but she knew their father felt it was a respectful way to serve customers—plus, Margaret did too.

"What message?" Margaret put on her own apron, snugly tying it around her waist.

"That it's business as usual. They can't stop us." Colleen patted her blonde curls back into place.

"Shh!" Margaret turned the volume up on the radio. "The news is coming on."

They both huddled near the radio, listening as the broadcaster interrupted the regularly scheduled soap opera, giving updates on yesterday's tragedy. Because Britain had declared war against Japan, they played an excerpt from Churchill's speech.

"And the White House has announced the loss of one old battleship and a destroyer, which was blown up in Hawaii."

"An *old* battleship?" Colleen whispered. The USS *Arizona* was an "old" battleship from the previous war.

"Hush." Margaret frowned, turning the volume up louder. But that was all the broadcaster said about that, and suddenly the soap opera was playing again.

"Which old battleship?" Margaret asked Colleen, as if she should know the answer. "Why won't they tell us the name of the old battleship? It wasn't in the newspaper either."

"There are a lot of battleships in Pearl Harbor," Colleen told her. "Remember, Dad said so." To her relief the bell on the front door jingled. "Sounds like a shopper." She turned the radio's volume down.

The store was surprisingly busy that morning. Some customers were simply doing their regular Monday shopping. But others seemed fretful, filling their baskets to overflowing, as if they suspected going into war would mean a short supply of provisions. Colleen knew she had to say something when Mrs. Gardner insisted she needed a hundred pounds of flour. "Excuse me," she said. "I'll need to check with Margaret."

She hurried to the back where Margaret was cutting and wrapping meat. They'd moved the radio back here so that she could listen for any updates, but Colleen turned it down to quickly explain the situation with Mrs. Gardner. "Do you think we should limit purchases? In case we run out? It seems only fair—I mean, to our other customers."

Margaret bit her lip. "Maybe so."

"But how do we do it?"

"Let's just tell customers that they can only purchase what seems reasonable for, say, a week's time," Margaret suggested. "No more."

"Okay." Colleen frowned at the beef loin on the butcher block. Normally she hated to handle these bulky bloody pieces of raw meat, but right now it sounded easier than dealing with Mrs. Gardner. "Why don't I take over back here?" she offered.

"Really?" Margaret looked shocked.

"Yes." Colleen took the meat cleaver from her sister, nudging her toward the sink. "I've done it before. Dad showed me how."

"But you despise—"

"Not as much as dealing with hoarders," she said quietly. After lifting the cleaver high, she swung it down with such force that the loin steak fell neatly away.

"Nicely done." Margaret hurried over to wash her hands.

Colleen was just finishing wrapping steaks when the radio program was interrupted by the announcement that President Roosevelt was about to speak. Wiping her hands on her apron, she unplugged the radio and ran it out into the store, quickly plugging it back in. "Listen!" she yelled as turned up the volume. "The president is about to speak."

All the customers stopped shopping, hurrying over to the front counter to listen as the president began his speech.

"Yesterday, December 7th, 1941—a date which will live in infamy— the United States of America was suddenly and deliberately attacked by naval and air forces of the Empire of Japan. The United States was at peace with that nation and, at the solicitation of Japan, was still in conversation with its government and its emperor looking toward the maintenance of peace in the Pacific."

The president went on to describe the negotiations with the Japanese ambassadors, which seemed to be taking place at the very same time Japan was attacking Pearl Harbor. He briefly described the damage, similar to the other news sources, mentioning that "very many American lives have been lost." He even mentioned what they'd read in the *Chronicle* this morning, that American ships were reported to have been torpedoed "on the high seas between San Francisco and Honolulu."

A woman let out a gasp, as if this was news to her, but someone else hushed her and they all continued to listen.

"Yesterday, the Japanese government also launched an attack against Malaya. Last night, Japanese forces attacked Hong Kong." And now he listed the other islands subjected to Japanese attacks, including Guam, the Philippine Islands, Wake Island, and Midway Island.

"No matter how long it may take us to overcome this premeditated invasion, the American people in their righteous might will win through to absolute victory."

One woman let out a little "Hurrah!" and others quietly clapped.

"Hostilities exist," their president continued. "There is no blinking at the fact that our people, our territory, and our interests are in grave danger. With confidence in our armed forces, with the unbounding determination of our people, we will gain the inevitable triumph—so help us God."

At the president's announcement of the state of war between United States and the Empire of Japan everyone cheered loudly. As the radio returned to its regular broadcast, everyone began to talk at once. They all knew someone who was affected by yesterday's tragedy.

"I just wish they would tell us *which* battleship was sunk," Colleen exclaimed hotly. "Peter is on the USS *Arizona*, and we can't find out if his ship was hit or not."

"I think many of the ships were hit," an old woman said sadly.

"Yes, but the news says one battleship was sunk," Margaret explained. "But they won't name it."

"The military probably doesn't want to release too much information," another woman said gently. "Until families of the victims are notified."

"And in the meantime?" Colleen demanded. "What are we supposed to do?"

"Pray," Mrs. Spencer told her.

Colleen wanted to say she wasn't sure she knew how to pray, but instead she bit her tongue.

"And I want you to know that I am praying for your brother too," Mrs. Spencer assured Colleen and Margaret. "Peter is a dear man. We all miss him here at the store." She turned to friends. "We'll all pray for him, won't we?"

Of course they all agreed, and although Colleen tried to act as if this was very comforting—and it was on some level—it still didn't answer their questions. Which battleship had been sunk—and more importantly, how was Peter?

The shoppers thinned out in the afternoon, but Colleen preferred being busy. Less time to think. And so, between customers, she made herself useful by cleaning and facing the shelves—a chore that none of the family much enjoyed—but by the time she finished it up, she felt satisfied.

"Nice work." Margaret came over to admire a shelf of canned foods, all lined up like neat little soldiers, labels facing out, a narrow gleaming strip of wood shelf beneath them. "Dad would be pleased."

"Mind if I take a cigarette break?"

Margaret frowned. "Truthfully?"

"No." Colleen smirked. "I'll be out back."

As she puffed in the alley, Colleen wondered how Margaret could stand it day after day. Working in the family store was pure drudgery. Oh, she knew it was necessary drudgery. All the family was expected to put in their time—and had been for as long as she could remember.

But if working at the store was the only thing Colleen had to look forward to in life...well, she wasn't sure what she'd do. Mostly she was proud of herself for not complaining. Not yet anyway. She wasn't sure how long she could keep it up. Of course, with this upcoming war, it was possible that people would have to do things they didn't want to do. Like Peter. She smashed her cigarette butt beneath the heel of her spectator pumps and went back inside.

"Molly's here," Margaret announced as Colleen came into the front part of the store. "She wants to work this afternoon."

"Good for Molly." Colleen joined them, playfully tugging one of her baby sister's golden braids. Molly's hair color was almost identical to Colleen's—well, before Colleen had started using peroxide on hers. "Don't you know that fifteen is far too old for pigtails?"

Molly smiled. "Patrick likes them."

Colleen laughed. "That's because he wants you to remain a little girl forever."

Molly's smile faded some. "Sonja Henie wore pigtails in her last movie."

"Only when she was skiing." Colleen gave Molly a suspicious look. "Don't tell me...you left your skis outside, right?"

Molly wrinkled her nose. "Since you're such a big tease, I suppose I won't tell you who called for you today."

A customer took her basket to the counter, and Margaret left to write it up. But now Colleen's interest was piqued. "Sorry, sis. Who called?"

"A young man." Molly's pale brows arched.

"Yes?" Colleen was fairly used to young men calling for her. This had been going on, much to her family's aggravation, since she was about Molly's age. Of course, Colleen had quit wearing pigtails long before she turned fifteen.

"He called on the telephone, about half an hour ago. Dad hung up on him without asking his name."

"Oh." Colleen frowned. "That figures."

"And then a stranger came to the house," Molly continued somewhat mysteriously. "I think he might be the same man who called on the phone." Her blue eyes lit up. "He was a very handsome man."

"Did he resemble Gary Cooper? Only younger?"

Molly nodded. "Yes, now that you mention it."

Colleen was surprised to feel a rush of interest to learn that Geoff Conrad had kept his promise to call on her. But, remembering that he had planned to call on her after he'd enlisted, her pleasure vanished. That must mean he'd done it.

"What's wrong?" Molly asked. "Don't you like him?"

"I like him well enough." She shrugged. "But he's about to go off to war."

"Oh." Molly frowned.

"Who's about to go off to war?" Margaret asked as she joined them.

"A friend." Colleen was craving another cigarette now.

"A man friend." Molly explained about the handsome stranger looking for Colleen. "So I told him that she was working here today." She glanced at Colleen. "I hope you don't mind."

Colleen looked down at her frumpy green apron, which was now dirty, and glumly shook her head. "Why should I mind?"

"I told him that I was heading down here," Molly continued. "And that I could give you a message."

"What message?"

Molly glanced over her shoulder. "That a young man is waiting outside to see you."

Colleen looked out the big front window and there, leaning against a lamp post, wearing a neat dark suit with his arms folded in front of him, stood Geoff Conrad. "Why didn't you say so?" Colleen fumbled to untie her apron, wadded it up, and handed it to Molly.

Molly giggled, and Margaret peered over her shoulder to see him.

"I'm taking a break," Colleen told them and, grabbing her jacket, headed outside. Resisting the urge to smooth her hair or check her face, she hurried toward Geoff, trying to understand exactly why she was so happy to see him.

"Colleen!" he exclaimed. And then, like they had been going together for years, he swooped her up into a big hug, swinging her around so that her feet left the sidewalk. "I'm so happy to see you."

She laughed breathlessly as he planted her back down on the ground. "What on earth are you—"

"I told you I was going to call on you today." He was still grasping both her hands. "And it wasn't easy to track you down. But I did."

She nodded. "You sure did."

"And now I must insist that you agree to go to dinner with me tonight."

"Tonight?" Colleen frowned. Did he realize it was Monday? Who went out to dinner on a Monday?

"Yes. I need you to go celebrate with me, Colleen."

"What are we celebrating?" She knew she wasn't going to like his answer.

"I went to the navy enlistment office first thing this morning. I was the first one in line, with a bunch of other guys behind me.

There were even newspaper photographers there. I might be in the *Chronicle* tomorrow." He grinned. "Anyway, I passed my physical exam. And then I passed my academic exam." He grabbed her up in another enthusiastic hug. "I've been accepted into the Navy Air Corp, Colleen!" He released her, still grinning. "I report for training on Wednesday. And in no time, I expect to be flying around in a trainer plane. Isn't it exciting?"

"You report *this* Wednesday? Just two days from now?" Colleen felt a strange clutch in her chest. But in the next instant, she questioned her reaction. After all, she'd had lots of beaus before...and she barely knew this guy. What was wrong with her?

"Yes, this Wednesday. That's why you *must* go out to dinner with me tonight. I was going to get reservations for the Fairmont, but I wanted to talk to—"

"But it's a Monday," she told him. "The restaurant may not be open."

He frowned. "Then we'll just go tomorrow night."

She nodded with uncertainty, trying to think of an excuse to get out of this.

"We *will* go tomorrow night," he firmly insisted. "You'll get all dressed up, Colleen. To the nines. And we'll paint the whole town red."

She couldn't help but smile at those images. Geoff Conrad was a man after her own heart. Frighteningly so.

"Are you done with work now?"

She shrugged. "I could be."

"Great. I never had lunch today and I'm starving. How about if we ride the cable car down to the wharf and get something to eat?"

Colleen had skipped lunch too.

"Come on," he urged. "I have less than three days in this beautiful city. I want to enjoy it."

"Okay."

"Perfect." He grabbed her hand. "Time's a wasting."

"Let me tell my sisters first." She pulled away from him. "I'll be right back." As she went into the store, she felt she was making a mistake. She probably should just tell him no. The smart move would be to send this soon-to-be navy pilot packing before things got difficult—for both of them. And yet she couldn't seem to stop herself—she was caught in a wave that was sweeping her away.

Six

B ridget felt as if she were wrapped in layer upon layer of thick, heavy gauze as she stood in the college breezeway, just staring at her best friend's anxious face. "Did I hear you right?" Bridget finally asked Virginia. "Did you really just say *that?*"

"I'm sorry to be the bearer of bad news," Virginia told her. "But I know you wanted to know."

"You know for a fact that the *Arizona* is the battleship that they keep mentioning on the news? You *know* that the *Arizona* was bombed by the Japanese attack? That it has been sunk in Pearl Harbor?"

"That's what my brother told me."

"How did her hear it?" Bridget demanded.

"Joe's friend Larry works for the *Chronicle*. He saw it on the telegraph last night."

"But it hasn't been in the newspaper...or on the radio." Bridget remembered how just this morning her dad had sounded so certain that of all the battleships, the mighty USS *Arizona* was probably just fine. He was sure of it.

"Apparently the military brass wanted to keep the bad news under wraps for a while."

"But why?" Bridget asked.

"Maybe they don't want the Japanese to know they did such damage." Virginia scowled. "Or maybe they need to notify the families first. I really don't know."

"Did Joe's friend say anything about the men...the crew...the ones on the *Arizona*?"

"Just that there were more than a thousand sailors and marines onboard." Virginia's tone softened. "It's so sad."

Bridget barely nodded, still trying to absorb this bad news. "What about Peter?" she said quietly, more to herself than to Virginia.

"I don't know...." Virginia seemed to stand taller. "But I do know this, Bridget—there's a desperate need for nurses right now. As soon as I finish today's final, I'm going downtown to enlist in the ANC."

"Oh...right...." A hard lump grew in Bridget's throat. She wasn't sure she could hold back her tears as the same three words kept echoing inside of her brain. *What about Peter? What about Peter? What about Peter?*

"Bridget?" Virginia peered curiously at her. "Are you all right?"

Bridget knew she needed to get control of her emotions. Nurses were supposed to be strong and stoic and capable. At least on the exterior. "What about your board exam?" she asked Virginia, hoping to reroute her emotions. "How can you enlist as an army nurse if you haven't even passed your boards yet? I thought they only took registered nurses in the ANC."

"I already told my recruiter that I'm scheduled for my boards in January. She said it's not a problem. Well, as long as I pass." She frowned.

Bridget nodded. "Right."

"How about you?" she asked eagerly. "Do you want to enlist now too?"

"Yes," Bridget declared. "But first I need to focus on today's final exam. I need to pass it...and then the boards."

"Oh, Bridget, you're at the top of our class. You've worked so hard, taking heavy loads of classes year round. Good grief, you'll have finished a whole year faster than me. You could be blindfolded with one hand tied behind your back and still pass today's test."

Bridget rolled her eyes. Virginia wasn't Irish, but she sometimes had the gift of blarney.

"And then we'll have almost a month to prepare for the boards. We can study together and quiz each other. I'm sure we'll pass with flying colors—and be warmly welcomed into the ANC."

Bridget let out a long sigh that was more about Peter than concern for the boards or being accepted as an army nurse. "I need to focus right now." She rubbed the center of her forehead. "I need to get through today's exam, Virginia."

"Oh, Bridget. Now I'm sorry I told you about the *Arizona*." Virginia looked truly contrite. "I should've waited until after our—"

"No." Bridget firmly shook her head. "If I'm going to be an army nurse, I'll have to toughen up. And you knew how badly I wanted more information about Pearl Harbor. It was frustrating not hearing the details about what's going on over there. I appreciate you telling me."

"Well, good luck with your final." Virginia glanced at her watch. "Not that you need luck. I'm the one who should be worried."

"You'll do fine," Bridget assured her. "We should probably get to class."

Virginia suddenly hugged her. "And, really, I'm so sorry about the *Arizona*. But I'll bet that Peter is perfectly fine. My brother said that Pearl Harbor is a really shallow bay. Some of the boats originally reported as sunk were only partially submerged with their hulls resting on the bottom of the bay. Maybe that's the case with Peter's ship. For all we know, Peter is sunning himself on the beach right this minute—and counting his lucky stars."

Bridget couldn't help but smile at the image of a sunny beach with stars above it. Maybe Virginia was right. Peter might be perfectly fine. And so, as she walked to class, she knew she must push thoughts of Peter and Pearl Harbor to the recesses of her mind for now. She needed to set her mind to focus. *Focus*, she told herself, *focus!*

The exam was probably good medicine. Not only did it successfully distract Bridget from worrying about Peter, but she felt a real sense of accomplishment when she turned it in earlier than the other students. Not because she'd finished it quickly, but because she knew she had aced it.

And this meant she was finally done with nursing school. Well, except for the boards next month. But it was satisfying to know that she had completed her schooling in less than four years and that she would soon be a registered nurse! While other classmates, like Virginia, had taken long summer breaks, Bridget had continued her schooling during the summer in order to finish college sooner. And now that the United States was plunged into war, she felt grateful. And she felt ready. Not only did she feel ready, she felt impatient.

As she waited for Virginia to finish her exam, praying that her dear friend would do well, Bridget made up her mind. She would go with Virginia to the recruiting office and enlist today. Really, what was the point in waiting? She knew it was what she wanted. And she knew that Peter would be proud of her.

Margaret had been pleased that Colleen was up and ready to go to work again on Tuesday. And since the store was even busier than it had been on Monday, an extra set of hands was most welcome. But by midafternoon, it slowed down some.

"Do you mind working on the produce for a while?" Margaret asked Colleen as she led her to the backroom. She fully expected her sister to balk at being stuck by herself doing menial labor. After all, she was the social butterfly of the family.

"That's fine. I don't mind."

Margaret hid her surprise as she pointed to the crates of vegetables that still needed to be cleaned and trimmed then stocked in the store. She'd started on it yesterday, but with all the distractions had been unable to make much progress. "Our produce section is looking pretty bare." She picked up a head of untrimmed lettuce. "You remember how to do it, right?"

"Yep. But can I have a new pair of rubber gloves?" Colleen fluttered her fingers in the air, showing off her coral red nail polish. "I just did these."

"For your *big* date with Geoff?" Margaret asked in a teasing tone.

"Well, he is taking me to the Fairmont for dinner and dancing." Colleen reached up to adjust the bandana scarf that was wrapped around her head. She had actually pinned up her damp hair while Margaret drove them to work.

"Looks like you're pulling out all the stops." Margaret frowned. "But I still say it seems a bit over the top, Colleen. I mean, you barely know this guy."

"That's true." Colleen sighed. "But I do like what little I know." She winked.

Margaret extracted a fresh pair of black rubber gloves from a storage cabinet, handing them to Colleen. "Well, you certainly stayed out late enough with him last night. I was certain you wouldn't be able to get out of bed this morning."

Colleen laughed. "I'll admit that I barely made it." She pulled on a rubber glove. "And yet, here I am."

"So what did you two do all night anyway?"

"What did we do...?" Colleen tugged on the other rubber glove with a dreamy look in her eyes. Margaret suddenly wished for Molly's camera. What she wouldn't give for a photograph of her stylish, glamorous sister in her dirty green apron, ugly black rubber gloves, head scarf, and no makeup. She could probably use if for blackmail. "We rode the cable car down to the wharf," she said wistfully.

"A noisy cable car...well, that must've been romantic."

"Geoff loves San Francisco." Colleen picked up a floppy head of lettuce and a big knife, expertly whacking off the stem end then peeling back the floppy outer leaves. "He grew up on a farm with his widowed mother and grandparents," she continued as she washed the trimmed lettuce in the deep sink. "But every time they came to the city, he always wanted to ride the cable cars. So we went down to Fisherman's Wharf. And there we got a walking shrimp cocktail." She sighed. "It was delicious."

Margaret suppressed the urge to roll her eyes.

"And then we got a bowl of clam chowder." Colleen smacked her lips. "Yummy." And she continued to tell about how they did very ordinary things, but made it sound as if it was a truly magical evening. So much so that Margaret started to feel jealous. She was relieved to hear the front door bell jingling.

"I'll go see to that," she told Colleen. "Keep up the good work."

Colleen held up another floppy head of lettuce. "I most certainly will."

Margaret felt an odd sort of concern as she went to see to the customer. Was Colleen in love? And how was that possible? She'd only known this Geoff guy for two days. No one could fall in love that quickly. Besides that, he was about to leave for the Navy Air Corps. How would Colleen have a chance to get better acquainted with him once he was gone?

Margaret had sneaked a peek at the striking stranger yesterday afternoon. And she had to agree with Molly—he did look like a young version of Gary Cooper. Perhaps even slightly more attractive. But that had concerned Margaret even more. Sure, Colleen could easily fall head over heels for a Hollywood-handsome fellow. But what were the chances it was the real thing? Or that it would last? What if Colleen wound up getting hurt?

Perhaps it was for the best that Geoff was leaving for pilot training so soon. Less chance that Colleen would get overly involved. Margaret felt a wave of relief as she realized this was simply a temporary relationship. A little fling. Why shouldn't the glamorous couple enjoy their big fancy date? It would give Geoff something pleasant to remember when he was far from home, fighting in the war. Nothing wrong with that.

Margaret waited on the customer then busied herself with the produce case, removing some of the older vegetables and washing it down. She'd just gotten it ready to be reloaded with fresher items when Colleen came out with a full cart of vegetables.

"Here we go," she said cheerfully. And together they began to load the case.

"You did a nice job on these," Margaret said as she laid a shiny cucumber on the pile of others.

"Thanks. It's funny, because I used to hate chores like that—I remember how Dad used to tease me for not wanting to get my hands dirty—but I actually kind of liked doing it today."

Margaret thought that Colleen was finally growing up. But she knew better than to voice this. Especially since Colleen was so adept at *acting* grown-up. With her sophisticated hair and makeup and fancy clothes, not to mention her cigarettes, she was often mistaken as the older sister. But it was nice to think that Colleen was starting to mature. Either that or she was in a good mood simply because she was looking forward to her fancy date with Prince Charming tonight.

"When is your date?" Margaret asked absently.

"Geoff's picking me up at seven." Colleen paused to check her watch. "So, if you don't mind, I thought I'd head for home around five."

"Molly promised to be here at four again today, so you can leave even sooner if you want."

"Okay." Colleen set the last head of lettuce in place then put her hands on her hips. "It looks pretty, doesn't it?"

Margaret laughed. "Yes, it does. But it's funny to hear you say it."

"Margaret?" Colleen peeled off her rubber gloves. "Can I ask you something?"

"Of course."

"When did you know you were in love with Brian?"

Margaret chuckled. "Honestly?"

"Yes," Colleen said eagerly. "When did you know?"

"Probably in third grade."

Colleen laughed. "Not like that. I mean as a grown-up. When did you know for sure?"

Margaret pursed her lips, trying to remember. "I'm not really sure, Colleen. The truth is I feel like I've always been in love with him."

"That is so sweet."

Margaret frowned.

"What's wrong?" Colleen adjusted the tomatoes on top of the pile, perfecting the display.

"I wish Brian wasn't enlisting."

"But it's better to enlist. That way he gets a choice. At least that's what Geoff says. But then he wants to be a navy pilot. You have to enlist for that."

"I just don't want him to go." Margaret sighed. "I thought maybe he'd be exempt...you know, because he's in college."

"Are you worried this will put the brakes on your wedding plans?"

"I had really been wishing for a June wedding." She sighed. "But it feels selfish to say that. I mean, in light of everything. The war... and there's Peter...I wish he'd send us a telegram or something."

"Me too." Colleen nodded. "I try not to think about it—and being busy helps—but it's always hanging there in the back of mind. I hate this not knowing...and I worry...what if he's been hurt? What if he's in the hospital? In pain? By himself?"

"I know. I have the same thoughts. And the only thing I can do about it is to pray." Margaret sighed. "I've been praying a lot."

"I wish I knew how to pray better."

"Maybe this war will teach you."

Just then the doorbell jingled. Molly called out "Hello," and the conversation changed to blackout curtains. "Mam made a list." She handed it to Margaret. "It's what she needs to finish our blackout curtains. The city is under mandatory blackout as of today."

"So we've heard." Margaret looked at the list.

"Mam said to have Jimmy deliver them as soon as possible so—"

"Jimmy is already out on deliveries. I don't expect him back for about an hour," Margaret told her. "We have most of these things in the backroom. But you'll still need to go to the hardware store. And I've heard they're running out of some things. Mam should've called this morning."

"Dad won't let her use the phone."

Margaret grimaced.

"Why don't I gather up what we have here," Colleen offered. "And I'll stop by the hardware store and take it all home straightaway."

"Good idea." Margaret handed her the list.

"Dad said to make sure you close the store in time to get home before dark," Molly continued. "And Mam said don't forget to turn off all the lights in the store when you close tonight, Margaret. Including that Coca-Cola display sign in the window."

"Yes, good thinking."

"And Dad's working on some tin cans to make little hoods for the Buick's headlights."

"Hoods for headlights?" Colleen slipped Mam's list in her trouser pocket.

"So the beam from the headlight goes down." Molly cupped her hand to show them how it would work. "And can't be seen from the sky."

"Very clever." Colleen checked her watch. "Well, if I'm going to get what Mam needs to finish those curtains, I better go."

"Have a good time on your date," Margaret said.

"You have *another* date tonight?" Molly asked.

"Geoff is taking me to the Fairmont for dinner."

"The *Fairmont?*" Molly's eyes grew wide.

"It's his last night here for a while. He leaves for Coronado tomorrow."

"What's Coronado?" Molly asked.

"It's the naval base in San Diego, where they train pilots." Colleen slipped into her jacket. "So it's our last date...well, until he gets some leave. And who knows when that will be."

"Oh, well, have fun then."

"If you get home before dark, like Dad says, I'll still be there." Colleen got her handbag from beneath the counter.

"Good," Molly said eagerly. "I want to see what you're wearing."

"So do I," Margaret admitted. And hopefully she'd have enough time to speak frankly with Colleen before her big date. Because, after hearing Colleen's questions about being in love, Margaret felt seriously worried. Colleen really could be setting herself up to be hurt. Margaret wished there was something she could say to prevent it. Not that Colleen would listen.

Too bad Peter wasn't around...Colleen usually listened to him.

Seven

As Colleen left the hardware store with a bag of blackout supplies, she tried to estimate how many dates she'd been on. But it was useless. Even before she turned sixteen—the official age when Dad proclaimed his girls old enough to date—she'd snuck out on dates. She'd probably been on a hundred dates by now, with nearly as many guys. And yet she didn't remember looking forward to a date as much as she was looking forward to this one.

Of course, this happy anticipation simply made her feel guilty. Wasn't it wrong to be this excited about a date when your brother was stationed on an island that had been severely bombed just two days ago? Of course, if she went with her dad's reasoning, Peter was just fine. Although the way Dad stayed glued to the radio and the telephone...well, she wasn't so sure.

Once again, she wished she was better at this praying business. Oh, it wasn't that she couldn't think of words to say. It was more that she wasn't sure God was listening. Or if he was listening, he wasn't listening to the likes of her. Perhaps it was better that people like Molly and Margaret did the praying. They were good at it.

But thinking of Peter made Colleen wish that he could meet Geoff. She felt certain that Peter would approve of Geoff. He would appreciate Geoff's enthusiasm about flying airplanes. And, like Peter,

Geoff was joining the navy. She wondered if there was any chance their paths would cross. Wouldn't that be something!

As she went into the house, Colleen could hear her parents' voices raised, as if they were having an argument. Although they used to argue occasionally, she hadn't heard too many disputes since her dad had gotten sick. Hearing them now concerned her.

"Hello?" she called out from the front room. "Anyone home?"

"Oh, you're here." Mam emerged from the kitchen with a startled expression. Her face was flushed, and she was wringing a dishtowel in her hands.

"I got the stuff on your list." Colleen held out the bag.

"Thank you." She used the towel to blot what looked like tears.

"What's wrong?" Colleen's words were quiet.

"Nothing is wrong," Dad said gruffly as he came out of the kitchen.

"But Mam's crying." Colleen looked from one to the other. "Did you hear something about Peter?"

"No." Her dad shook his head, going over to his easy chair to sit. "It's Bridget."

"Bridget?" Fear clutched Colleen's chest. "Did something happen to Bridget?"

"She's joined the *army!*" Mam exclaimed, breaking down into fresh tears. "She's going to war!"

"As a nurse," Colleen added, keeping her voice calm. "Not to carry a gun."

"She told you about it?"

"Yes." Colleen nodded. "I think it's wonderful that she wants to serve her country by caring for wounded soldiers. You should be very proud of her."

"Exactly what I was saying." Dad picked up his newspaper,

waving it in the air for emphasis. "They say right here in today's *Chronicle* that nurses are needed—more than ever now."

"But what if she gets hurt on the battlefield?" Mam shook her dishtowel in the air. "We've already lost Peter and now—"

"We have not lost Peter!" Dad shouted. "That's what I keep telling you, woman! Don't you go saying we have lost him when we don't know that it's true. It's like tempting fate, Mary. Can't you see that?" With a flushed face, he started to cough, covering his mouth with his handkerchief and shaking his head.

Mam let out an exasperated groan as she returned to the kitchen.

"Where is Bridget?" Colleen asked.

"She said she was taking a walk," her dad said sadly. "But I'm sure she couldn't stand to hear your mother going off like that. Can't blame Bridget, either. If I were in better shape, I'd take myself for a walk too."

Colleen went over and patted his shoulder. "Mam will cool off, Dad. Eventually. Just give her time."

He stuck his nose in the newspaper, nodding glumly. "Time's about all we got right now...but the waiting is killing me."

Colleen picked up the bag and went into the kitchen. "Bridget knows what she's doing, Mam." She set the bag on the kitchen table and then hugged her mother. "She's an intelligent young woman. Very sensible and dependable. The army is lucky to get her. And I'm certain she will be very safe wherever she goes."

Mam nodded somberly. "Yes, I'm sure you're right, Colleen. It's just that I wasn't expecting it. And I've been so worried about Peter. It was as if something inside me just snapped when Bridget told me her news." She sniffed. "If you see her, will you tell her that I'm sorry?"

"Of course. How about if I tell Dad that too?"

"Yes, yes...now I better get busy or we'll not be having any supper tonight."

Colleen quickly explained that she wouldn't be home for the evening meal and, before her mother could question this, she darted out. Pausing in the front room, she reassured her dad that his wife was returning to her normal self. Then, not wanting to be questioned by him regarding her plans for the evening, she hurried up to the room she shared with Molly.

As Colleen got ready for her date, she felt sorry for Bridget. She could just imagine how hurt Bridget would be that their mam rained on her parade like that. Especially after Bridget had worked so hard to get through nursing school. And yet she could understand her mother's concerns. Hadn't Colleen felt just like that when Bridget told her sisters about her plans on Sunday?

As Colleen carefully rolled her silk stockings up her legs, she thought that Sunday now seemed very far away. Had it only been three days ago that they'd sat in church and heard the news about the Japanese attacking Pearl Harbor? It felt like a different lifetime.

Colleen removed her topaz blue satin gown from the closet and held it up. Margaret had helped her to sew this dress last year, but the off-the-shoulder sweetheart neckline and fitted bodice was still very much in vogue. And the long full skirt, just above her ankles, was still quite stylish. She loved the swishy sound of the fabric when she moved in it. Perfect for dancing. And her delicate black ankle-strap heels that she'd gotten on sale before Thanksgiving looked absolutely perfect with it. She went over to the full length mirror on the back of the door and scrutinized her image.

Her shoulder length blonde hair looked just fine. The quick bobby-pin job in the car had been a success. It was wavy and glossy, curling under just above her shoulders. But should she put it up in a French twist instead? Wouldn't that look more sophisticated?

Strangely enough, she wasn't sure. Maybe her sisters would have an opinion. As she went to the bathroom to apply her makeup, using a softer than usual touch, she wondered if Margaret might loan her pearl earrings. Because, for some reason, Colleen didn't want to be too flashy tonight. And her usual glitzy costume pieces just didn't seem right.

Not bad. Not bad at all. Some people thought Colleen resembled Ginger Rogers—and that was a compliment, for sure—but Colleen would prefer to look like that new Scandinavian actress she'd been reading about in recent movie magazines. *Ingrid Bergman.* She was a classic beauty. Very sophisticated, and Colleen predicted she would be a hit in the United States.

"Oh, look at you," Molly said as she came into the bedroom. "I love that dress on you, Colleen. That blue matches your eyes perfectly."

"It matches yours too," Colleen pointed out. "Maybe someday you'll get to wear it."

"Really?" Molly's eyes grew wide.

"I want to see too," Margaret pushed open the door, coming into the small room to inspect Colleen. "Very pretty. Geoff should be impressed."

"But you don't have on earrings," Molly said.

"My earrings are all so flashy," she confessed. "I was sort of wishing for pearls tonight." She looked hopefully at Margaret.

"Promise not to lose them?" Margaret asked.

Colleen held up her hand like a pledge.

"Why don't you get them?" Margaret said to Molly.

As soon as Molly left, Margaret cleared her throat. "I can tell you really like Geoff, Colleen. And that makes me want to say something."

"Say something?" Colleen turned from removing her short fur

coat from the closet.

"I just wanted to warn you to be careful, Colleen."

"Careful of what?"

"Of your heart."

Colleen laughed.

"You know that Geoff is leaving tomorrow," Margaret continued in a serious tone. "He'll probably be overseas soon. And you barely know him."

Colleen frowned. "What are you saying exactly?"

Margaret held up her hands in a helpless gesture. "I don't know. But I just felt like if Peter were here, well, he may warn you to be careful."

"I know what Peter would say," Molly announced as she held out the earrings. "He would say, 'You're a very pretty girl, and you shouldn't let the boys take advantage of you.'"

"Really?" Colleen looked at Molly in surprise.

Margaret looked shocked too. "Did Peter say that to you?"

"He did." Molly nodded firmly. "Peter told me a lot of boys go after pretty girls because they think a pretty girl is like a trophy or a prize. They don't really care about the girl. They just want her around because she's pretty. And Peter didn't want any of his sisters to be treated like that."

Colleen couldn't help but laugh. "And Peter, as usual, is right. But I assure both of you, Geoff is not like that. I've known enough of the other kind of boys to know a good one when I meet him." She frowned. "I just wish he wasn't going off to war."

"Speaking of Peter's opinion of boys." Margaret tipped her head. "I think I hear someone at the door."

"I'll get it." Molly took off running with Margaret behind her. Meanwhile, Colleen checked out her image in the mirror one more time. Her short coat was only dyed rabbit fur, but it was well-made and a good design, and actually looked rather nice with her topaz satin. She was ready for her big night. But first she needed to make a graceful exit—and that might be a challenge. She could hear her dad grilling Geoff now. Normally, Colleen was quick to slip out the door before her date had the opportunity to knock and come inside. Naturally, this aggravated her parents.

She slipped into the front room where Geoff and her dad were standing face to face. Geoff's back was to her, but she could see that he had on a very nice looking suit. She wouldn't feel overdressed. That was a relief.

"You know the city is in a blackout tonight," Dad grimly informed Geoff. "You can't be driving around town with your headlights burning."

"I know about the blackout, but other cars are using their headlights," Geoff politely told him. "I think it may be dangerous to drive without them."

"I made some hoods." Dad went over to his chair to get the tin cans he'd been fussing with today. "You can put them on with this electrical tape." He handed the works over to Geoff.

"Oh, Dad." Colleen came over to join them. "Geoff doesn't need to—"

"No, you're dad's right," Geoff told her. "I'm grateful to use these, Mr. Mulligan. Thank you very much." He examined them more closely. "A very innovative idea too."

Her dad grinned, and Colleen knew that Geoff had nearly won him over.

"You look beautiful," Geoff told Colleen. He held out a small white box. "This is for you. Feel free to wear it or leave it here for your mother."

"Speaking of our mother." Colleen nudged Molly. "Want to invite Mam out here to meet Geoff?"

Molly took off like a shot, and Colleen peeked into the little box. "An orchid!" she exclaimed. "How elegant. I'd love to wear it." She turned to Margaret. "Would you help me get it on just right?"

They had just pinned the orchid to her bodice when Mam emerged from the kitchen. She'd removed her apron and smoothed her hair as she peered curiously at Geoff. Colleen introduced them.

"I can see where Colleen gets her good looks," Geoff told her mother. And, although Colleen sometimes forgot that she actually did resemble her mother, she appreciated the genuine smile it brought to her mother's face.

"Oh, go on with you." Mam waved a hand.

"It's true," he said with sincerity. "You've got the same eyes and coloring."

"Well, you two better get going," Margaret said. "You'll need to give yourself plenty of time to get to the Fairmont, due to the blackout. You'll have to drive more carefully."

Grateful for Margaret's intervention, Colleen told her family good night and soon they were out the door. "Watch your step." Geoff reached for her arm. "It's very dark with the blackout."

She looked around in wonder at her neighborhood. Other than a few slits of light here and there, all was dark. Even the streetlamps were off. "It's weird, isn't it?"

"Yes. But it's not as much of a blackout when you get downtown. I suspect some businesses will receive warnings about their lights tomorrow." He opened the car door for her. "You get comfortable while I attempt to attach these blackout hoods."

"Oh, you don't have to—"

"I want to," he told her.

Colleen felt glad for her dad's sake. It would please him to know that Geoff had really used his contraptions. Geoff had easily won her family over. To be fair, he was quite an improvement over some of the guys that she'd brought home in the past. But it was also bittersweet. She finally found a guy who felt like a keeper, and he was going off to war tomorrow. Colleen chided herself as Geoff got into the car—she was not going to think about that now. Tonight was about sending Geoff off in style. And that was exactly what she planned to do. What happened after that...well, like Scarlet O'Hara, Colleen would have to think about that tomorrow.

Eight

When Bridget left the house shortly after her mother went to pieces, she had no idea where she was bound. She just wanted to get away. As far away as her legs would take her. But once it started getting dark—and no streetlamps came on—she began to feel uneasy. It wasn't that she was frightened. And it wasn't that she expected San Francisco to be bombed by the Japanese, although there seemed to be plenty of people with that very concern. She was worried that she might become lost.

But when she finally made it back to her own neighborhood, she still wasn't ready to go home. And so she decided to pay a visit to the Hammonds' house. It was only a few blocks away from hers, and it had been like a second home for as long as Bridget could remember. Mr. Hammond and her dad were old friends from the old country. She'd heard their tale enough times to repeat it back to them. The two had emigrated as strapping young men back in late 1911. Partly to escape the "troubles" brewing there, partly for the adventure, but mostly to make their own stake in the "land of opportunity."

"We sailed out of Belfast just five months before the sinking of the great Titanic." They liked to brag about seeing the mighty Titanic in the docks, as if they'd nearly been part of that fateful voyage. "Our ship was made by the same ship building company—Harland and Wolff. But she was smaller...sturdier." The two men were full of stories. Whether they were completely true or part blarney was anyone's guess. But the two Irishmen had been young and energetic back then, filled with major expectations and minor wealth. And because Mr. Hammond had relatives in San Francisco, that became their destination.

Bridget's dad found a job at a grocery store that had, at that time, been owned by his future wife's family. The rest was history. The young couple had fallen in love and, after years of working together at the store, her parents had taken over the business for Bridget's aging grandparents. Meanwhile, with the help of a generous uncle, Mr. Hammond opened a tiny cobbler's shop in a good location downtown. The small business grew over the years into a respectable leather goods store that managed to survive the recent depression. And now Mr. Hammond was eager to hand it over to Brian when he finished college. Although Bridget suspected that plan, like so many others, would be put on hold now. Until the war ended.

"Bridget Mulligan!" Mr. Hammond exclaimed happily as he opened the door. "Bless my soul! I thought maybe it was the Japs knocking at me door. Come in, come in. We're just sitting down to supper."

"Oh, I'm sorry. I totally forgot what time it—"

"Nonsense." He gripped her by the arm. "Come in and sup with us. We haven't had the pleasure of your company for a long time. Mother!" he called. "Bridget is here. Lay another plate."

Mrs. Hammond came out of the kitchen with a flushed face. "Oh, Bridget, I'm so happy to see you." She hugged her. "It's been too long." She escorted her into the kitchen where the small wooden table was already set with three places. "It's only stew and biscuits tonight, but there's plenty. And I've got a berry cobbler in the oven." She glanced at the rooster shaped clock above the stove. "And Patrick should be home any minute now. He doesn't always eat supper with us, but he promised to be here tonight."

"I really didn't mean to barge in on you—"

"Not another word about that from you." Mrs. Hammond helped remove Bridget's coat. "You're as welcome as the rain, darling, and I'm sure you know it."

Bridget nodded—she did know it. "Thank you."

"And there's my boy now," Mrs. Hammond said cheerfully. "Just in time too." She tipped her cheek toward her son, waiting as he plunked a kiss on it.

"Good evening," he politely told Bridget as he removed his overcoat. "I didn't know we were having company."

"Bridget isn't company," Mrs. Hammond scolded. "She's family."

He laughed. "Yes, of course."

Before long they were seated at the table and Mr. Hammond was saying grace. With her head bowed, Bridget questioned herself. What was she doing here? She should be home with her own family. And yet...it felt like a refuge being here.

As they ate, the conversation hopped around the recent war-related events. Mr. Hammond told them of a reported attack of a lumber ship off the coast last night. And Patrick described how the blackout looked downtown.

"So much going on." Mrs. Hammond passed the butter to Bridget. "I can hardly keep up."

"And I suppose you've heard that Patrick enlisted in the navy yesterday," Mr. Hammond told Bridget.

"I knew he planned to enlist." She smiled at Patrick. "Congratulations."

"Thanks. I just gave notice at work, and my boss promised I'd still have a job when I return."

"That's grand news." Mr. Hammond spread butter on his biscuit.

"I guess." Patrick sounded uncertain. "But maybe I'll want a different job by then. Who knows?"

"Don't you like working for the insurance company?" Mrs. Hammond asked.

"I liked it at first—because I needed a job," he told them. "Work was scarce a couple years ago when I took it. But I'm not sure I want to work there forever."

"Oh, well, you don't need to figure it all out now," Mrs. Hammond assured him.

"And maybe you'll decided you want to work with me," Mr. Hammond said hopefully. "Brian has big plans to grow our store. Well...after the war anyway."

"I'm just glad the navy doesn't want you until *after* Christmas," Mrs. Hammond said. "Brian will be home soon too. It will be good to have the whole family together...before...." Her smile faded. "Well, before my boys are shipped off to...God knows where...and to face God knows what." Her voice cracked.

"Now, now, Mother." Mr. Hammond reached across the table to pat her hand. "Just remember that both Bridget's daddy and myself went off to fight the Hun in 1915. And Riley and I both made it back home in one piece. Our boys will too."

She nodded. "Yes, yes, I'm sure you're right."

The table grew quiet and Bridget decided it was her turn to speak up. "I enlisted too," she said meekly.

"What?" Mr. Hammond's spoon clanked against his soup bowl.

"In the ANC. That's the Army Nurse Corp," she said quickly. "I'll be an army nurse."

"Oh, my." Mrs. Hammond slowly shook her head.

Bridget explained how she and Virginia finished their final exam that morning, how they were so excited about nearly completing their nursing degrees, and how they wanted to help the servicemen. "And so we decided to enlist. It just seemed the right thing to do. And the military needs nurses badly."

"Congratulations," Patrick told her. "I think it's great what you're doing. And I know I'll be thankful—as a serviceman—to know there are nurses like you and Virginia ready to assist...I mean, if I ever needed it."

"But you're in the navy," his mother reminded him. "Bridget will be an army nurse."

"Why did you pick the army?" Mr. Hammond asked.

"Virginia said the need is greater in the army right now. She thinks we'll be positioned on the European front. Not right away, of course." She explained how they would have to pass their board exams then complete boot camp and special training. As they were finishing up supper, she confessed one of the reasons she'd run away from home tonight. "Mam was really upset to hear I'd enlisted."

"Well, that's understandable," Mrs. Hammond said gently. "It's hard enough to see a son go off to war. But a daughter. Well, I don't even have a daughter, but I can imagine." She reached for Bridget's hand, clasping it. "You Mulligan girls are the closest thing I've ever had to a daughter...and I must admit it's not easy to think of you going overseas, Bridget."

"But don't you think Bridget will make a wonderful nurse?" Patrick offered.

"Of course!" Mrs. Hammond nodded eagerly. "And the army will be blessed to have her." She squeezed Bridget's hand. "I'm sure it will be very exciting. Promise you'll stay in touch, darling. We'll all want to know how you're doing."

"I promise." Bridget sighed. "There's something else...something I need to talk to someone about. Just not my parents. Not yet anyway. It's the real reason I couldn't go home tonight." Bridget felt the lump in her throat again.

They all got very quiet, looking at her with concerned and curious expressions. "Go ahead, darling," Mrs. Hammond urged her. "We're like family. You know that. You can tell us anything."

"Okay." Bridget felt her chin trembling. "It's just that I—I'm not sure. Not sure I can say this without crying."

"You go ahead and cry if you need to," Mrs. Hammond told her. "Tears are good for the soul."

In a voice that cracked with emotion, Bridget quickly poured out the news about the USS *Arizona*. "And—and that means that most of the men on board—the vast majority of them—did *not* survive. So—so that means that Peter—Peter might not even be alive."

"Oh, darling." Mrs. Hammond went over and gathered Bridget in her arms, holding her close as she sobbed. And then Mr. Hammond and Patrick came over too. All of them huddled together while Bridget cried freely. And by the time she got control of her emotions, she realized they all were crying.

"I've been so worried about Peter." Mr. Hammond removed his handkerchief, blowing his nose.

"Why don't we go into the front room?" Mrs. Hammond wiped her tears on her apron. "To talk a bit more."

After they were seated in the front room, Mr. Hammond cleared his throat. "I'm so sorry to hear this sad news, Bridget. So very sad. Now, let me get this clear—your parents *don't know* about it yet? They're unaware that the *Arizona* was the battleship that sunk? The one we've been hearing about in the news?"

"I'm sure they don't know...not yet anyway." She explained how she'd learned this first from Virginia, then picked up a few more pieces of devastating news at the army recruiter office. "I'm sure we weren't supposed to hear it. But we did. And I had planned to tell my family, but Mam got so upset when I told her I'd enlisted, well, I just didn't have the heart to tell her the rest of it. And so I took a walk. And that's why I ended up here."

"And good that you did," Mrs. Hammond said. "That's a heavy load for one young person to bear."

"But we don't know for sure that Peter is—is gone," Patrick said quietly. "We can't give up hope yet."

"That's true." Bridget barely nodded. "It's possible that he may be wounded. He could be in a hospital. And, quite honestly, that was part of my motivation to enlist today. I thought I'd want Peter to have the best nurse available...if he was hurt."

"Yes, dear. I can understand that." Mrs. Hammond sighed deeply.

"I know I need to tell my parents." Bridget glanced at her watch. "I probably should go and tell them right now."

"Let me go with you," Patrick offered suddenly. "That might make it easier."

"Yes," his dad agreed. "That's a good plan."

Mrs. Hammond agreed and as they all stood, Bridget looked gratefully at Patrick. "Thanks. I think it really would help if you came with me. If you don't mind."

"Not at all. You know Peter is like a brother."

"I know. This way if I fall apart again...well, maybe you can help explain it." She felt close to tears as she pulled on her coat. "I want to be strong, but it's hard."

"Of course it is." Mrs. Hammond hugged her again.

"And, remember, you don't know for sure about Peter," Mr. Hammond said as they stood by the front door. "It may be that he wasn't even aboard the ship Sunday morning. After all, the ship was in port. Peter might've had leave. He could be just fine."

Bridget sighed. She wanted to believe that...but she knew it wasn't realistic. Facts were facts. They had to be faced. But at the same time she didn't want to dispute this with him. She didn't want to destroy what little hope he still had left. Especially right before his own two sons were preparing to go to war. Instead, she thanked them again, and she and Patrick stepped outside.

"It's so dark out here." Bridget felt around, grasping the metal porch railing as they cautiously went down the steps. "It'll be a wonder if people don't get hurt stumbling around in the dark like this."

"I heard that one of the first fatalities in London—even before the Jerrys started bombing—happened to a man who was outside painting a curb in the nighttime. I guess he was painting it white so that people could differentiate the sidewalk from the street during the blackouts, but it was so dark out that he got run over by a car."

"That's so sad. Let's stay on the sidewalk tonight."

"Right."

Bridget's eyes adjusted to the darkness somewhat as they walked up the hill toward her house. Still, everything around her felt strange—like she was in a different town, living a different life. Maybe this was how it would feel when she was sent overseas in a few months. Maybe she should get used to strangeness.

"I realize that it's possible Peter is dead." Patrick spoke quietly, slow and deliberate. "I've known the possibility existed ever since the news about Pearl Harbor. But somehow I just cannot believe it, Bridget. Something inside me refuses to accept that could happen to Peter. It just feels impossible to me."

"I know what you mean," she confessed. "Maybe it's because, no matter what, Peter will always be alive inside of us. Our memories and all that...well, those never die."

"That's true. But even beyond that, well, I just can't accept that Peter could be gone from this world. I guess I won't be able to accept it—not until I know it for a fact."

"That's probably good." And it was probably equally good that Patrick was going to help her break this hard news to her parents. It sounded as if he might be able to put a hopeful spin on the whole thing. That would help a lot.

Because Bridget's hope had dwindled significantly this afternoon, and she was afraid she wouldn't be able to revive it. Of the four Mulligan girls, Bridget was the realist. She was pragmatic and practical, a problem solver. And the truth was, the more she thought about the attack on Pearl Harbor, the less likely it seemed that Peter was alive.

As painful as it was to admit this to anyone, including herself, Bridget felt she was simply being realistic. Besides the odds stacked against her brother's survival, there were other reasons for her doubts. The fact that Peter hadn't gotten word to them was concerning. Bridget hadn't told anyone about this, but a conversation she'd overheard at the recruiting office had seemed to seal Peter's fate. At least in her mind.

She hadn't meant to eavesdrop, but her ears perked up when she heard the two army officers talking about Hawaii. One officer mentioned receiving a telegram from Oahu on Monday. It seemed a confirmation had been sent, declaring that his brother was in the hospital, but alive and expected to recover. This was the third day since the sinking of the *Arizona,* and for her family to hear nothing from Peter seemed to confirm that he was not okay. But she had no intention of pointing this out to anyone. And if Patrick could help her break this news—and keep hope alive at the same time—she would be grateful. Because hope might be all her family had to hold on to right now.

As Bridget led Patrick into her house, she could tell her parents were relieved to see her. Not only that, they were pleased to see she was with Patrick. Nothing would make her parents happier than if she married him. Mrs. Hammond and Bridget's mother had been "secretly" discussing a double wedding for years now. Brian and Margaret. Patrick and Bridget. And it wasn't that she didn't have great respect for Patrick—she did—but she thought of him more as a brother than a boyfriend. And she suspected he felt the same.

"Bridget has heard some difficult news," Patrick began after they sat down in the front room. Margaret turned the volume down on the radio, and Molly set down her pen. "And I came with her tonight to help her tell it." Patrick glanced at Bridget as if he was unsure of how to proceed.

"What is it?" Dad demanded.

"My friend Virginia—I mean her brother, Joe," Bridget began meekly. "Joe's friend—his name is Larry—he works at the *Chronicle*. And he—he heard something." And now the tears began to fill her eyes again. "About Peter's ship." It was too late, she was crying again.

"Bridget heard that the battleship, the one that was sunk, the one we've heard about in the news, was the *Arizona*."

Mam gasped. "Peter's ship?"

"The one with more than a thousand casualties?" Margaret asked.

"The *Arizona? Sunk?*" Dad looked from Bridget to Patrick with troubled eyes. "You're certain of this?"

"I don't know if we can be certain of anything," Bridget said sadly. "Until we hear from someone."

"But Peter may be okay," Molly declared. "Not everyone on that ship died. Maybe Peter wasn't even on the ship when the Japanese attacked. He might've been on the island, exploring somewhere. He wrote to me about some of the places he'd been to in Hawaii.

When he had his leave. Maybe he was on leave on Sunday." Molly was crying now. She held the paper she'd been writing in front of Bridget, as if it was some kind of proof. "This is my letter to him. And I'm going to finish it. And I'm going to send it. Because he's Peter—he has to be alive."

"I had the same thoughts," Patrick gently told Molly. "I'm not ready to give up on Peter either." He tapped on his chest. "I can still feel him in here. I think he's alive."

"Yes!" Molly nodded hopefully. "Patrick is right. We can't give up on Peter. We've got to believe he's alive. We've got to keep praying for him. I've lit a candle at Old Saint Mary's every day for him. And I'll keep doing it every day too." She looked around the room, pointing at the rest of them. "You all need to do it too. We can't give up on Peter."

Bridget wished she could share in her little sister's optimistic hope, but she knew it was too late for her. Bridget's hopes were like the San Francisco streets right now—dark and bleak. Extinguished.

Nine

Colleen felt like she was starring in her own glamorous movie as she and Geoff danced to the three-piece band that was playing at the Fairmont Hotel. Even though the music was a bit more sedate than some of the lively tunes she was accustomed to dancing to, it was absolutely perfect for this evening. Almost as perfect as being in Geoff's arms.

For a boy who'd grown up on a farm, Geoff was a surprisingly good dancer. And an attentive and interesting companion. The only fly in the ointment was knowing that he was shipping out tomorrow. That was all wrong! But Colleen was trying not to think about that.

She hadn't expected the restaurant to be overly busy tonight due to the recently declared war, the city's blackout, and the fact that it was only Tuesday. But to her a surprise, a number of servicemen in uniform, along with their wives and sweethearts, had filled the restaurant almost to capacity. In fact, she was impressed that Geoff had been able to get them a table at all.

"That's because I'm a guest at the hotel," he'd explained earlier.

"A guest?" she'd questioned him.

"Yes. I'd been staying with my buddy Rick these past few nights—sleeping on his lumpy sofa in his tiny apartment. But when I realized this was my last night in the city, well, I decided to live it up a little.

So I got myself a room here, and that helped with getting dinner reservations for us."

Now if Geoff had been a different sort of fellow—like some of the bums she'd gone out with in the past—she might've felt concerned over the fact that she was dining in a hotel with a man who had booked a room. But after only three days, she felt certain that Geoff was a gentleman. She had no reason to think otherwise.

"This has been the best night ever," Colleen told him as they returned to their table after a dance. Their dinner dishes had been cleared and the white tablecloth glowed with the flickering golden light of the lamp in the center. Very romantic.

"I must agree," Geoff told her, reaching for her hand across the table. "Thank you for giving me all these nice memories to take with me."

"Thank *you.*" She sighed. "I just wish that you weren't leaving so soon."

He nodded. "I've had the same thoughts. But the need for pilots is dire out there. Especially ones who already know how to fly." He grinned. "Who knew I'd be such a hot commodity?"

"I would." She giggled. "You're a good guy, Geoff. I feel very lucky that our paths crossed on Sunday."

"It seemed like fate."

Their waiter returned to their table now, asking if they wanted dessert and coffee. Of course, Geoff insisted they did. He didn't even bother to ask Colleen if she agreed—instead, he asked the waiter to bring them the specialty of the night. And then, unless she imagined it, Geoff seemed to wink at the waiter.

"Let me guess," she said after the waiter left. "He's going to bring something flaming to the table?"

Geoff laughed. "Well, that would be exciting. To tell you the truth, I'm not even sure what the special dessert of the night is, but I heard it's good." He looked deeply into her eyes now, squeezing her fingers gently within his own and sending ripples of pleasure through her. "Besides, anything to make this evening last longer is good with me."

Colleen heartily agreed. This was an evening that she wished could go on forever. She suspected the other couples in the restaurant felt the same. In fact, the very air seemed to be charged with romance and excitement tonight. As if everyone here was savoring every minute of this magical evening and, like her and Geoff, they were stretching it out as long as possible.

The waiter set a silver coffee carafe on the table, carefully filling their china cups and promising to return shortly with dessert.

"I don't want tonight to end," Colleen said wistfully. "Everything is so perfect."

He nodded. "I know."

"But I feel a little guilty," she confessed.

"Guilty?" Geoff looked worried. "What for?"

"Your family," she said quietly. "I wondered if you should've been with them tonight...instead of with me."

"Oh that." He grimaced. "My mom and grandparents may agree with you there, but I called them and explained that I'd met someone very special."

"You told them about me?"

"Of course."

She felt another flutter of excitement rushing through her.

"And my recruiter said that I'll get to go home for a few days at Christmas. So I'll see my family then." He looked earnestly into her eyes. "And I hope I'll get to see you then too, Colleen."

"Of course, you can see me." She nodded eagerly. "Say when and where and I'll be there."

"Really?" He looked hopeful. "What if I wanted to take you home to meet my mom and grandparents? Would you be good with that?"

Colleen felt momentarily speechless. Had he just said he wanted her to meet his family? Did he know what that sounded like? What that could mean? Instead of questioning him on it, she simply nodded. "I'd love to meet them."

And now the waiter was bringing their desserts, carefully setting what looked like chocolate cake in front of them with a mysterious grin. "Enjoy!" He winked at Geoff.

Curious as to what was going on, Colleen picked up her fork.

"Be careful there." Geoff grinned. "Watch out for that cherry on top."

"What?" Colleen looked down at the cherry garnish on top of her cake and was surprised to see that it was glittering in the candlelight. "What is that?" She stared wide-eyed at what appeared to be a sparkling diamond ring balanced right on top of the cherry. And before she could say anything, Geoff had dropped down to one knee.

"Colleen Maureen Mulligan," he said with his eyes locked with hers. "I love you. I think I loved you from the instant we met. And, although I know this must seem very hasty to you, I know what I want and more time will not change that. Colleen Mulligan, will you marry me?"

Colleen was truly speechless now. Was this really happening?

Geoff's smile was fading now. "If you're going to turn me down, please, be quick about it, Colleen. I'll under—"

"No," she told him. "I'm not turning you down, Geoff. I'm just in shock." She took in a deep breath. "Yes, I will marry you, Geoff Conrad. Yes!"

And now he took her into his arms, kissing her so passionately it felt like her world was spinning. "Here." He plucked the ring from the cherry. "Let's see if it fits. If it doesn't, the jeweler promised to adjust it." He slid the ring onto her finger, and they both stared down at it.

"Do you like it?"

"I love it," she proclaimed, looking back into his eyes. "And I love you, Geoff." They kissed again, and suddenly Colleen was aware that they were being watched—and just like that the other couples began clapping and cheering, as if they'd been in on the whole thing.

"I think we should seal this with a dance," Geoff whispered in her ear.

As they joined the others on the dance floor, a sweet familiar song began to play. As she listened to the tune of "I'll Be Seeing You," Colleen could hear the lyrics playing in her head. And she knew that it was no coincidence. She felt certain that after Geoff was gone, she would be seeing him in all the old familiar places...she knew that she would be looking at the moon but seeing Geoff. And, once again, it was bittersweet. But, she decided as she felt his strong arms around her and imagined a lifetime with this remarkable man, it was mostly sweet.

Margaret hadn't intended to wait up for Colleen. At least not past midnight. But she had fallen asleep on the sofa, so when she heard footsteps tiptoeing through the front room, she jerked to attention. "*Colleen*," she whispered sharply. "What time is it?"

"Oh!" Colleen jumped. "I didn't think anyone was still up. What are you doing out here?"

"Waiting for you." Margaret shook her finger at the clock. "It's nearly three in the morning. What're you doing staying out so late? Mam and Dad will throw a fit."

"Not unless you tell them." Colleen bent down to slip off her shoes. "And not when they hear my news." She giggled.

"Come on." Margaret tugged Colleen by the arm, guiding her down the hallway and pausing by her own bedroom. It was the same room she'd shared with Bridget for years. Until Peter had left. Since then both she and Bridget finally got their own private bedrooms. But one night of sharing wouldn't hurt. Besides, Molly had school in the morning—and she'd been so upset over Peter. She needed her sleep. "You're bunking with me tonight, sis."

"Okay." Colleen sighed. "But I'm not sure I'll be able to sleep."

Margaret nudged Colleen in ahead of her and then closed the door and turned on the light. "Now tell me, what are you babbling about? What *news?*" Margaret removed her bathrobe, hanging it on her bedpost. "And please, don't tell me you've gone and joined the WACs or something. Mam and Dad can't take much more."

"The one time they can be glad I'm nothing like Bridget." Colleen tossed her fur jacket onto the chair then unzipped the side of her gown, letting it drop to the floor in a satiny heap of topaz blue.

"Bridget was out a really long time, walking, after Mam overreacted. And then—" Margaret stopped herself as she watched Colleen carefully removing the pearl earrings she'd borrowed tonight. At least she hadn't lost them. That was something. But what was that glittering on her finger? Margaret went closer, leaning in to examine what looked like a diamond ring. With a fairly big diamond too. "Colleen Mulligan!" she exclaimed. "What on earth is *that?*" She pointed to the ring.

"Oh that?" Colleen fluttered her fingers in front of Margaret's nose in a showy way. "Just a diamond."

"Yes, I can see that. But *what* does this mean?"

"Oh, Margaret!" Colleen beamed at her. "Geoff proposed tonight. And I accepted."

Margaret felt like a slight puff of wind could topple her. "Wh–what?" She sank down on her bed, trying to understand what Colleen had just said. Was she dreaming?

"It was so romantic." Still in her white lacy slip, Colleen sat down on the chair. "Everything about tonight was just perfect. Amazing. And Geoff is so romantic."

"You're engaged?" Margaret stared at Colleen in wonder.

"Yes! Isn't it wonderful?"

"You barely know him," Margaret said quietly. "You met him two days ago."

"*Three.*" Colleen admired her ring. "It's a little big, but Geoff said the jeweler would adjust it for me."

"You know a man for three days," Margaret continued, "and you agree to marry him?"

"I know, it sounds crazy. But when you know something is right—well, you just know that it's right."

"But you're only eighteen and—"

"I'll be nineteen in February."

"Yes, fine. But you've only known him for three days."

"But he's wonderful, Margaret. You've met him. Don't you think he's wonderful?"

"I don't even know him."

"Mam and Dad liked him," Colleen persisted. "And Molly—"

"Speaking of Mam and Dad," Margaret interrupted, suddenly remembering the main reason she'd been waiting up for Colleen—besides wanting to be sure she made it home okay. "We've had some news. About Peter."

"Peter?" Colleen looked up from her ring in alarm. "Is he okay?"

"Bridget found out that it was Peter's ship—the *Arizona*—that was sunk in Pearl Harbor. That was the ship that had more than a thousand men...men who lost their lives on Sunday."

Colleen's brow creased. "Peter's ship? It sank?"

Margaret nodded glumly.

"But we don't know for sure that—that—" Colleen's voice cracked. "Just because the *Arizona* sank doesn't mean that Peter died. Does it?"

Margaret shrugged. "The truth?"

"Yes, of course," Colleen insisted.

"The truth is that more men died on the *Arizona* than survived. And if Peter did survive, he is probably injured."

"Oh." Colleen wrapped her arms around her middle, rocking in the chair. "Poor Peter."

"Like Molly keeps saying, we all need to pray for Peter. I plan to stop by Old Saint Mary's on our way to work in the morning. To light a candle for him."

"Yes, of course. I'll do that too. Geoff and I went there on Monday night so I could light a candle for him. But I got so busy today...." She looked sadly at her new ring. "I forgot."

"Well, it's late." Margaret tossed a nightgown at her. "I'm going to bed. Turn off the light when you're done." Margaret got into bed, but now she didn't feel the least bit sleepy. And it was only partly due to her concern for Peter. She couldn't believe that Colleen was engaged. What was wrong with that girl? How could she spend three days with a man and then know he was the right one to marry? It not only sounded impossible, it seemed all wrong.

Margaret had been seriously dating Brian since her senior year in high school. For more than three years now. Not three days, mind you, *but three long years!* And she'd been in love with Brian for much longer than that. Sometimes it felt she had spent her whole life waiting for Brian to come around.

Oh, she knew he needed to finish his college. And that had been the plan. Her plan, anyway. That they would marry after his graduation—hopefully in June, even though that was probably pushing too much too soon. But now it seriously irked her to find out that Colleen was engaged. After three days!

Meanwhile she and Brian were not getting any closer to that place. And she wasn't getting any younger either. Knowing that Brian planned to enlist—or maybe he'd already enlisted—she wondered if they'd ever get engaged. One thing she did know, Brian was not impulsive. Not in the least. For that matter, she wasn't exactly impulsive either. Although if he would get around to popping the question, she wouldn't have to think twice about accepting.

But everything was changing so quickly these past few days. So many new distractions, worries, and responsibilities, all thanks to this war. Her chances of getting engaged to Brian seemed slight at best. As Colleen turned off the light, Margaret envisioned herself as a wrinkled old maid—the poor spinster aunt who managed the family grocery store then went home to her cat.

It was not a happy picture.

Ten

Molly was the first one to spot the diamond ring on Colleen's finger the next morning. Well, besides Margaret, who already seemed to know. "Is that what I think it is?" Molly quietly asked as Colleen filled her coffee cup in the kitchen.

"Shh." Colleen put her forefinger over her mouth, glancing over to where their mother was dishing oatmeal into bowls.

Margaret handed Molly two bowls of porridge. "Not yet," she said quietly.

Molly pursed her lips, nodding, but as she carried the bowls to the dining table, she knew what this meant. *Colleen was engaged!* Of course, it seemed impossibly fast. But then Colleen was always full of surprises. She liked spontaneity. And Geoff had seemed very nice. Still, after the drama of last night—Bridget's announcement and the news about Peter's ship...well, Molly wasn't sure how much more this family could take.

"Here you go." She set the bowl in front of her dad and sat down. His brow was furrowed as he read the headlines in the morning paper. Like the last few days, everything on the front page was related to the war. She wanted to ask if there was anything there about the *Arizona*, but at the same time wasn't sure she wanted to know. Last night when she'd finished her letter to Peter, she had convinced herself that until she heard that news from a reliable source—like President Roosevelt on the radio—she was not going to believe the *Arizona* had been the one to sink. The rest of her family could think what they wanted, but she was going to keep believing that Peter was okay. And she would mail her letter to him on her way to school. It was the second one she'd written to him since Sunday.

She bowed her head, said her silent blessing, asked God to watch over Peter, then crossed herself and started to eat. Breakfast at the Mulligans' on weekdays was a casual affair, everyone heading off in their various directions at various times. Although Margaret hadn't gone to the store yet...and Bridget was done with nursing school. So everyone, for a change, was still in the house. Well, everyone but Peter.

"Isn't it time for you to be heading off to school?" Dad laid down his paper and looked at Molly as if he'd just noticed her sitting there.

"I have plenty of time." She glanced toward the kitchen, where she could hear her mother talking to Colleen. Did Mam know about Colleen's news yet?

Bridget came to the table with her oatmeal and coffee, sitting down beside Molly. "I'm going to work with Margaret this morning," she said absently.

"What about Colleen?" he asked. "Isn't she helping out there this week? Maybe you should stay home and help your mother."

"I'm not working this morning," Colleen announced as she joined them, setting a basket of blueberry muffins on the table. "But I do have an announcement to make." She sat down in her usual place, but only with her coffee. "As soon as Mam gets in here." She glanced toward the kitchen. "And if you don't mind, I'm in a hurry this morning."

"I'm coming." Mam came out with her bowl, followed by Margaret.

Colleen waited for them to sit down. "Okay, now that you're all here, I'll tell you my news." She held up her left hand, wiggling her fingers in the air, showing off the glistening diamond. "I am officially engaged!"

"*What?*" Dad set his coffee cup in the saucer with a loud clang.

"Colleen Maureen!" Mam exclaimed. "What on earth are you saying?"

"Geoff proposed last night. And I accepted."

"That boy you only just met?" Dad scowled. "Are you *daft?*"

"Riley!" Mam scolded.

"Seriously?" Bridget stared at Colleen. "You're going to get married?"

"Well, not right away, of course," Colleen explained as she stood. "Geoff is being sent to San Diego to start his pilot training. The navy was eager to get him into training since he already knows how to fly. And they really need pilots right now. He's getting shipped out this afternoon."

"But it's not even eight o—"

"I need to go right now, Dad. I promised I'd see him off today. But I just wanted my family to know my good news." She beamed at them. "I'm so happy. Really, I am!"

"But you hardly know the—"

"I have to go," she interrupted her mam. "I promise you can ask me more about it all later. Grill me as much as you like after he's gone." She was pulling on her blue peplum jacket—with shoulders so wide it made her narrow waist look even smaller as she fastened the brass buttons in front. With her matching flared skirt and black pumps, Molly felt her sister was as stylish as a film star. No wonder

Geoff had fallen in love with her.

"Don't forget my hat," Margaret pointed to the buffet table where she'd set a striped hatbox.

"Don't worry, I won't." Colleen chattered about how she and Geoff had dined and danced at the Fairmont last night, using the mirror above the buffet to make adjustments to Margaret's new blue and black hat, adjusting the fascinator scarf to look very sophisticated. And then she pulled on her gloves and reached for her handbag.

"You look very pretty," Molly told her.

"Thank you." Colleen continued smiling brightly at everyone.

"Are you walking down to the docks in those high heeled shoes?" Mam frowned skeptically at her feet.

"No. Geoff is picking me up in his car."

"But you said he's going on the ship today," their dad blustered. "How can he just leave his car behind and—"

"He's leaving his car with me." She picked up her handbag.

"But we don't have room for another car in our—"

"I'll explain it all later," she called as she headed for the front room. "Geoff is probably already here—and we don't have much time." She waved and hurried out.

"Well!" Dad huffed. "You'd think the young man could at the very least come in here and speak to us directly."

"Colleen said that he wanted to," Margaret told them. "But she insisted it wasn't necessary. They're going to breakfast together and then she'll drop him off at the ship."

"And I suppose this means that you approve of all this?" Dad scowled at Margaret as if she were somehow to blame.

"I, uh, I wouldn't say that I approve exactly." Her voice sounded shaky. "I—I'm not sure what I think." She stood. "Excuse me." She practically ran from the room.

"What's wrong with her?"

"What do you think?" Mam said sharply. "Margaret has been waiting for Brian to propose marriage for years now. And there goes her younger sister, beating her to the altar."

Dad coughed, using his napkin to cover his mouth, then turned to Bridget with a perplexed expression. "You know, I had expected something like this from you."

"Wh—what?" Bridget stopped her spoon in midair. "What do you mean?"

"Last night when you didn't come home for supper...and then you showed up here with Patrick in tow. Well, that got my hopes up. For some reason I felt certain that you two kids had come to your senses—I thought, by golly, my oldest daughter has gotten herself engaged." His lower lip protruded in a slight pout. "And let me tell you, I was ready for some good news like that. I was ready to call Jack Hammond and invite him over here to celebrate with me—we'd open up a bottle of good Irish whiskey and drink to our children. But, no, no..." Dad pushed his chair back, wheezing as he stood. "Instead you brought more bad news to this house."

"I'm sorry, Dad. I only—"

"I'm tired now. Need to rest." He coughed loudly, then shook his head. "Excuse me."

"There, there..." Mam quickly got to her feet. "Let me help you, Riley."

After their parents were gone, Molly turned to Bridget. "Don't feel bad," Molly quietly said. "It's not your fault."

"It sure feels like my fault." Bridget looked close to tears. "I wish I had never told them about Peter's ship. What difference would it make if they didn't know the truth?"

"You did what you felt was right, Bridget. Dad's just feeling low right now. And the news about Colleen...well, you must admit it's a little shocking."

"Yes, of course. And on the heels of me enlisting...and the news about Peter. It all feels like very bad timing." Bridget stood, picking up her bowl and coffee cup. "Hearing Dad say that almost made me wish that Patrick and I were engaged."

"Really?" Molly picked up some of the other dishes. "Would you really want to marry Patrick?"

"Oh, it's a silly idea. But it would make Dad happy." Bridget shrugged as she went into the kitchen. "And like Margaret is always telling me, a girl could do worse."

"That's for sure." Molly followed her. "If I were grown up, I'd want to marry Patrick. I think he's awfully sweet."

Bridget actually smiled now, which made Molly feel better. "Maybe Patrick will wait for you." She set her dishes by the sink.

"Oh, that's silly." As much as Molly admired Patrick, she felt certain she'd never have a chance with him. After all, he was more than seven years her senior.

Bridget ran some water, rinsing the dishes. "Patrick will be shipping out after Christmas. That would be awfully quick to pull off an engagement." She chuckled. "Well, except for Colleen."

"Maybe you and Patrick will be stationed near each other," Molly suggested. "You could have an overseas rendezvous. Wouldn't that be romantic?"

"You're such a little dreamer." Bridget tugged a braid. "But don't forget he's joined the navy and I enlisted in the Army Nurse Corp. I doubt our paths will cross."

"But would you want them to cross?"

Bridget pointed to the clock. "You better get a move on, Molly.

You'll be late for school."

Knowing Bridget was right, Molly grabbed her coat and hat and book bag, as well as Peter's letter, which she stuffed in her pocket. Then yelling "good-bye," she took off running. It would only take an extra minute or two to swing by the mailbox on her way to school—and even if she was tardy, it would be worth it to get his letter sent today. She felt certain Peter could use some encouragement.

Colleen felt a bit selfish as she waited for Geoff outside. She knew that her parents would be upset that she hadn't dragged her fiancé into the house again. But, really, after seeing them getting so upset—questioning everything about her happy news—why would she want to subject Geoff to their inquisition? Besides, her time with Geoff was so limited. There so was much to do before he shipped out.

She spotted his Ford coming up the street and, waving, she went down the steps. Everything about her life felt slightly unreal—like she was still starring in a romantic movie. She'd wanted to pinch herself when she woke up this morning, after less than three hours sleep, wondering if it wasn't all just a sweet dream.

"There she is," Geoff said cheerfully as he sprinted around his car to sweep Colleen into his arms again. "My girl!" He landed a kiss on her lips, so passionate that it tingled clear down to her toes. When they finally parted, she extracted a fresh hanky from her handbag, using it to gently clean her coral lipstick off his mouth.

"Are you ready for this?" He helped her into his car.

"I'm not sure." She felt a rush of nerves. "What if they don't like me?"

"Of course they'll like you." He smiled with confidence, leaning down to move a corner of her skirt inside the car. "I love you, Colleen. That's all they need to be concerned about."

As he went around to the driver's side, she wasn't so sure. Geoff was his widowed mother's only son, and the only grandchild of his elderly grandparents. Her parents seemed very upset by her good news—and she was one of five siblings. What if it was five times worse with Geoff's family?

"Don't worry," he said as he drove. "Even if by some chance my family hated you—and that is not going to happen—I wouldn't care a bit."

"But you'd have to care," she told him. "Family is important. Even if I don't always agree with my family, I still love them. I may not do what they want, but I care about what they think." She giggled, realizing that sounded contradictory, but she knew what she meant.

"You're right, Colleen, I suppose I do care about how they react to this. But, no matter what they say, I want to marry you. Don't forget that."

Although Colleen was still caught up in this moment—relishing that she and Geoff had miraculously found each other and that he truly seemed like her Mr. Right—she still felt a thread of uncertainty. It had all happened so fast—even for her. And if she allowed herself to think about it too hard, well, she probably harbored a few doubts. Tiny ones, to be sure, but they were there just the same. And she had wondered, if Geoff wasn't headed off to pilot training and then to the battlefield, would she have agreed to marry him so quickly? Was this decision reckless? Would she regret it later?

But when she turned to look at him, her doubts nearly vanished. "I'm so happy." She sighed and leaned back into the seat. "It might not make sense to anyone else, Geoff, but I am truly happy."

"I love hearing that," he told her. "I am too."

As he drove through the city, Colleen told him the news about the *Arizona*. "But we don't know anything for sure," she said quickly. "Molly and I both think he must be okay. We're not giving up hope."

As he drove them through the suburbs, Geoff quizzed her about her childhood in the city. Then she asked him about growing up on a farm. There was so much to learn about each other—and so little time to do it. It seemed that even the smallest stories were interesting. As he drove through the countryside, past a meadow with horses, Geoff told her about how he used to dream of being a cowboy.

"As a teen, I wasn't afraid to ride anything. A mule or a bull or a bronco—didn't matter. I didn't think anything could throw me." He chuckled. "But then I got tossed off a cranky old bull at a local rodeo with all my friends watching. Hurt my pride almost as much as it hurt my hind-end. I looked up to see Hank Gardner's yellow biplane flying up above the rodeo grounds. He's my crop-duster friend—the first guy to ever take me flying. And that's when I decided I'd rather fly a plane in a loop-the-loop than get thrown from an animal again."

He turned onto a gravel road, slowing down. "This is my grandparents' property," he explained. "It's not a big farm. Just under three hundred acres. Been in my family ever since my great grandpa purchased it in the 1850s. Not long after the California gold rush. As the story goes, he came out here from Pennsylvania to make his fortune in the mines. But as it turned out, instead of making his money mining the gold, he made it by mining the pockets of the gold miners." He chuckled. "He wasn't a thief though. Great Grandpa hung up his pick ax in order to sell food and goods to the miners.

That's how he got rich."

"Sounds like a smart man." Made of tan-colored bricks with dark green shutters, the two-story farmhouse coming into view looked sturdy and substantial. He turned into the drive around that cut through the big lawn in front, parking beneath one of the large oak trees.

"Welcome." He grinned at her.

"It's very pretty." She suddenly felt uncomfortable. "Everything looks well cared for. Very nice."

"There's a lot to keep up here. I've done my part over the years, but Grandpa has a few hired hands too. Not as many as he should have. He's a stubborn old cuss. Thinks he can still do everything he did when he was younger. Grandma keeps reminding him to slow down, but he doesn't listen."

"How does your family feel about you enlisting?" She stared up at the handsome house.

"Oh, you know...they respect my decision and that I'm doing my patriotic duty...but, well, they are not really on board." He turned off the engine. "If you know what I mean."

"Well, everything has happened so quickly. I can understand how it might be hard on the older generation. It's certainly been hard on my parents." She didn't even want to think about that right now. "I just think young people adjust to these sorts of changes better. We're more adaptable."

"I agree." He reached over for her hand, giving it a squeeze. "Anyway...just be yourself around them, Colleen. I already told Mom we could only stay about an hour, so at least it will be over quickly."

"Right." She smiled nervously as he helped her out of the car. As they walked up to the house, she reminded herself of how she usually performed pretty well under stress. Some of her friends called her the "cool cucumber." And, of her sisters, she was usually the one to keep it together. Hopefully she would be able to maintain herself like a polite young lady now. Be the well-mannered girl that her mother had worked so hard to bring up. Colleen did not want to let Geoff down. But the truth was, as he opened the shiny black door to the tall handsome house, Colleen Maureen Mulligan felt completely out of her element. Who did she think she was anyway?

Eleven

B efore going to work at the store, Bridget went to say good-bye to her dad. Partly to apologize and partly to check on his health. She found him lying in bed with his eyes closed and breathing heavily, but it was his slightly grayed skin tone that concerned her most. Something was seriously wrong.

"It's me," she said quietly as she sat in the chair by his bed. "Just relax, I want to take your pulse and check your vitals."

His eyes popped open. "There's no need for—"

"Hush, Dad." She gently took his wrist. "Just humor me while I play nurse. Okay?"

"Okay," he said in a husky voice, closing his eyes again.

His heart rate was elevated and, although she didn't get the thermometer, she could tell that he was warm to the touch. "That cough of yours?" She pushed a curly strand of gray hair away from his forehead. "It seems to be getting worse."

"Nah, it's just the same," he assured her. "It's just I've been overdoing it some. I worked on those hoods for the headlights and then helped your mother put up the blackout curtains. I must've worn myself out."

Bridget wasn't so sure, but not wanting to worry him, she simply nodded. "Well, then you better take it easy today, Mr. Mulligan."

"I will do just that."

She leaned down to kiss his cheek. The stubble revealed that he hadn't shaved this morning. He'd probably been too tired. She knew the past several days had been hard on him. Harder than he would admit. Too much happening, too many worries in regard to his children...it was all taking a toll on his health. She considered loosening his collar but was surprised to see that it was already loose. Had he been losing weight? And she hadn't even noticed? She knew better than to question him on this. It would simply rile him, stirring up his defenses.

"I'm sorry I was the one to bring you bad news last night, Dad," she said softly.

"Oh, Bridget, I'm sorry I said what I did this morning." He closed his eyes, coughing again. "It's not your fault, darling. None of it. And I wouldn't want you to go getting yourself hitched to Patrick Hammond—even though he is a fine young man—just to make your old man happy. That was a foolish thing for me to say. I hope you'll forgive me."

"Of course I do." She patted his cheek. "Well, as long as you promise to really rest up today. No sneaking out of bed as soon as I leave. Otherwise, I'll stay home and play nurse, and Margaret will be on her own at the store today. At least until Jimmy gets there, but that won't be until after three."

"No, no, you go with Margaret." He frowned at the alarm clock on his bedside table. "And you better get going too, if you girls plan to open on time."

"You take care now." She forced a smile, but as soon as she closed the bedroom door, she felt a stab of very real concern. Hurrying to the kitchen where her mam was just starting to wash the breakfast dishes, Bridget prepared her words.

"Dad is sick," she said solemnly.

"I know that." Mam continued filling the dishpan with water.

"Mam, he is very sick. I don't know why the doctor hasn't—"

"The doctor has prescribed rest for him. But your stubborn father overdoes it and then he gets worse. You know that, Bridget."

"*Mam*," Bridget said urgently. "I think Dad has tuberculosis."

Mam looked at her with frightened eyes. "Tuberculosis?"

"Has he been tested for it?"

"I don't know." She turned off the tap.

"He needs to be tested. As soon as possible."

"You really think it—"

"I don't know why I didn't question this sooner." Bridget shook her head. "He's got so many of the symptoms—I just never noticed. He's had fever and chills. His cough never seems to go away. He's even lost weight. I can't believe I missed it before."

"Oh, dear. What do we do?"

"Talk to his doctor."

"His doctor might listen to you—better than me," her mother was saying as Margaret came into the kitchen.

"Whose doctor?" Margaret was pulling on her coat.

Bridget quickly explained.

"Tuberculosis?" Margaret's eyes got big. "Isn't that terribly contagious?"

Bridget nodded solemnly. "If it turns out that I'm right, if Dad has TB, we'll all need to be tested. If any of us tests positive, we could be contaminating others." She pursed her lips tightly, knowing this could put an end to her dreams of joining the ANC.

"What about working at the store?" Margaret asked. "We could be passing the disease to others and not even know it."

"Bridget, you need to call Dr. Thompson right now." Mam was

already flipping through her little black book of phone numbers.

"You're right. But he's probably not in his office yet." Bridget followed her mother out to the front room.

"I'm calling his home number." She was already dialing.

"Until we know if Dad has tuberculosis, we probably shouldn't even be working at the store," Margaret quietly told Bridget.

"But maybe I'm wrong. Maybe Dr. Thompson already tested Dad for TB. Maybe he doesn't have it." She listened as her mam asked for Dr. Thompson.

"My daughter needs to speak to you." Mam handed the receiver to Bridget.

Bridget quickly identified herself, explaining her concerns about her dad. "I wanted to know if you'd done a tuberculosis test on him."

"Oh, I'm sure I must've done that, Bridget."

"He has all the symptoms, Dr. Thompson," she said urgently. "And if he does have TB, that means that our whole family has been exposed. And, as you know, we work at the store. We handle food and deal with customers daily and that—"

"Yes, I see your concern. I'm about to head to the office. I'll check his file as soon as I get there."

"And please call us back as soon as you find out. Until we know for certain that Dad doesn't have TB, I feel it's wise to keep the store closed. I'd hate to think that our family could start an epidemic."

He agreed that was a prudent plan.

"He's checking on it," Bridget told her mother.

"Did he say not to open the store?" Margaret asked with concern.

Bridget just nodded, and now their mother began to cry. "I just don't know how much more I can take," she said as they led her to the kitchen, sitting her down at the table. "I feel as if God has turned his back on our family." She covered her face with her hands, sobbing.

Bridget and Margaret tried to comfort her, but Margaret looked close to breaking down herself—much like Bridget felt. Still, Bridget reminded herself, she needed to be strong. For the sake of her family as well as her nursing career, Bridget needed to learn to control her emotions, to keep a stiff upper lip, to function in the midst of chaos if necessary. And if all the recent challenges were meant to be a training ground for this, she should be grateful.

Unfortunately, she did not feel gratitude—she felt anguish.

Instead of surrendering to distress and grief, Bridget fixed her mother a cup of tea and urged her to drink it. "We will deal with whatever this is," she said calmly. "After all, we are family. We have each other." She patted her mother's back. "We are the Mulligans. We will pull through."

It took nearly an hour for the doctor to call back. Bridget, who'd been sitting by the phone, quickly answered. "I'm sorry to say that your father has not had a tuberculosis test," he admitted sadly. "I don't know how that happened. I'm certain I requested one. But I hired a new nurse last fall. Perhaps it slipped beneath the cracks. I'm very sorry."

"When can you test him?"

"I am coming over there as soon as I hang up," he said somberly. "I'll test Riley myself—and anyone else who is in the house. I'll see you in about thirty minutes."

She thanked him and hung up, telling her mother and Margaret the news.

"Oh, dear." Mam looked close to tears again. "This isn't reassuring."

"No, but we need to know."

"What will we do if he has tuberculosis?" Margaret asked.

Bridget was about to declare it was almost certain that he did, but stopped herself. She was not a doctor. It might possibly be something else. She didn't always need to be the bearer of bad news. And sometimes it was true—that what you didn't know wouldn't hurt you—but not usually.

"What if we have tuberculosis too?" Margaret's voice sounded shriller than usual, as if she was on the verge of breaking. "What will we—"

"We will simply deal with it," Bridget said calmly. "People face serious illnesses all the time. And I've been trained to treat illnesses. It is not the end of the world, Margaret. Modern medicine is amazing. They are coming up with new discoveries every day." She tried to sound more confident than she felt. The truth of the matter was that there was no known cure for tuberculosis. Certainly there were sanatoriums around the country. Generally in high arid places. Not San Francisco. And, from what she'd heard, the best sanatoriums were not inexpensive. And the patient's stays were not brief. And this information would not be helpful to her family right now.

As Colleen sat primly in the Conrad's parlor, one silk-stockinged leg tucked gracefully behind the other, back straight, pleasant expression on her face, every hair in place...she knew she was in over her head. Not only was Geoff's family much wealthier than hers, they were better educated too. A fact Geoff's mother seemed intent on driving home.

"I really had hoped that Geoff would finish his schooling before marrying," she said directly after Geoff announced their engagement. No "congratulations" or "when did this happen?" or "have you set a date?"

To Colleen's relief, Geoff reassured his mom that he had every intention of getting his degree. "After the war ends," he declared.

"I'm afraid that's easier said than done." His mother pursed her thin pale lips, which Colleen felt would look prettier with just a touch of rose lipstick. Not that she was going to say this. "And if you're married, trust me, son, it will be more challenging than you think."

"Then it will be *my* challenge," he said firmly.

His mother turned to Colleen. "When Geoff's father began courting me, I was still in college," she said. "I had one year left and we decided it wise for me to finish." She glanced at her in-laws, seated across from her. So far they'd been rather quiet, which Colleen had interpreted as disapproval. "I think you appreciated that we waited."

"Oh, well..." the elder Mrs. Conrad spoke gently. "To be honest, I didn't know how important it was for a woman to have a college diploma back then. Don't get me wrong, I think education is important for everyone. I earned my teaching certificate when I was nineteen, and I even taught in a one-roomed schoolhouse for two years before I married Geoffrey." She reached for her husband's hand. "But I don't know that my education helped me too much in regards to being a farmer's wife."

"I don't know that it hurt any." He grinned at her. "I like intelligent women."

"Colleen is intelligent," Geoff told them.

"You have known her for *how long?*" His mother's brows arched.

"Some things you know instantly," he said.

"What were your plans?" his mother asked Colleen. "I mean before you got engaged. You already said you had no interest in college. So had you simply planned to get married and—"

"No," Colleen interrupted, instantly regretting it. "I had never planned to get married at all. I mean I might've considered getting married...someday, when I was older. But it wasn't in my immediate plans. And about college, well, you see, my parents had already put my older brother through two years of business school, and my oldest sister is just finishing nursing school. She almost has her RN degree. And then my dad got sick...and even if I wanted to go to college, I'm not sure we could afford it. Right now my other sister has taken over managing our family's store, and I help her sometimes." She glanced over at Geoff, knowing she was rambling, but no one said anything, so she continued. "And if I really did what I've always dreamed of doing, well, I'd go to Hollywood and pursue an acting career."

Geoff's mother looked slightly stunned and Colleen wished she hadn't said that. *What was she thinking?*

"And she would probably succeed at it," Geoff said defensively. "You should hear her sing. Or see her dance." He beamed at Colleen. "She's really something."

"That's interesting." His mother straightened the front of her brown cashmere cardigan. "How does your family feel about these, uh, Hollywood aspirations?"

"Some of them—like Molly and Peter—think I could do it. But Margaret and Bridget are more...practical. And Mam and Dad, well, they just think I'll grow out of it."

"And will you?"

Colleen glanced at Geoff. "I don't know. But I know that when I'm with Geoff, I don't think about becoming an actress."

"You mentioned several siblings," his grandmother said. "How many are in your family?"

Relieved for the change of topic, Colleen told her.

"That's a big family," she said. "Very different than what Geoff grew up with."

"Her brother was in Pearl Harbor," Geoff solemnly told them.

"He was a sailor on the battleship that was sunk."

They expressed their regrets and concerns, and then Geoff told them about how Bridget had enlisted to be an army nurse. "The Mulligans are definitely doing their part for the war effort."

"That's easier done when you have five children," his mother said stiffly. "Our family has already contributed to this country's war effort." She looked at Colleen. "Did Geoff tell you that his father gave up his life for our country in the previous war?"

Colleen looked at Geoff in surprise. "No...I knew his father had passed on. I didn't realize..."

"So you see why we are reluctant to let Geoff become a navy pilot." She sighed deeply. "And we know that pilots are at the greatest risk...for fatalities."

"Oh, Mother." Geoff grimaced. "Let's not go down that road again. You knew I'd made up my mind to enlist as a navy pilot—even before our country decided to go to war. And now that we are in a war, I'd much rather be enlisted than drafted. At least I have a choice this way."

"And I bet you'll be one of the best—if not the very best—navy pilot out there," Colleen declared. She looked directly at his mother now. "And I would think it would be much more helpful to Geoff to feel that all his loved ones are fully behind him when he goes to the battlefield. Don't you?"

"Well, I...I haven't really given it much thought."

"Colleen is right," Geoff's grandpa said. "We all need to back Geoff in his effort to do this." He reached over to shake Geoff's hand. "Congratulations, son. Both in your endeavor to be a navy pilot and your engagement to a very beautiful girl."

"Yes," the grandmother chimed in. "Congratulations to both of you."

Geoff thanked his grandparents, but his mother just sat there like a stone. For a very awkward moment no one said a thing. And then Colleen knew it was her turn to speak up.

"I cannot imagine what it would feel like to lose your husband in war," she said quietly to Mrs. Conrad. "I hope to God I never find out. But I do know what it feels like to have a brother over there... in harm's way...and not knowing if he is...dead or alive. But I'm very glad that even though I didn't want him to go—in fact, I even told him that when he first enlisted—I eventually gave him my full support. And I even wrote him a couple times—and trust me, I'm not usually much of a letter writer." She glanced nervously at Geoff. "Although I will try to improve at that. Anyway, all this to say, that I'm very glad my brother knew that I was behind him. That his whole family was behind him. I think that's the best thing we could've given him...under the circumstances."

Colleen sighed. She'd never actually thought of it quite like that before, but she knew it was true. She had been vehemently opposed to Peter's enlisting at first. But her love for her only brother had forced her to stand behind him. And even though she wasn't much good at praying, she had lit several candles for him. Last night, after hearing about the *Arizona*, she had even prayed several Hail Marys for him before falling asleep. Like Molly, she was hoping for the best. What more could she do?

Twelve

Molly's feet felt heavy as stones on her way home from school on Friday. So much had happened this week, so many upsets and changes and concerns...would anything ever be the same for her family? Or for the world in general? Instead of going directly home, she stopped by Old Saint Mary's and purchased two candles—one for Peter and one for Dad. She lit them both and then slid into a pew and knelt down.

Sincerely praying for her two loved ones, Molly pleaded with God to help them through their current trials. And then she entrusted Peter and Dad into God's care, asking for God's will to be done. But then, feeling slightly desperate, she made a backup prayer, asking for a miracle—begging God to make everything right again, to help Peter and Dad and to restore her family to what it used to be. Finally, encouraged and satisfied, she crossed herself and stood.

As Molly exited the pew, she noticed how many bowed heads were present today. And so many candles burning—more than she recalled ever seeing before. Was it because the whole world—not just the Mulligans'—was falling apart? And if so, would God really be able to put it all back together? Her current-affairs class had discussed the Third Reich and the Nazi regime this afternoon—and it had been truly horrifying. Much more serious than the challenges facing her own home. So much so that she almost felt guilty for troubling God with her personal worries now.

As she walked through the sanctuary, Molly considered asking Father McMurphey his opinion on these matters, but she could see he was busy with several people waiting for the confessional booth and, although she probably had some minor sins to confess, she didn't feel it was anything worth standing in line for. Especially since she needed to get home to see what the news on Dad might be. Dr. Thompson had promised the results of the tuberculosis test by the end of the day. Not just for dad, but for all of them.

Hurrying up Kearny Street, Molly rubbed the spot on her arm where she'd been injected with the TB test two days ago. It had hurt some at first but was only a pin prick by the next morning. And today there'd been no traces of anything. Fortunately, her mother and sisters had experienced similar reactions and, according to Bridget, this was good news. But their dad, who'd remained sequestered in his room these past two days, refused to talk to anyone about the condition of his test. Not even Bridget.

But after praying for both Peter and Dad, Molly felt hopeful as she went into her house. "Hello?" she called out, dropping her book bag at the hall tree.

"In here." It sounded like Bridget.

Molly went into the kitchen where Bridget was just pouring a cup of tea. Molly greeted her as she peeled off her coat, taking a seat at the kitchen table and helping herself to one of the coconut macaroons on the plate in the center. "Mam made Dad's favorite cookies?" She took a bite. "Does that mean we're celebrating?"

"Want some tea?" Bridget asked in a flat tone.

"Sure." Molly looked up at her, knowing the answer before she even asked. "Did you hear from the doctor?"

Bridget nodded solemnly, setting a cup of steaming amber tea in front of Molly and bringing her own cup and saucer to the table as well. "The good news is that you, Margaret, Colleen, Mam, and I are all fine."

"But Dad?"

"Has TB."

Molly's heart sunk. "What does that mean? I mean, I know what it means...Dad has tuberculosis. But what does it mean for Dad? Is there medicine? Will he get better now that we know what's wrong with him?"

"There's no medicine. The only treatment is rest...in a sanatorium."

"What is a sanatorium exactly?"

"A place where TB patients can be isolated—to keep the disease from spreading. TB is very contagious. We're very fortunate no one else contracted it from him." Bridget sighed. "But it's imperative he be kept away from the public."

Molly frowned to imagine her sweet dad locked up in a jail cell type of room. "But what's it like inside a sanatorium? Is it kind of like a prison?"

"No, not at all. At least not the place where Dad will be. It's more like a hotel. But it's a medical facility located at a higher elevation so the patients get fresh clean air and sunshine. Dad will need lots of rest and nutritious food and good nursing care...and in time he'll get better." Bridget looked down at her tea.

"How long does that take?"

Bridget sighed. "A long time."

"A month?"

"More like six months, although it could take a year or more."

Molly felt shocked. A whole year without Dad in the house. And how would they pay for it? "Is the sanatorium terribly expensive?"

"Fortunately, for Dad, it won't be." Bridget scowled. "Dr. Thompson feels guilty about not diagnosing this sooner. Oh, he didn't say as much, but I know he feels responsible that Dad's TB has progressed as much as it has. I'm sure that's why he's arranged to cover most of the expenses for Dad's treatment in a sanatorium in the Sierra Nevadas. He was probably afraid we would sue him for malpractice."

"Oh." Molly stared glumly at her tea. None of this was the kind of news she'd been hoping to hear.

"All things considered, it's not so terrible." Bridget reached for a macaroon.

"How can you possibly say that?" Molly frowned.

Bridget shrugged. "Things could be worse."

"It's just that I was at Old Saint Mary's this afternoon.... I lit a candle and prayed for Dad. And I know it sounds silly, but I really believed God was going to give us a miracle."

"Maybe the miracle is that no one else was infected with TB, Molly. Do you know how horrible that would've been? Imagine if Mam or you or any of us had to be in the sanatorium." Bridget shuddered. "I can barely stand to think about it. And, really, it's good to finally know what's wrong with Dad. It's kind of like a miracle that Dad's treatment expenses will be mostly covered." Bridget's halfhearted smile was not convincing. She was just as worried about Dad as Molly felt. Maybe more so.

But Molly considered Bridget's theory. In a way, her sister was right. Except that this was not the kind of miracle Molly had hoped for. "I prayed for a miracle for Peter too," she said quietly, almost wishing she hadn't. What if Peter's miracle was as disappointing as Dad's?

"Good for you," Bridget told her. "We should all be praying for a miracle for Peter. I've been praying that we'd hear something from the navy soon." She took a sip of tea. "I've heard that other families have received telegrams from the war office...regarding Honolulu. Not good news. But we've heard nothing."

Molly felt a tinge of hope. "Maybe that's good news, Bridget. If we don't get a telegram from the war department, it may mean that Peter is okay."

Bridget finished her tea and, nodding, stood. "Maybe so."

"Where's Mam?"

"With Dad. Packing his stuff."

"When is he going?"

"Dr. Thompson wanted to arrange for a car to pick him up this afternoon, but we insisted on waiting until tomorrow so that everyone can see him and say good-bye. I'll drive him to the sanatorium in the morning."

"Can I go with you?" Molly asked eagerly.

"No. The only reason I can go is because I'm a nurse. Or nearly. We really need to keep Dad away from everyone. Even when you see him to say good-bye, it will have to be from a safe distance."

"Oh. Do Margaret and Colleen know about this yet?"

"I called the store and told Margaret. She's closing early. They should be home any minute now. I told Mam we girls would fix dinner tonight. Margaret's bringing home a rib roast. And Colleen wants to bake an apple pie. Dad won't be able to join us at the table, but we want to make tonight feel happy...for his sake. Mam doesn't want any long faces. She thinks that'll make Dad feel worse. I already warned Margaret." Bridget pointed to a pile of potatoes. "Want to start peeling those for me?"

"Sure." Molly put the last piece of cookie in her mouth, but it now tasted more like sawdust shavings than coconut. She rinsed it down with her tea and then went to work on the potatoes. As she peeled, she wondered what life in the Mulligan house would be like without Dad around. Even though he could sound gruff at times, they all knew it was mostly for show. And before getting sick, his humor had kept them amused on a regular basis. Even when they'd made fun of his silly pun jokes, they had still laughed.

She dropped a peeled potato into the pot of salty water, realizing that without Dad and Peter, they would be a house of five females. And then, after Bridget left—possibly as soon as next month—there would be only four females. And if Colleen married Geoff, like she planned on doing, it was possible that she would move down to San Diego. And then there would be just three of them—Mam and Margaret and her. As much as Molly loved Margaret and Mam, it sounded awfully bleak compared to what their family used to be. Plus, if Margaret got her way, she'd be married to Brian by summer—if not sooner. Then it would be just Molly and Mam. Molly could barely stand to imagine what that would be like.

Molly glanced over to where blackout curtains were still hanging over the kitchen window. Mam had probably been distracted over her worries over Dad and forgotten to take them down. And since it would be dusky in about an hour, there seemed little point in removing them now. But because of the heavy dark curtains, the kitchen felt dim and gloomy...sort of dead. Just one more part of this new "war-era" life—it felt like everything was slowly being blacked out.

As she hurried about the store, getting it ready to close early, Margaret wanted to throw something. Instead, she slammed the front door, turning the lock so firmly that the key got stuck. And instead of trying to ease it out, like she knew she should, she kicked the door so hard that the glass rattled and the bell jingled.

"Do you need help?" Colleen asked.

"*No*, I do *not!*" Margaret gritted her teeth, twisting and tugging on the stubborn key.

"Excuse me." Colleen reached past her, gently jiggling the key before she turned it and slipped it out of the lock. "Here." She dropped the brass key in Margaret's hand.

"Thanks," Margaret growled. "Let's go."

"I'm ready when you are," Colleen said.

"How can you be so cheerful?" Margaret demanded as she reached for her coat. "Oh, yes, I remember now. Colleen's world is wonderful. She's engaged to a navy pilot and—"

"Geoff isn't a navy pilot yet." Colleen pulled on bone colored leather glove.

"Even so!" Margaret glared at her younger sister. "It's all just so unfair."

"What is unfair?" Colleen asked as they made their way to the backroom, turning off the lights as they went.

"*Nothing!*" Margaret followed Colleen out, pausing to lock the backdoor, making sure not to get the key stuck again. As they got in the car, Margaret attempted to compose herself. It wasn't prudent to drive in an angry state of mind. Peter had told her that once.

"What's wrong?" Colleen asked in a surprisingly gentle tone. "I mean, besides this news about Dad, which isn't good, but it's not unexpected either. Bridget warned us that he would probably test positive for TB. And at least Dr. Thompson is paying for his care. Or most of it."

"It's not just that," Margaret snapped back at her. So much for controlling her anger.

"What then?"

"It's *everything.*"

"Oh...right." Colleen let out a long sigh. "I'm well aware that it's been a bad week. And I suppose it was insensitive of me to get engaged...and to have the gall to be happy about it."

Margaret rolled her eyes. "Well, you have to admit that your happiness is sort of...well, it's sort of a slap in the face to some of us."

"Really? That's how you feel about Geoff and me? Like our engagement is a slap in your face?" Colleen sounded slightly indignant now.

"You know that I've been waiting for Brian to propose to me, Colleen. Wouldn't you think that I'd be less than enthused to see my baby sister getting a big diamond ring first? But, really, that's just one part of it. I mean, think about it—first the news about Peter... and then Dad. What's next? Remember what Mam always says, how trouble comes in threes? So which member of our family will be struck down next? Bridget perhaps? She's heading out the battlefield the first chance she gets. What if something happens to—"

"Oh, Margaret, don't go looking for trouble."

"I'm just saying what everyone else is probably thinking."

"You really need to stop being so overly dramatic." Colleen chuckled. "Besides, that's usually my job. Remember?"

Margaret still hadn't turned the key in the ignition. And now, with tears filling her eyes, she was afraid she wouldn't be able to see well enough to drive safely. "It's just that—that I'm so upset—about everything, Colleen. I just—just don't think I can go home and put on a happy face—like Mam wants and—" Her words were choked out by sobs.

"Oh, Margaret." Colleen reached over to hug her. "I'm sorry this is so hard on you."

"It's just that—no—nothing is going right."

"Poor Margaret." Colleen patted her back. "I always expect you to be the strong one. You're always so controlled and responsible and reliable. I sometimes forget that you have feelings too. I'm sorry you're feeling so sad."

"And I feel selfish for some of my feelings," Margaret confessed. "I'm upset that Brian probably won't propose to me now that he's decided to enlist in the service. And yet that seems such a small thing compared to—compared to Peter and Dad."

"But it's a big thing to you, Margaret." Colleen opened her car door. "Now you need to get out and let me drive. You're in no condition to be behind the wheel."

Margaret didn't even argue with her as she got out and switched seats. "Just be careful, please," she muttered from the passenger's side.

"I will." Colleen started the engine and cautiously backed out. "I am actually a very good driver," she said. "Geoff tested me out before he let me drive his car."

"I still don't see why you didn't want to keep Geoff's car like he'd suggested." Margaret got out her handkerchief to wipe her tears.

"Dad was right. We really don't have room to park two cars at home. Besides, I didn't think Mrs. Conrad liked the idea of me having her son's car." She made a little groan. "She wouldn't even let me drive it when I returned to the farm to get her. Of course, it was probably because she was mad that Geoff hadn't let her come with us to the city, to tell him good-bye. Anyway, she insisted on taking his car keys when I drove the car back to the farm. I honestly thought she was going to make me walk back to the city, Margaret."

"What? That's awful."

"When I explained that she either had to drive me home or I would be keeping his car, she got in the car. But it was the most unpleasant experience, Margaret. The silence was so thick I really could've cut it with a knife. And when Mrs. Conrad dropped me off at our house, she didn't even say good-bye."

"She sounds terribly rude."

"She is." Colleen poked Margaret in the arm. "Be thankful that *your* in-laws are so sweet. You're so lucky to get the Hammonds."

"That's true." She blew her nose. "Well, that is if Brian and I ever do get married. Did you know that he finished his exams on Wednesday? But he didn't want to come home until Saturday? I bet he doesn't even want to see me." She felt the tears coming again.

"He's probably busy, Maggie. Give him time. He'll come around."

"I don't know." She sniffed. "What if he found someone else?"

"Brian loves you," Colleen assured her.

"I thought he did."

"He does!" Colleen insisted. "Why else would he be willing to wait all these years to marry you?"

"I thought I was the one waiting on him." Margaret sighed.

"He was waiting too."

"I just feel so confused right now." Margaret took in a deep breath, trying to steady herself, especially since they were nearly home now.

"Everything is just a little out of balance these days," Colleen said philosophically. "I think we all need to be ready for the unexpected with this war. It's like the Axis have knocked the whole world off its axis." She laughed. "Hey, that's pretty good, don't you think?"

"It sounds like a pun Dad would make. At least when he was healthy, anyway."

"So, speaking of Dad, we really do need to put on our party faces tonight, Maggie. Do you think you'll be all right? I could drive around a little bit if you need more time."

Margaret pursed her lips. "I think I'm okay now." She glanced at

Colleen, realizing that her little sister had not only been a comfort just now, but her driving had been much better than usual too. Maybe she was growing up. Maybe that was one potential benefit of this war. It would force all the Mulligan girls to grow up.

Thirteen

Although she had kept her thoughts to herself, the happy-family dinner party had felt like a complete sham to Bridget last night. But, really, what were their options? And at least they had all given it their full effort and now, thankfully, the charade was over.

As Bridget drove toward the mountains with her dad, sleeping like a baby amidst the blankets and pillows she'd padded into the backseat, she wondered at the role she'd been recently given by her family. With Peter and Dad both out of the picture, it felt like the others were now looking to Bridget for direction. Of course, it made sense because she was the oldest of the girls. Plus she was competent with medical issues, like the one they'd faced today. But she had no intention of taking over as the *head* of the family. It wasn't that she wouldn't be capable. It was simply not practical.

Bridget knew she'd be shipping out of the country in about a month. She'd be far from home and unable to help with much of anything. Someone else would have to take the leadership position. Ideally, she felt, it should be Mam. Except that their mother never seemed overly strong. Even when Dad first got sick, Mam had been reluctant to take the reins. Bridget figured that was simply because their dad had always been such a sturdy father figure. And although Mam was good at following his lead, she was not ideally suited to take over for him. For starters, Mam seemed to have difficulty making even some of the simplest decisions.

That had been made painfully clear this morning when she couldn't even decide which blankets to give Bridget for Dad's makeshift bed in the car. Mam, worried about TB germs, had already started to launder the bedding from their bedroom. And she seemed worried about "infecting" other pieces of bedding. As distressed as their mother was about her husband's illness, she almost seemed relieved that he was going. Of course, Bridget knew this was out of concern for the rest of the family. Finally, Bridget had simply ripped the bedding from her own bed, promising her mother that she'd wash it herself when she got back. Really!

Bridget glanced at the rearview mirror, relieved to see her dad was still sleeping peacefully. She knew this was due to the barbiturate Dr. Thompson had prescribed for the three-hour journey. He had recognized Mr. Mulligan's anxiety yesterday, his reluctance to being "locked up" in a sanatorium for so long. Who could blame him?

She just hoped that Dad would be awake enough for her to tell him good-bye at the sanatorium. But if not, she'd already made a note for him. Perhaps that would be the easier way. Poor Dad.

It was close to noon when Bridget pulled in front of the sanatorium, and Dad was still soundly sleeping. Even getting out of the car didn't rouse him. Grateful for the opportunity to go inside and explain the situation, Bridget was relieved when the head nurse ordered her to remain in the waiting room to fill out Dad's paperwork. Meanwhile the nurse got a pair of orderlies and a stretcher, and it wasn't long before Dad, still sleeping, was wheeled past.

Bridget got the personal belongings that he'd been allowed to bring and, sticking her note on top, she left them at the front desk. "Is it possible for me to look around?" Bridget explained that she was a registered nurse, "or almost," and that she just wanted to see the place from a professional perspective. And, although that was partly true, she mostly wanted to be sure she was leaving her dad in a good place.

A quick tour revealed that the facility was clean and well-managed. The staff appeared professional yet caring. And, although the patients seemed glum—which wasn't surprising—they were bundled up in sturdy beds that had been rolled onto an exterior veranda that overlooked the snowcapped mountains. All in all, it was not bad. Certainly not a prison like Molly had feared. Bridget would be able to reassure her family that Dad was in good hands.

Finally, satisfied that there was nothing more to do here and seeing that her dad was still resting comfortably, Bridget left. But as she drove away from the sanatorium, she wept. No, it was not very nurse-like behavior, but she couldn't help it. As senseless as it seemed, she felt like a neglectful mother who had just abandoned her sickly child. But she knew that there were no other options. From this point on, when it came to her father's health, all she could do was pray. As she drove home, she not only prayed for Dad to get well, but that someone in the medical field would discover the cure for tuberculosis. Soon!

Molly didn't know what to do about her mother. Margaret and Colleen had gone to work at the store and, although Molly had longed to join them—especially since she knew they could use an extra set of hands on a Saturday—Margaret had insisted that, with all the disinfecting that needed to be done, Mam had needed her more.

But now it was nearly noon and her mother was still crying. Oh, she was trying to hide it from Molly. She was quietly holed up in her bedroom, where she'd been supposedly "getting rid of the tuberculosis germs." But when Molly peeked into the bedroom, she saw her mother sitting in the chair with a heap of Dad's clothes piled around her on the floor, and a limp striped tie dangling from her hands, silent tears streaming down her cheeks.

Molly didn't know what more she could say, what more she could do, and so she quietly closed the door then went straight to the telephone. Without even pausing to think about it, she dialed the Hammonds' phone number and quickly explained her dilemma to Mrs. Hammond. "I'm sorry to trouble you, but I just don't know—"

"Don't you worry about troubling me, child. I'm on my way," she said gently. "It's no wonder your dear mother is upset."

Feeling guilty for tying up the telephone line, even for less than two minutes, Molly quickly hung up. For the past week, due to Dad's insistence, they'd all avoided the telephone like the plague. And even though Dad was gone, it still felt right to continue doing so. For all she knew Peter might try to call them today. Oh, she hoped so!

Before long, Mrs. Hammond arrived and, after a bit, managed to coax Molly's mother to take a walk with her. "And then you'll come home with me for lunch," she said as she helped Mam into her winter coat.

Molly mouthed *thank you* to Mrs. Hammond and then, greatly relieved to have her mother out of the house and in the hands of a caring friend, Molly returned to the long list of disinfecting tasks that Bridget had made for them last night.

It was around two o'clock when the doorbell interrupted Molly from mopping the floor of her parents' bedroom. Since she was the only one at home, she dropped the mop and hurried to answer it. A fellow not much older than her dressed in a Western Union uniform was standing on the stoop, a telegram in his hand. Molly felt her heart lurch as she remembered how her mother had reacted to a similar delivery man bicycling down their street just yesterday afternoon. "What do you want?" Molly asked him.

"Telegram for Mr. and Mrs. Mulligan," he solemnly announced.

"They're not here," Molly declared. She suddenly wished this redheaded young man would disappear—along with the telegram in his hand.

"Can you sign for this, please?" He held out his pad, waiting for her to sign.

"I—uh—I don't—"

"If I don't deliver it now, I might not be able to get back until—"

"Yes, yes," she breathlessly agreed. "I'll sign." With trembling fingers, she grabbed the pencil and signed on the line he pointed to. And then, feeling sick inside, she took the thin paper envelope from his hand.

"I, uh, I'm sorry if it's not good news," he mumbled. Then turning away, he hurried down the steps and hopped onto his bicycle.

Molly just stood there, watching him ride away into the gray San Francisco fog. For a moment, she wondered if she were overreacting. Perhaps this telegram was *good* news. It was possible. But the young man had said he was sorry... Did he know that this telegram carried bad news? She bit her lower lip and, blinking back tears, stared down at the yellow envelope. What to do? What to do?

Without closing the front door, she returned to the house and, walking around in a foggy daze, roamed from room to room as if she thought some family member might be lurking in a closet until she realized—she was alone. She looked down at the telegram again, wondering if she should just open it, but then seeing her parents' names in bold print, she knew that would be wrong.

As she went to the phone, she considered calling her mother at the Hammonds', but remembering Mam's state of mind this morning, Molly decided to call the store instead. Margaret would know what to do. She could handle whatever this was. But the store's phone line was busy. Molly slowly counted to twenty then tried again. Still busy. Probably a longwinded customer placing a delivery order.

Molly hung up the receiver with a loud clang that echoed through the house. She stared at the telegram—yellow was such a happy color. Shouldn't it contain happy news? Maybe the delivery boy had simply assumed it was something bad. Really, he was only a delivery boy, how should he know what was inside a private message? What if the telegram was from Peter? What if he'd sent it to reassure them that he was just fine? It was possible. Maybe he'd been unable to communicate with them sooner because he'd been injured and convalescing in a hospital. Or perhaps he'd been shipped out into active service on the high seas.

She picked up the phone again, but instead of calling the store, she dialed the Hammonds' number and to her relief, she heard Patrick's voice on the other end. She quickly blurted out the upsetting news of the telegram delivery and how she didn't want to upset her mother, but felt she needed to tell her. "It may be from Peter," she said hopefully. "Informing us he's okay." She waited, but when Patrick said nothing, her chest tightened. "Patrick? Are you still there? Can you hear—"

"Yes, yes," he assured her. "I'm here. Sorry about that, Molly. So... you didn't open the telegram?"

"No, of course not. It's for Mam and Dad."

"Let me get your mother," he said quickly. "Hold on."

As she waited, Molly felt her heart racing all over again. *What if it was bad news?*

"Molly?" Patrick's tone was urgent. "Your mother wants you to open the telegram and read it to her over the phone. Can you do that?"

"Yes. Of course. But I need to set the phone down to open it." With shaky hands, she used the ivory letter opener to carefully slit open the telegram and then, without looking at the words that appeared pasted inside, she picked up the receiver.

"Molly?" her mother was saying with urgency. "Are you there?"

"Yes." Molly stared down at the telegram then, and seeing the first sentence and the words *deeply regrets*, she let out a scream. "Oh, no!"

"Molly? What is it?" Mam demanded. "Tell me."

"It's—it's about Peter." Molly's voice cracked with emotion.

"Read it to me!"

Molly's voice sounded low and gruff as she solemnly read the words of the despicable telegram, but she burst into tears before she could finish the last sentence. Not that it mattered. Her mother's cries and sobs were so loud, Molly knew she was no longer listening.

December 12, 1941

The US Navy Department deeply regrets to inform you that your son Peter James Mulligan, Seaman First Class, USN was lost in action in the performance of his duty and in the service of his country. The department extends to you its sincerest sympathy in your great loss. To prevent possible aid to our enemies please do not divulge the name of his ship or station. If remains are recovered they will be interred temporarily in the locality where death occurred and you will be notified accordingly.

"*Molly!*" Patrick was on the other end again. "Are you okay?

Molly?"

Molly could no longer speak—all she could do was cry out her brother's name. "Peter! Peter! Peter!"

"I'm on my way," Patrick said firmly. "Hang up the phone, Molly. Just sit down. Take some deep breaths. I'll be there in a flash."

She mechanically did as instructed. Falling onto her father's favorite armchair, she collapsed into uncontrollable sobs, crying so hard that her whole body shook, and she felt certain she would never be able to stop.

She didn't look up as Patrick entered their house or protest when he gathered her up in his arms, carrying her like a baby out to his car. She continued sobbing as he drove to his parents' house, and she was still shaking violently as he gently deposited her onto the front room sofa where Mrs. Hammond was waiting. Mrs. Hammond hugged and rocked her like a newborn, insisting she drink some milk and swallow a pill. Molly could hear her mother crying in another room.

Fourteen

B y the time Molly woke up, she suspected by the blackout curtains blocking the windows that it must be nighttime—and that
she was still on the Hammonds' front room sofa. Feeling slightly
blurry and confused, Molly sat up and looked around.

"You're awake," Patrick said quietly.

She blinked and nodded. "What time is it?" she asked in a hoarse
whisper.

"Nearly eight."

"I've been asleep all this time?"

"You were so upset that Mom gave you one of her sleeping pills.
I don't think it was such a good idea. It obviously knocked you for
a loop."

Molly sighed deeply, trying to remember the events of the afternoon—but only one fact seemed to matter. "I can't believe it. That
Peter is...*dead.*" She whispered the last word.

Patrick sat down across from her, his hands hanging between his
knees with the saddest expression she had ever seen on his face. He
slowly shook his head. "I can't believe it either."

She remembered the first sentence of the telegram—almost word
for word. "Do you—do you think it could be a mistake?" she asked
with a splinter of hope. "Is it possible that...?"

"Anything is possible." But the flatness in his voice told her the truth. He believed the words in the telegram were true. And despite the longing in her heart, she did too.

"I've lost my only brother." She felt her eyes misting up as she looked at Patrick, absorbing the fact that he could be hurting as much as she. "And you've lost your best friend."

He simply nodded.

Molly pushed the crocheted afghan off of her legs, swinging her legs down to the floor. Her family would be in pain too. She should be with them. "Where are my shoes? I need to go home." She stood up but, feeling lightheaded, starting to tumble.

Patrick leaped from his chair to catch her. "Easy there, Molly Girl."

His words sounded just like Peter—and once again she broke into sobs. Not as uncontrollable as before, but just the same, she couldn't stop. Patrick continued to hold her, steadying her, and gently stroking her head—just like Peter would do when he wanted to comfort her. "We're going to be okay, Molly," he said in a husky voice. "We're going to make it through this...somehow. We've just got to be strong."

Molly took in a deep breath and stepped back. "I know." She sniffed, trying to get control, not wanting to act like a baby.

He picked up a fresh handkerchief from a side table, handing it to her. "But it'll take time...and effort." He went over to get her saddle shoes, handing them to her one at a time, waiting as she slipped them on and tied them. "I'll take you home."

"Thanks." She looked around the dimly lit room. "Where are your parents?"

"At your house. Mom made dinner for your family. They already ate, but everyone is there now. Even Brian. Margaret picked him up at the train station this afternoon."

"I need to be with them." Molly glanced around. "Did I have a coat? I can hardly remember now. Except that you, well, carried me out of my house. Uh, thanks."

"I forgot to grab your coat. But I'll find something for you to wear home."

Molly felt numb as she stood by the front door waiting for him. She could feel an aching hole inside of her...for Peter. But it was a strange consolation to have Patrick helping her like this. In a way, it was like having Peter here, and she was grateful.

"How about this?" Patrick held out his red and white letterman jacket from high school. It was identical to the one that Peter used to wear. "It'll be too big, but it'll keep you warm." As he slid it over her shoulders, the satin lining felt cool yet comforting.

"Thanks," she murmured as she fastened the snaps down the front.

"I can drive if you want," he offered as he opened the door. "Or we can walk."

"Yes...I think maybe I'd like to walk." Even though she knew she should be with her family, it would be so hard. Everyone would be distraught—she could hardly imagine how much grief must be filling the Mulligan house right now. She wasn't even sure she could face it.

"Maybe we can talk about Peter while we walk." He paused on the front stoop, giving them time to adjust to the darkness.

"I'd like that."

"Be careful on the steps. It's so dark you can barely see them." He took her arm, looping it around his own as he guided her down to the sidewalk. But once they were on the sidewalk, he continued to keep her arm tucked snugly into his. Again, it was a comfort... and it reminded her of her brother.

"Peter was my best friend for as far back as I can remember,"

Patrick said as they walked. "And even though he was only five months older than me, I looked up to him like a big brother. He was always strong and brave...and wise."

"He was wise," Molly agreed. "He always had the best advice. Out of anyone in my family, even Mam and Dad, if I had a problem or question, I'd usually go to Peter. And he always seemed to have time for me. And even though he was protective of me, he never treated me like a baby." She sighed. "I guess it was no secret that out of my siblings, Peter was always my favorite."

"I'll tell you a secret."

"What?"

"You were Peter's favorite too."

"Really?"

"Absolutely. I heard him say it more than once, Molly. He told me you were special. He saw something in you that stood out."

Molly didn't even know what to say, but Patrick's words touched her deeply, and eventually she spoke. "I will treasure that always, Patrick. Thank you. And I'm not just saying this because of what you said, but because I know Peter loved you like a brother. It showed in his face and his voice whenever you popped over to our house. In fact, I remember feeling a little jealous. I was afraid he liked you more than me."

Patrick gave her arm a squeeze. "We were lucky to have him, Molly. Even if it was for just a short time."

"I know."

"And as hard as it is to accept this, I do believe that God knows the number of our days. And whether we can understand it or not—at least this side of heaven—God is in control."

Molly felt uncertain. She stopped walking and peered up at him, barely seeing his features in the darkness. "Do you believe that God controlled the Japanese planes that dropped the bombs on Peter's ship?"

He blew out a loud sigh. "Now, that's a tough question, Molly. But here's what I believe...first of all, I believe the Japanese forces did an evil thing and—"

"Then why didn't God stop them?"

"I believe it's because God allows us to have the freedom to choose. The Japanese chose to do evil. But beyond that, I believe that if God had wanted Peter to survive the sinking of the *Arizona*, he would've done it."

"Then why didn't he?" she demanded.

"I'm afraid that's one of those questions that won't get answered on this side of heaven."

"You sound just like Peter."

"I'll take that as a compliment."

"You remind me a lot of him," she said quietly. "And I'm sorry to sound so doubtful about these things. I really don't want to question God. But it's so hard to figure this stuff out."

"I know. I feel the same way. I mean, Peter was a special guy, and I can understand why God might want him with him in heaven. But, personally, well, I think we could've used him down here even more."

She nodded firmly. "That is exactly how I feel."

"And just for the record, I don't think it's wrong to feel like that. I think God must understand."

For some reason this was reassuring. They walked in silence for a while, and Molly ran these ideas through her head. And then Patrick started talking about Peter again and they took turns, sharing various memories. Although some of her pain was lessening, she still had a deep ache inside her chest.

"I just can't imagine life without him in it," Molly declared when they were about a block from her house. "It feels so dark and bleak. Like the night will never end and the sun will never rise again."

"I know what you mean. But they say it's always the darkest before the dawn, Molly. I'll admit I've never felt such darkness. It's as if the whole world is experiencing a giant blackout. And when I think that there are thousands of loved ones feeling the same kind of anguish we're feeling right now—and that's just for Pearl Harbor. But our country's involvement has barely begun. You can be sure there will be a lot more pain and grief before it's over with."

Molly turned to look at Patrick and, unable to make out his expression in the darkness, a shock of fear ran through her. "Oh, Patrick, I almost forgot that you're getting ready to ship out too." Using both hands, she clutched tightly to his arm as if she could keep him from going. "What if something happens to you too?"

"Nothing is going to happen to me," he firmly told her.

"How can you say that?" She gasped. "Peter said the exact same thing, Patrick. He was so certain. Please, don't say nothing will happen. It may be bad luck."

"No, I think it's good luck. Nothing bad will happen to me," he declared. "It's like lightning doesn't strike the same place twice. I'll be fine, Molly. I know it deep down. So, please, don't worry."

"How can I not worry?"

"Well then, when you feel worried for me, why don't you pray?"

"Like I prayed for Peter?" she challenged him. "How did that help anything?"

"I'm sure Peter appreciated your prayers," Patrick said gently. "And don't forget that Peter must be very happy—in heaven—right now."

"I know I'm being selfish," she admitted. "Peter probably is happier in heaven. But I still wish he were here. And I wish you hadn't joined the navy. And I wish there was no such *thing* as war!"

"And 'if wishes were fishes, we'd all have a fry.'"

Despite her gloom, Molly almost smiled. "Peter used to say that same thing."

Patrick stopped walking just a house down from the Mulligans'. "Peter told me something before he left for Hawaii. I hadn't planned to tell you, but I guess I will now."

"What?" she asked eagerly.

"Well, Peter didn't know that I was going to follow his lead and join the navy too. We didn't even know for sure that the US would actually enter the war. But before Peter shipped out for Honolulu, he told me he was concerned about leaving you behind. I think he knew you would miss him a lot. And he was more worried about you than for your sisters or your parents. So anyway, he asked me to help keep tabs on you while he was away."

"He did?" It was a bittersweet sort of comfort, but a comfort all the same.

"Yep. And I gave him my word, Molly." He sighed. "And I plan to keep my promise...somehow."

"Thanks, Patrick. I do appreciate it." Of course, she knew he'd be gone soon... His promise to Peter would be broken.

"I'm aware it'll be difficult to keep close tabs on you while I'm in the navy, Molly. So I'm thinking that maybe you and I can stay connected through letters. Do you think you'd like to write to me when I'm overseas?"

"I *love* writing letters," she eagerly told him. "I wrote to Peter all the time." She sighed. "I kept on writing...even after the Japanese attacked Pearl Harbor."

"I know. So anyway, I promise to stay in touch. I'll answer every letter you write to me—although it might take awhile for my letters to make it to you. I'm not sure how reliable overseas mail will be. But it'd be great to hear from you. You can keep me posted on all the happenings with your school and the store...and your parents and your sisters."

"I'll do that," she agreed. "I promise." At the mention of her sisters, Molly remembered Bridget...and how her parents, as well as the Hammonds, hoped that Bridget and Patrick might marry one day. "And I plan to write to Bridget too," she told him. "And maybe you'll be writing to her yourself, but in case you don't or in case she doesn't write back too regularly, well, I can keep you informed of what she's doing and where she's stationed and everything."

"Great! You can be like my personal home-front war-time correspondent," he said as they went up the steps to her house. "I'm already looking forward to your letters."

As Molly reached for the doorknob, unsure of what they would find within the walls of her house and bracing herself for more sadness and tears, she suddenly faced an even more troubling question—what would this news do to Dad?

On Sunday afternoon, Bridget had found herself making the trip into the mountains once again. But this time, her mother and three sisters joined her. And if yesterday's journey had seemed sad, this one was a thousand times worse. Her family was in deep pain and, although she was supposed to be a "healer," there was nothing she could do to alleviate their anguish.

Few words had been said since leaving San Francisco. And, in a way, it was a relief to her. Especially after last night. So many tears... so much deep sorrow...so much agony. Bridget had remained fairly cool, exercising more self-control than any of them. Something that would make her profession proud—but at the same time made her feel guilty. She had barely shed a tear at the news of her brother's death. When the phone call came to the store in midafternoon, Margaret and Colleen had instantly gone to pieces. Meanwhile, Bridget had politely but firmly ushered the customers out, explaining it was a family emergency, then locked the front door. With her sisters sobbing inconsolably in the backseat, Bridget had driven them home.

But she had not cried. Bridget told herself it was because she had already known he was gone. In her heart she had known that Peter did not survive the sinking of the *Arizona*. From the moment Virginia had told her, Bridget had intuitively believed it was true. But with so much going on, she was unable to share it with anyone in her family, and so she'd had to bear it alone. Hoping against hope that she was wrong, Bridget had simply buried it deep within her. As if her denial would make it so. Then, even as she'd held the wrinkled telegram in her hands yesterday, slowly reading and rereading the words, she had been unable to cry.

Instead, she had argued with her mother.

"He has the right to know!" Mam declared.

"But it may slow down his healing," Bridget protested, knowing that it could be worse than that. Bad news like this could kill him!

"But I promised Riley," Mam told her. "I told him, one way or another, I would let him know any news about Peter. I will not break my word to him."

Despite Bridget's urging, Mam had made her decision last night. She wanted the family to tell Dad this sad news in person. Bridget knew it wouldn't be easy but agreed with her mother—it would be better to have his family around when he heard the news. After dinner, Bridget had called Dr. Thompson, interrupting his bridge game but insisting it was an emergency. She'd solemnly informed him of Peter's demise and Mam's insistence to tell Dad.

Dr. Thompson had been sympathetic and had even agreed to call the sanatorium. Due to the circumstances, the doctor in charge had agreed to their request. Dr. Thompson had called back shortly afterward, informing Bridget that the Mulligans would be allowed one hour together in an isolation room. "But with no personal contact with Riley," he had warned her. "We are bending the rules as it is."

Bridget had promised to keep her family in line, but now that they were waiting for the nurse to bring Dad to see them, she was not so sure she could keep that promise. And seeing Dad's hopeful smile as the nurse pushed his wheelchair into the isolation room where his family was waiting, she felt her heart breaking all over again.

Clearly, her dad assumed this was purely a social visit—a pleasant surprise! But his smile soon vanished when he noticed their somber expressions. Dad was no fool. He knew all was not well.

"What's wrong?" he demanded. "What has happened? Tell me!"

"It's Peter." Mam handed him the telegram, reaching for her handkerchief. "He's, he's—" She broke into fresh tears, and Molly, bless her heart, wrapped her arms around her to comfort her.

"Wh—what?" Dad stared at the rumpled piece of paper. "Peter?"

"Peter didn't make it, Dad." Bridget's fingers knotted together. "We just heard about it yesterday afternoon."

"We've lost him." Margaret's voice cracked with emotion. "Our Peter is gone."

Dad's whole face seemed to crumble as he broke into tears, and despite Bridget's warnings to her family, Colleen ran to him, wrapping her arms around his shoulders. And before long, they were all clustered around him. Once again, everyone was crying. Everyone except Bridget, although she tried to appear as if she were.

To her relief, their sobs were less emotional than last night, but, other than Bridget, there wasn't a dry eye in the room. Even Dad's nurse dabbed at her eyes—and never once told them to keep a distance from her patient.

"We're not supposed to have contact," Bridget reminded her sisters and mother. "I promised Dr. Stratton we'd keep our distance."

"Yes, yes," the nurse agreed. "That's true."

"I cannot believe it." Dad used the disposable tissues provided by his nurse to wipe his eyes. "Peter...*gone?* It doesn't seem possible."

And now, like they'd done last night, they talked about Peter, sharing favorite memories and saying how brave and strong he was, and how they would have to be strong and brave now too. They all expressed how Peter would always be their hero and how they would try to make him proud. When the doctor tapped on the glass door and pointed to his watch, Bridget announced that their one-hour visit was up.

"I'm sorry to interrupt," the balding doctor told Bridget as she opened the door. She introduced Dr. Stratton to her family, and he shook Mam's hand. "I'm so very sorry for your loss, ma'am." He glumly shook his head. "Clearly your family is facing some hard trials these days. You have my deepest sympathy."

"It is true...we are amidst hard times," Dad said firmly. "But we are the Mulligans—and in honor of the memory of my only son, Peter James Mulligan, we will be strong too. We will make our boy as proud of us as we have been of him. Peter gave his life for our country—and in our own ways we will all give of ourselves too. Maybe not on the battlefield, and hopefully not with our lives."

"That's right," Molly declared. "We will all do our part for the war effort."

"We most certainly will." Dad nodded to the doctor then pointed at Bridget. "Our Bridget here is going to be an army nurse." Now he pointed to Colleen. "And this one is engaged to a navy pilot. Or nearly a navy pilot." Dad started to cough now. He was obviously tired, and Bridget hoped he would be resting soon.

"And that's not all." Colleen pointed at Margaret. "Her beau is going to serve as well," she declared. "He'll ship out after Christmas."

"And there's Patrick too," Molly added. "He's almost like family. And he's going into the navy right after Christmas too. Everyone will be doing their part."

"I can tell that you Mulligans are a force to be reckoned with," Dr. Stratton said. "But if Dad is going to get well, you'll have to abide by our rules from now on. No more family visits. Your father needs his rest."

Bridget knew Dad was more than a little worn out. Despite his bravado, he looked gray and his cough sounded worse. "Don't worry," she assured the doctor. "We plan to abide by your rules. All we want is for Dad to get well."

Good-byes were said, with kisses blown from a cautious distance as the nurse, accompanied by the doctor, wheeled their father away.

"Oh, dear." Mam let out a little choked sob. "I'm glad Riley is being so brave about this—probably for our benefit. But I fear he'll be in deep grief as soon as the reality of everything sets in. I hope and I pray it's not his undoing." She shook her forefinger at her daughters. "And you girls remember to pray your rosaries for your dear old dad—morning, noon, and night."

"Why don't we pray for him right now?" Molly suggested.

"Yes," Margaret agreed. "Let's all say a silent prayer for Dad." And right then and there, they Mulligan women all bowed their heads and silently prayed.

But as they walked back to the car, Bridget knew that her mother's fear was legitimate. Wasn't it exactly what Bridget had attempted to tell her last night? She'd learned it in school—patients always recovered more swiftly and completely when they remained in good spirits. If Dad should allow this sad news about his only son to pull him down, it could very well take him to the depths. And where would they all be then?

"We need to plan some ways to stay in touch with Dad while he's in the sanatorium," she told her family as she drove toward San Francisco. "Ways to encourage him. I think we should send letters and packages regularly—at least for two or three months—to help him get past this. I won't be able to help much since I'll be busy with the ANC. But would someone else like to organize this?"

"I will!" Molly offered eagerly.

"Perfect," Bridget told her. "It's in your hands, Molly." And she knew that, of all of them, Molly was the one who would follow this through. Molly would do all that she could to encourage their dad. She might be the baby of the family, but this girl with her heart of gold could be trusted.

Fifteen

M argaret removed yesterday's page from the daily calendar next to the cash register and sighed. "Can you believe Christmas is only four days away?" she said absently as she tidied up the countertop. Knowing the store would be extra busy with Christmas around the corner, Margaret had brought both Colleen and Molly with her this morning, coming early to get the store ready for a busy Saturday. She could've used Bridget too, but everyone felt she should remain home with Mam, who was still deeply grieving. Plus, Bridget needed time to study for her board exams, which were less than three weeks away. But at least Jimmy was coming in for a few hours today. That would help.

"It sure doesn't feel like Christmastime to me." Molly stopped sweeping, leaning onto the broom handle with a sad expression.

"Christmas will definitely be different for our family this year." Colleen paused from straightening up the colorful packages of Christmas candy on the promotional display shelf.

"Maybe we should just cancel it altogether," Margaret suggested. "I mean, for our family. Who would care?"

"I wouldn't care," Molly glumly agreed. "But it's not just Christmas, Margaret. Nothing is the same anymore. Nothing's like it used to be. And it feels like everything is going to keep changing... and changing and changing."

"A lot has happened these past couple of weeks." Colleen adjusted the smiling Santa Claus image on top of the display.

"That is an understatement." Margaret checked her watch to see that they still had about ten minutes before opening time. Despite the unwelcome idea of the "happy holidays," she'd been grateful for the busyness in the store. Waiting on customers was highly preferable to missing Peter. She grabbed the feather duster, busying herself with dusting the dry goods shelf and trying not to think about her brother.

But not thinking about Peter seemed to simply remind her of Brian Hammond. And that was another thing she wanted to block from her mind. Because from what Margaret could see, her old beau had no intention of proposing marriage to her anytime soon. Perhaps never.

Brian had been home for a full week now, but he clearly had no interest in spending any time with her. She continued moving around the store, carelessly swooshing the feather duster back and forth. Margaret had only been alone with him once since he'd come home, and that was only because she'd picked him up at the train station. To be fair, Brian's neglect might have something to do with her, although that seemed a paltry excuse. But between running the store, which had been busier than ever this past week, combined with her family's recent difficulties, including Peter's funeral yesterday, there had been little time for much of anything or anyone else.

She tossed the feather duster beneath the counter then reached for the glass cleaner and cloth, heading for the meat case. Even so... it did not feel like Brian was even trying. It all seemed to add up to one thing—*Brian had fallen out of love with her.* But he didn't want to admit it. Naturally, he would be reluctant to hurt her when he knew she was still grieving over Peter. But she wished he'd just get it over with. Although she had nothing to base this on, she suspected that some pretty college coed had stolen Brian's heart. But it seemed that he could, at the very least, just tell her!

"Bridget offered to work for me on Christmas Eve day," Colleen said as Margaret furiously scrubbed the smudged glass front of the meat case. "I forgot to tell you."

"Why can't *you* work that day?" Margaret asked sharply. She stood up straight, instantly regretting her tone. Why was she snipping at Colleen? Especially considering how hard Colleen had been working at the store recently.

But Colleen seemed unruffled. "I just learned that Geoff has a few days of leave for Christmas. He asked me to join his family out on the farm for Christmas Eve."

Of course, this just aggravated Margaret further. Why should Colleen gallivant about with her beau while other people were in pain? "What about *our* family?" she demanded.

"Geoff and I plan to spend Christmas Day with our family," Colleen assured her.

"But Christmas Eve?" Molly shook the broom at Colleen. "Our house already feels empty without Dad and—and Peter. But now you too?"

"She's right," Margaret agreed. "It'll be bleak enough as is...one less person will make it far worse."

"But you'll have the Hammonds there with you," Colleen reminded her. "That will fill the house up just fine."

"It won't be the same," Molly declared stubbornly.

Colleen tweaked one of Molly's pigtails. "I'm sorry, sweetie, but that's the way the cookie crumbles."

"I don't like crumbly cookies." Molly scowled as she snatched her braid back from Colleen's fingers.

"Tell you what." Colleen smirked at Molly. "I'll see if Geoff and I can make a late showing at our house. Would that work for you?"

Molly nodded glumly. "I guess so."

"But on one condition." Colleen winked at Margaret like she was concocting a plan with her, although Margaret had no idea what she meant.

Molly frowned. "What?"

"You have to let me do your hair, little sis. I get to make you look more like a sixteen-year-old—and less like a six-year-old."

"I'm not sixteen yet," Molly protested. "Besides, I do *not* look like a six-year-old!"

Despite her gloomy mood, Margaret felt amused. "I must agree with Colleen, Molly." She waved her hand from Molly's head down to her toes. "Pigtails, denim coveralls, and saddle-shoes—how old are you?"

"I planned to work in the backroom today, cutting meat and cleaning vegetables," Molly protested. "Did you expect me to wear a dress?"

"Even so, you still look like a juvenile most of the time." Margaret had been chiding Molly about her work wardrobe lately, warning her that she wouldn't be allowed to work the cash register dressed like a delivery boy. "Even Jimmy makes fun of you."

"Who cares what he thinks?" Molly frowned.

"I take it back." Colleen put a hand over her mouth. "You don't look like a six-year-old, Molly. You look more like a three-year-old."

"Maybe I don't want you home for Christmas Eve after all," Molly retorted.

Colleen snickered. "Sure you do, baby girl. And I think you want me to give you a new look too. In fact, I'm certain you do. You just won't admit it."

Molly folded her arms across her front, and her blue eyes glistened as if she were close to tears. Suddenly Margaret felt sorry for her little sister. They'd all been through so much these past couple of weeks. And, really, Molly had been holding up surprisingly well. Margaret hated to see her fall apart just as the customers started to come in. Maybe she should intervene.

"You do want my help, don't you?" Colleen playfully tickled Molly's ribs, making her smile. "Come on, sweetie, you can be my Cinderella and I'll be your fairy godmother. It'll be fun. I promise."

"I suppose it might be interesting." Molly shrugged. "I guess I can sacrifice myself for the sake of the family. I'm sure Mam will appreciate having you home for Christmas Eve."

Margaret pointed to the clock behind the counter. "Opening time." She jingled the keys as she hurried to the front door, relieved that she would now have customers to distract herself with. Two older women were already waiting. She unlocked the door, politely greeting both the women and stepping aside to let them enter. "It's chilly out there," she said as she shut the door against the wind.

"Oh, dear Margaret." Mrs. O'Brian's tone was sympathetic. "That was such a lovely service at Old Saint Mary's yesterday. Your brother was truly a fine young man. The world was a better place for Peter Mulligan, and I am grateful to have known him. If only for a short while. I'm so sorry for your loss." She clasped Margaret's hand, squeezing it between her two hands.

"I feel the same way," Mrs. Jones agreed with her friend. "It seems the old saying holds true. 'The good die first.'"

Margaret bristled slightly as she thanked them for their condolences. She turned away, pretending to tidy up a display of cans so they couldn't see her face. She truly wished that customers would quit talking about Peter. Well, at least *some* of them. She knew that many were well intentioned. But she hated it when certain customers acted as if they'd been Peter's close friends, when Margaret knew otherwise.

Oh, she knew there were many customers who'd been genuinely fond of her brother. But there were others, including Mrs. Jones, who'd been openly critical of Peter's management skills after he took over for Dad last summer. Some of them had acted as if Peter had deliberately tried to cheat her, but Margaret knew that her brother had never been anything but completely fair with everyone. Still, she couldn't very well say *that*.

But, she decided as she set the last can of green beans on top of the pyramid, the customer was *not* always right. It was simply that Margaret needed to make them feel as if they were! In the meantime, she would try to keep her own thoughts to herself. No room for Irish tempers to flare at the store. Not just days before Christmas.

"I thought you might not be open today," Mrs. O'Brian said as Margaret rang up her purchases. "But I wanted to give you my business if you were."

"We appreciate that." Margaret set the yams on the scales. "If we weren't in the business of selling food that can spoil, we might've considered closing the store until after Christmas," she admitted.

"When young Jackie Roberts was killed in the automobile accident, they closed Roberts' Fine Furniture for nearly a month out of respect," Mrs. Jones stated in what seemed a deprecating tone.

Margaret had to bite her tongue, simply nodding as she put the yams into a paper bag. "Colleen," she called over her shoulder. "I could use some help up here."

Margaret was just finishing up Mrs. O'Brian's order when Colleen joined her. "You can take over for a bit," Margaret said briskly. "I need to check on something in the backroom."

Colleen looked a bit confused but said nothing as Margaret hurried away. And she hadn't lied to Colleen because she *did* need to check something—her temper. It had taken all her self-control not to hurl the yams at Mrs. Jones's head. What was wrong with people? Margaret was still counting to ten—for the sixth or seventh time—when Molly came to the backroom, peering curiously at her.

"Are you okay?" Molly asked with concern.

Margaret pursed her lips, emphatically shaking her head.

"So it's not a good time to talk?" Molly asked with wide eyes.

Again, Margaret shook her head.

"So should I tell Brian to come back another time?"

"What?" Margaret demanded.

"He just came into the store," Molly explained. "He wants to talk to you. Should I say that you're—"

"Tell him I'll be right out." Margaret was already removing her apron and wishing she'd worn something prettier than her plain gray skirt and white blouse. "I could use a break." As Molly hurried away, Margaret took a moment to check her image in the tiny bathroom mirror, smoothing her hair and even putting on a bit of lipstick. Her hands were trembling as she blotted her lips with a piece of tissue.

Then taking in a deep breath, she went out to face him. If he was going to break it off with her, she wanted to remain as calm as possible. If it was even possible. Mam always said bad things came in threes. First there was Dad's diagnosis of TB, then the telegram about Peter...her third catastrophe would probably be Brian breaking her heart. She should simply prepare herself.

"Hello, Brian," she said briskly. "Did you want to speak to me?"

He looked uneasy, confirming her worries. "Yes. Are you terribly busy right now?"

She glanced around the store, relieved to see it was still only

Mrs. O'Brian and Mrs. Jones and nearly finished at the cash register. "Colleen and Molly can handle it."

He made a nervous smile. "Can you get a cup of coffee with me?"

"I'll get my coat." She turned from him and, feeling sick to her stomach, she went over to Colleen. "I'm taking a break," she murmured. "You're in charge."

Colleen just nodded, but her eyes were compassionate as she rang up Mrs. Jones's apples. "Take as long as you need, sis."

Margaret grabbed her coat and handbag and hurried outside where Brian was just lighting up a cigarette. For some reason it didn't bother her too much that Brian smoked. Not like it did when she caught Colleen puffing like a chimney. Despite all the glamorous starlets that smoked, the habit just did not seem feminine.

"Let's go to Marty's." He pointed down the street. "Okay?"

She just nodded, feeling too nervous to speak but trying to think of ways she could respond to him when he announced he was breaking it off with her. She wouldn't throw coffee in his face—even if she wanted to. Because that could seriously hurt him. But she would do something dramatic—something to show him how badly he'd hurt her.

Instead of putting his hand under her elbow as they walked, like he used to do, he seemed focused on smoking. And he looked almost as nervous as she felt. "Cold out today," he said briskly.

"Yes." She pulled her collar up more snugly around her neck, wishing she'd thought to get her scarf from her handbag.

"Here we go." He ground out his cigarette in the sand-filled container by the door then led her inside and over to a vacant table by the back wall. When he offered to help with her coat, she declined, saying she was still chilled. But really she wanted to have it ready for a quick exit.

Brian made small talk about yesterday's funeral service while they waited for the waitress to come. And then, when she did arrive, he ordered chocolate cream pie with his coffee, insisting Margaret do the same.

"No thank you," she said primly. "Just coffee for me."

"First of all, I need to apologize," he said after the waitress left. "You probably think I've been avoiding you, Margaret."

She tried to act nonchalant, although she was on the verge of tears. "I realize it's been very busy...for everyone."

"At first I was trying to give you time," he said slowly. "To grieve for Peter. And the truth is I was pretty upset about it too. I guess I still am. It's hard to take it all in...that he's really gone."

"I know." She paused as the waitress set their order down.

"It makes the war seem much more real, Margaret. Much more serious."

"It is serious." She poured cream into her coffee, wondering if she would even be able to drink any. As she stirred in a spoonful of sugar, she studied Brian. His reddish hair was cut shorter than usual, and his slightly ruddy face appeared very somber. But he still looked handsome. Maybe Brian Hammond wasn't everyone's cup of tea—but he was hers. Or at least she had hoped he was. Now she wasn't so sure.

"I wanted to inform you that I did decide to enlist." He took a sip of coffee. "I went into the enlistment office on Tuesday. I would've told you sooner, but your family was, well, in the midst of everything."

"So you're in the navy too?" she asked in a slightly absent way. She really wished he'd get to the heart of the matter—where did he stand with her?

"Not the navy, Margaret. Dad had been talking to an old military friend, and they both felt I'd get in with a higher ranking if I enlisted with the army. So that's what I did."

"You're in the army?" For some reason this felt unimpressive to her. Disappointing.

"Because of my college studies, I'll start out as a first lieutenant." That sounded more impressive. "Congratulations, Brian."

"Thanks. I'll be leaving for my training in Camp Roberts shortly after New Year's."

She took in a deep breath, knowing that she couldn't keep playing this game—it was time to cut to the chase. "Brian," she said urgently. "What is going on?"

"What?" He looked surprised. "I was just telling you about enlisting and—"

"No, I don't mean about the army. I mean what is going on with *us*? I can tell that something has changed. And I want you to quit beating around the bush about it. Tell me what is going on. *Now*." She pounded a fist onto the table so hard that their coffee cups jingled against the saucers.

"What do you mean? With us?"

"I know something is wrong," she declared hotly. "Something has changed. Did you find someone else? Do you have a girlfriend at college? Just *tell* me, Brian!"

"Margaret." He hushed her. "Keep it down. People are staring."

"I don't care," she continued. "Just tell me what is going on!"

"Nothing is going on," he said quietly. "Not like what you're saying. I don't have a girlfriend at college."

She felt slightly relieved but still uneasy. "Then what is it?"

"I don't know what you mean, Margaret." He actually did look somewhat bewildered now. "I was simply telling you about enlisting, and suddenly you are—"

"Because you've been avoiding me," she told him. "And I've got this feeling that things have changed between us. And it's nearly Christmas, and Colleen and Geoff recently became engaged and I had always thought...I had hoped..." She felt tears coming now. "Oh, never mind." She reached for her handbag, starting to get up. "If you don't know what I'm talking about, well, just *never mind!*"

"Wait, Margaret." He reached over to stop her. "Where are you going? Why are you so upset? Talk to me."

She reluctantly sank back down onto the chair. "Oh, Brian." She reached into her handbag for a handkerchief. "I think you know what I'm hinting at." She dabbed her eyes, wishing she'd kept herself more under control.

Brian reached across the table, taking her hand in his. "Margaret," he said gently. "I *know* you want to get married..."

She blinked, looking directly into his brown eyes. Was he about to do it? Had he brought her here to propose marriage and now she had ruined it all by throwing a fit?

"And I did want to talk to you about it."

"You did?" She tucked her handkerchief away, attempting a shaky smile.

"I decided that with me going into the army...and soon getting shipped off to, well, God only knows where... Well, I think we should wait."

"Wait?" she echoed meekly.

"Yes. It seems the prudent thing to do, Margaret."

"But...what if...what—"

"There are a lot of 'what ifs.' We don't know what the future holds. And it just feels wrong to tie you up with me when I'm about to—"

"But I want to be tied up with you." She clung to his hand. "I've been waiting so long, Brian. There's no one for me but you. Don't you understand that?"

He smiled, holding her hand in both of his. "That's good to hear, Margaret. And that is exactly why I know you'll still be here for me...when this war is over."

Her heart sank. Brian was determined to postpone their marriage again. "And what about finishing college?" she asked weakly.

"Yes, that's part of my rationale, Margaret. I'll still have college to finish up after the war. And then it will be time to get married. Does that work for you, darling?"

"Do you want an honest answer?" She pulled her hand away from his.

"Yes." He nodded eagerly.

"It does not work for me, Brian. As much as I love you, I am tired of waiting and waiting and waiting. And at the rate this is going, I suspect I will be old and gray before you're ready to get married and so..." She stood up, trying to maintain some composure. "I think perhaps it is time we called it a day. We're finished, Brian. Good-bye." And without saying another word, she walked out of the coffee shop, holding back her tears until she was a short way down the sidewalk—and until she felt certain that he was not chasing after her.

Well, that proved it, didn't it? If he really loved her—if he really wanted to marry her—he would chase her down, he would get down on one knee, he would beg her to become his wife...wouldn't he?

Sixteen

With Margaret's permission, Molly had been helping herself to items from the store to send to Dad at the sanatorium. She'd already sent one care package on Monday, and on the Sunday night before Christmas, she was putting the finishing touches on a special box that she and Bridget would deliver in person on Christmas Day. Molly knew they wouldn't be able to do more than simply wave at Dad from the isolation room when the nurse presented the Christmas box to him, but at least they would see his face. The only reason they'd been allowed this special privilege was because of all their family had gone through with losing Peter. And the only reason Molly got to go along was because she was in charge of the care packages.

"Very pretty, Molly." Colleen paused from getting a glass of water long enough to admire the colorful box that Molly had decorated with Christmas wrapping paper, ribbons, and glitter. "I'm sure Dad will like it."

"I know it's more than he can possibly eat himself." Molly tucked another orange into an empty corner. "But I plan to write a note suggesting that he share the spoils with his nurses and friends. Kind of a like a Christmas party in a box."

Colleen pointed to the big cellophane bag of chocolates sitting on top. "Dad will be popular."

Molly looked more closely at Colleen now, noticing her sister's red rayon evening dress and sparkly earrings. "Why are you all gussied up?"

"Geoff arrives tonight," Colleen lowered her voice. "We're going out on the town—just the two of us."

Molly glanced around the kitchen to see no one but them was in there. "Why are you whispering?" she whispered.

"I don't want Margaret to know."

"Oh..." Molly nodded with understanding. "Good thinking."

"I'm hiding out in here until seven. Then I'll just sneak out the back door. I told Geoff to pick me up on the street."

"That's thoughtful." Molly was well aware that Margaret was still upset over her breakup with Brian. She'd been almost unbearable at the store these past two days, but Molly and Colleen were trying to be understanding. Molly hoped it wouldn't take her sister too long to get over it. But it didn't seem likely.

"Yeah, I'd rather not upset her." Colleen slipped on her fur jacket, adding a filmy silk scarf around her neck and looking more like a movie star than ever.

"You look pretty," Molly told her. "I know Dad thinks you look like Ginger Rogers, but I think you look more like Lana Turner."

Colleen's eyes lit up. "Lana Turner? Really?"

"Tilt your head that way." Molly pointed, waiting while Colleen struck a pose. "Yeah, you really do."

"Well, thank you." Colleen beamed at her.

"And you're still spending tomorrow at Geoff's family's farm?" Molly asked. "But coming here in the evening like you promised?"

"That's right. But before I go with Geoff tomorrow, I'll transform you into a glamorous young lady."

Molly rolled her eyes. She'd half-expected Colleen would've forgotten about this by now. Although she was sort of glad that she hadn't. "How do you plan to do it?" she asked. "I really mean—*when* do you plan to do it? I'm supposed to work at the store, and you know how busy it can be on Christmas Eve with last minute—"

"You and I will go in with Margaret in the morning. Then Mam and Bridget will take over for us around noon. We'll come home and have the house to ourselves. And Geoff won't pick me up until 4:30." Colleen pointed to the kitchen clock. "And now I must go." She tugged a pigtail then blew a kiss, careful not to smudge her lipstick. "Keep up the good work, Molly."

With the kitchen to herself, Molly finished up Dad's package then went out to the front room where the radio was quietly playing. But the only one there was Bridget, and she had her nose in her big nursing textbook. "Where's Mam?" Molly asked quietly, almost afraid to disturb her.

"Bed." Bridget didn't even look up.

Molly was tempted to ask about Margaret but suspected she was holed up in her bedroom again. Just like last night. Home had turned into a lonely place and grew lonelier with each passing day. Knowing that she might get her head bit off, Molly tapped lightly on Margaret's bedroom door.

"Come in," Margaret growled.

"Hi, Margaret," Molly said cheerfully. "Want any company?"

Margaret sat up on her bed with a sour expression. "I am not what you would call good company, Molly." She reached for a handkerchief, blotting her eyes—she'd obviously just been crying.

"That's okay." Molly perched on the bench by Margaret's vanity table. "I finished the box for Dad. It looks really pretty."

"Good for you." Margaret looked like she was trying to sound more pleasant. "I'm sure it's very nice."

Molly listed all the things she'd put into the box, and Margaret actually looked impressed. "And Colleen told me that Bridget and Mam are going to work at the store tomorrow afternoon." Molly continued explaining Colleen's plan for transforming Molly into a young lady. "I actually thought she'd forgotten about it, but she hadn't. And I guess I'm kind of glad. I mean, most of my classmates look older than I do. And some of my friends tease me sometimes. Maybe it is time I grew up." Molly sighed. "But it's hard...you know... because of Peter."

"Because of Peter?" Margaret looked confused. "Why?"

"Oh, you know. Peter always liked me being the little sister. The baby. He never wanted me to grow up."

"Is that why you keep dressing like a little girl?"

Molly shrugged, feeling tears coming on. "I—I guess so. I miss him so much."

"Oh, Molly." Margaret got off her bed, came over to hug her.

"Will that achy feeling deep inside of me ever go away?" Molly asked between tears.

"I don't know."

"I just want everything to go back to how it was," Molly said sadly.

"We all do." Margaret sniffed. "But all we can do is go forward now."

Molly felt guilty. She'd come in here to encourage Margaret and now they were both crying. "I'm sorry about Brian," Molly said quietly. "I know he loves you, Margaret. But he just wants to be careful. You know how he is."

Margaret sat on the edge of her bed, barely nodding. "Yes. I know. And you're probably right."

"And you still love him, don't you?"

"Of course I do." Margaret sighed deeply. "I never should've said what I did to him. That was stupid."

"Can't you take it back?"

Margaret reached for the decorative pillow that she'd made, with Brian's initials embroidered in the middle of the heart, first punching it with her fist then holding it to her chest. "I would if I could, Molly. I'm just not sure that I can." She threw the pillow against the wall. "And I know you're trying to help me, but really I just need to be alone...to sort this out."

"Okay." Molly stood and, while backing out of the bedroom, got an idea. "Good night, Margaret."

Molly went back out to where Bridget was still glued to her book and, without saying a word, got her coat and went into the kitchen. She wrote a note, which she doubted would be read, saying that she'd gone to the Hammonds'. It wasn't even 7:30, but it felt later as she went out into the dark night.

Fortunately, the Hammonds lived only a few blocks away. And lucky for Molly the full moon made it easier to find her way down the darkened street. Hopefully no Japanese planes were getting ready to attack San Francisco right now. Just the same, she decided to run and, breathlessly arriving at the Hammonds' door, was welcomed by Patrick.

"What's wrong?" he asked as he led her inside.

"Nothing is wrong," she told him. "Well, not really wrong." She paused in the foyer to catch her breath. "I just need to talk to Brian."

Patrick looked surprised. "He's in the kitchen with Mom and Dad."

"Can I talk privately to him?" Molly asked. "It's about Margaret."

Patrick made a knowing nod. "Yes, of course. I'll get him. And then I'll keep the parents in the kitchen for a bit. Okay?"

"Thank you." She smiled gratefully.

Before long, she and Brian were seated in the front room and she began the speech she had rehearsed in her head just moments ago. "Brian, I know that Margaret gave you your walking papers yesterday morning," she said solemnly. "But I also know that she regrets it. Margaret really does love you. I'm not sure if you really love her or not. But if you do, I'm begging you to tell her. And I think that even if you don't want to get engaged, she will still take you back." She stopped long enough to catch her breath. "Because the truth is, Margaret is utterly miserable without you. But I'm afraid she'll never tell you so. And by the time you two figure it out, it'll be too late."

"It didn't feel like she still loved me when she said what she said," Brian told her.

"I'm not sure what she said to you, but I know she wishes she could take it back."

"You're certain of that?"

Molly firmly nodded. "I am."

Brian pursed his lips with a furrowed brow.

"And I know you probably don't like getting advice from a kid, but I do have some thoughts, Brian."

He looked at her with interest. "Such as?"

"Well, what would be wrong with being engaged before you go into the service? Wouldn't you like to have a girl at home? Someone who loves you and writes you letters and sends you cookies? Someone who prays for you? Who eagerly awaits your return?"

He frowned. "But what if...what if I don't make it back?"

Molly stiffened, carefully weighing her words. "Then wouldn't it be even more important that Margaret knew you loved her enough to be engaged to her? Wouldn't it be more comforting?"

"Maybe. But what if...what if I get hurt over there? What if I came back missing an arm or a leg or something?"

Molly looked evenly at him. "Margaret would still love you, Brian. I know she would love you no matter what. I can't think of any reason she would ever stop loving you. Well, unless you ever stopped loving her. You wouldn't, would you?"

"No, no, of course, not. I've always loved Margaret. I always will."

"Then why don't you *tell* her that? Why don't you ask her to marry you? Really, Brian, what on earth are you waiting for? You two aren't getting any younger, you know?" Just then Molly heard the sounds of laughter coming from the kitchen. And they both looked up to see Patrick and Mr. and Mrs. Hammond sheepishly listening from the doorway.

"Hip-hip hurray!" Mrs. Hammond cheered with enthusiasm. "Listen to the child, Brian. She makes more sense than you and Margaret put together."

"That's right," Mr. Hammond added as they emerged from the kitchen. "Molly has good sense. Listen to her."

"I agree," Patrick said.

"Okay, okay." Brian held up his hands. "You're all obviously ganging up on me."

"Because you need it." Patrick turned to Molly. "You should see how this guy has been moping around the house the past two days. Like he'd lost his best friend."

"That's what it felt like," Brian told them. "I guess you don't fully appreciate what you have until you lose it."

"Then don't lose it," Molly challenged him.

Brian nodded. "Okay. I won't." He looked curiously at Molly. "You don't happen to know Margaret's ring size, by any chance?"

Molly's eyes lit up. "As a matter of fact, it's the same as mine. She let me try on her birthstone ring awhile back and it fit perfectly."

Brian grabbed Molly's left hand. "Can I take this with me to the jewelry store tomorrow?"

Molly laughed. "Only if you take me with it." She thought for a moment then explained how she and Colleen were getting off work early. "If you picked us up at noon, we could go to the jewelry store with you, but then you'd have to bring us home."

"And Colleen is just the girl to help pick out a ring," Mrs. Hammond told Brian. "That girl has good taste."

And so it was agreed. They would all go engagement ring shopping tomorrow, and then Brian would present it to Margaret for Christmas. Molly thanked the Hammonds and was getting ready to leave when Patrick insisted that she shouldn't be walking alone in the dark.

"I'll see her home," he told his family. "Do you want me to drive?" he asked Molly. "Or shall we walk?"

"Walk, if you don't mind." She tugged on her coat. "There's a beautiful moon out tonight."

Patrick grinned. "Then walk it is."

"And I can return your letterman jacket when we get home," she said as they went outside. "It's still at my house, and there's been so much going on, I forgot to get it back to you."

"Maybe you should just take care of it for me," he said as they stood on the stoop, their eyes adjusting to the darkness which, thanks to the moon, was not quite so dark.

"Take care of it?" she asked as they went down the steps.

"Well, it'll just be hanging in my closet while I'm gone anyway. And since you're going to the same high school, why not just hold onto it for me? Maybe it'll remind you of your promise to write to me once in a while."

"I don't need a reminder," she assured him. "I *want* to write to you."

"Hang onto the jacket just the same, okay?"

"Okay." She nodded. "I'll take good care of it too."

He chuckled. "I know you will."

"Look at the sidewalk in the moonlight," she said suddenly. "It almost looks like it's yellow, don't you think?"

"By golly, it does," he agreed. "We're on the yellow brick road."

"This reminds me of when Peter took me to see *The Wizard of Oz*. It's funny because I wasn't even sure I wanted to go to the movie. But Peter insisted I had to go."

"Why didn't you want to go?"

"Because I loved the original Oz books so much, and I'd heard the movie had changed some things."

"Like Dorothy's shoes? They weren't silver like in the book."

"That's right," she eagerly agreed. "Did you read the Oz books too?"

"You bet I did. Peter was the one who got me started on them. I read every single one."

"Me too! Peter actually gave me his set of Oz books when I was in fourth grade. I think that's why I love reading—thanks to Peter and Oz."

Suddenly Patrick began to sing: "Follow the yellow brick road..."

Looping her arm into his, Molly joined in the song as they skipped and danced along the moonlit sidewalk until they reached the final line of the song: "Because of the wonderful things he does." And then they both laughed. But in the same instant a wave of guilt washed over her.

"Was that wrong?" she asked him.

"Wrong?" he echoed.

"Singing and laughing," she explained. "I felt happy for the first time since, well, you know...and suddenly I remembered what happened to Peter...and, well, it just felt wrong to be happy. Do you think it's wrong?"

There was a long pause where neither of them said a thing, with only the lonely sound of their footsteps on the moonlit sidewalk. Finally Patrick broke the silence. "I know Peter would understand that we're very sad to lose him, but do you think he'd want us to remain sad like this forever?"

"Probably not. I doubt that Peter would want us to be unhappy at all," she concluded. "But even so, it felt odd...like it was wrong."

"I know what you mean. But knowing Peter like we did, we know he'd feel badly to think his passing took our happiness with it. Don't you think?"

"You're right." She nodded grimly. "Peter wouldn't like seeing us unhappy. I'll try to remember that."

"It seems to me that if we give in to our grief...if we let this loss steal all the joy out of life...well, it's like letting the enemy win. And if the enemy wins, it dishonors that Peter gave his life for his country. Does that make sense, Molly?"

She considered it. "It does make sense. Even though I'm sad, I don't like the idea of the enemy stealing my joy. I really do want to remember this." She sighed. "I wish Mam could hear what you just said. It feels like she's fallen into a deep dark hole and can't climb out." She looked hopefully at Patrick. "Could you could tell her what you just told me?"

"If you think it would help her."

"I'm sure it would, Patrick. Especially since you were so close to Peter. And in some ways, you're so much like him." They were at her house now. "If you're not in a hurry, you could tell her tonight. She really needs to hear it."

"Do you think she's still up?"

"I'll find out," she said urgently. "And if she is, I'll encourage her to talk to you. If you don't mind."

"Not at all."

"Come inside." Molly eagerly grabbed his arm and, afraid they might lose this moment, tugged him into the house. "You can visit with Bridget while I check on Mam." She hurried through the front room. "Patrick is here, Bridget. Be a good hostess and offer him some tea or something, okay?"

Bridget looked up from her book, frowning curiously at Patrick. "Oh, hello there. What is going on?"

But Molly didn't pause to answer. Instead she went to Mam's bedroom where, to her relief, her mother was sitting in the chair by the window—just staring at the blackout curtain as if she were looking outside. "Mam?" Molly placed a hand on her mother's shoulder. "Patrick is here."

"Patrick?" Mam turned to look at Molly with a blank expression, almost as if she had no idea who Patrick was.

"Patrick. Peter's best friend. He wants to talk to you," Molly explained. "He wants to talk to you about *Peter.*"

"About Peter?" Mam was suddenly on her feet. "Yes, of course, where is he?"

Molly led her mother out through the front room and then, hearing voices visiting in the kitchen, she realized Bridget was actually making Patrick a cup of tea. Good for her!

"Here's Mam," Molly announced as she victoriously presented her mother to Patrick. Then, not wanting to stand around and watch, she picked up her dad's festive care-package and excused herself. Saying a silent prayer that Patrick's words might help her mother, Molly scurried off to her room.

Seventeen

Colleen knew Molly was up to something the next morning, but for the life of her, she could not figure out what. But her suspicions grew when Molly looked at the clock and announced it was time for them to leave. "Bridget and Mam are here," she told Colleen. "They don't need us to work anymore."

Seeing a small cluster of customers about to enter the store, Colleen was about to dispute this, but Molly grabbed her by the elbow and practically dragged her to the backroom. "Why are we using the back door?" Colleen asked as Molly shoved her coat and purse toward her.

"Shhh," Molly hissed. "Just come on, *please.*" Once they got outside to the back parking area, Colleen saw Patrick waving from his car, and Brian was sitting on the passenger side. "Hurry," Molly told her. "We don't want Margaret to see us."

"What is going on?" Colleen asked as they jumped into the backseat and Patrick took off. "I feel like a gun moll about to make our getaway."

Brian laughed. "Don't worry, we haven't joined the mob. Didn't you tell her, Molly?"

"Are you kidding?" Molly shot back at him. "She might've spilled the beans."

"What beans?" Colleen demanded. "Am I being kidnapped or something?"

"We're going ring shopping," Molly explained. "Brian needs our help."

"For Margaret?" Colleen asked hopefully. Molly nodded, and Colleen let out a happy shriek. "That's fabulous news!"

"See why I kept it under my hat?" Molly said smugly.

Before long, all four of them were perusing a jewelry store owned by a friend of the Hammonds, but Colleen was clearly in charge. Although she wasn't truly an expert in engagement rings, she knew more than the three of them put together. She showed the jeweler the ring that Geoff had recently given her, asking his opinion of the quality of the diamond. Using his magnifying scope, he studied it closely—and Colleen suddenly felt nervous. What if he told her it was no good or a fake?

"Very, very nice." He removed the device from his eye and smiled. "Wonderful clarity, nearly flawless, an excellent cut, and the platinum setting is beautiful." He winked at Colleen as he returned her ring. "Your man has excellent taste. This is a valuable piece."

Colleen sighed as she slipped the ring back on. She felt guilty for even questioning this. But it was nice to know Geoff had gotten her such a nice ring.

"Well, I doubt I can afford a ring as nice as Colleen's," Brian told the jeweler.

"Margaret wouldn't expect one like that," Molly assured him. "Besides, her taste is simpler than Colleen's."

"I'll tell you what I can afford." Brian leaned over the counter, whispering in the jeweler's ear. "Can I get something good for that?"

"Of course you can. Come over here." He led them to a glass case, and soon they were ogling a variety of rings, using Molly's hand as the model. Eventually, Colleen pointed to an oval solitaire set in yellow gold. "That looks like Margaret to me. Classic, pretty, elegant."

"I like it too," Brian said, holding up Molly's hand to examine it more closely.

"That's an excellent choice," the jeweler told them. He handed Brian the magnifying device. "Would you like a closer look?"

Brian inspected the stone carefully then nodded firmly. "This is the one."

While the jeweler wrote up the sale for Brian, the other three continued to look around the sparkly store, oohing and ahhing and exclaiming over some of the price tags.

"What kind of a ring do you want when you get engaged?" Colleen asked Molly.

"I don't know." Molly shrugged. "Fortunately I won't need to think about *that* for a long, long time."

"Well, that's a relief," Patrick said in a teasing tone.

Molly pointed to a pale blue stone. "And actually, I like my birthstone better than I like diamonds."

"What's your birthstone?" Patrick asked.

"Aquamarine," Colleen told him. "Molly's birthday is in March. My stone is a ruby, for July."

"All done," Brian announced as he held up a neatly wrapped package. "Ready to go?"

They quickly piled back into Patrick's car again. "Now, you girls better not forget that mum's the word," Brian warned them. "I want Margaret to be completely surprised tonight."

"Lucky for you, Geoff and I will be at his family's house until later," Colleen said. "Otherwise I might let the cat out of the bag."

"And you can trust me," Molly told him.

"That's true," Colleen confirmed. "Molly didn't let on about a thing." She nudged Molly with her elbow. "Who knew you were so good at keeping secrets? I wonder what else you've got up your sleeve."

"Here you go, ladies." Patrick parked in front of their house.

"Thanks so much for your help." Brian reached over the back of the seat to grasp Molly's hand. "Particularly yours, Molly. I owe you one."

Molly's eyes lit up. "I'm just glad that you and Margaret are finally getting engaged." She patted him on the back. "It's about time."

"I'll say," Colleen agreed as they got out of the car.

"See you later," Molly called out.

Then as they hurried up to the house, Colleen turned to Molly. "Why was Brian thanking you like that? Just because you let him use your hand to get the ring?"

"It's a long story," Molly said as they went inside.

"Well, you'll have time to tell me while I'm working you over," Colleen said. "I want to hear the whole story." She pointed Molly toward the bathroom. "The first thing you need to do is take out those little girl pigtails and give yourself a good shampoo then towel it mostly dry. Okay?"

Molly rolled her eyes but fortunately did not argue. While she was occupied in the bathroom, Colleen put together a plan. She'd wanted to do something like this for Molly's fifteenth birthday, but Peter had gotten wind of it and thrown a fit. To be fair, it hadn't really been a fit. He'd simply put his foot down, reminding Colleen and everyone that Molly was their last sibling and for that reason should be encouraged to fully enjoy her childhood. Naturally, Dad and Mam agreed—and Colleen's plan had been tossed aside.

But Molly would be sixteen in a couple of months. Already her friends looked more like young women than little girls. And Colleen knew that Molly got teased sometimes. It was time she grew up outwardly—especially since she always seemed so grown-up inwardly. And this might be Colleen's last opportunity to help her because, although her family was still in the dark, if Geoff got his way, they would be getting married soon. Last night he had suggested the day after Christmas. "That way you can come down to San Diego with me and get set up in the officers' family housing."

Colleen had been slightly shocked by his urgency, but it did sound exciting...and she did love him. No doubts about that. Still, she sometimes wondered if eighteen-and-a-half was a bit young for marriage. Although Mam had been younger than that when she married Dad, and they'd seemed to do okay.

"Here I am," Molly proclaimed as she came into their room with a pink towel draped around her shoulders.

"Wow." Colleen fingered Molly's curls. "I didn't realize your hair had gotten so long."

"It grows." Molly shrugged.

"Sit." Colleen pointed her to the vanity bench and reached for a hairbrush. As she worked it through Molly's thick hair, she knew what had to be done and, reaching for her scissors, she informed Molly. "We need to take some off."

At first Molly looked alarmed but then she simply shrugged again. "Okay."

Colleen was surprised, but wasting no time in case Molly had second thoughts, she began to snip. During the depression, Colleen had started cutting her own hair, as well as everyone else's in the family, and she wasn't half bad at it. Plus, she knew that Molly's thick blonde curls would hide anything that was less than even. "You're hair's a lot like mine," Colleen said as she snipped. "But thicker. And the color is nicer. You probably won't ever need to color your hair."

"Good grief, I hope not." Molly reached up to touch her hair. "I never want to use hair dye."

"I don't use dye, Molly, I lighten it with bleach."

She wrinkled her nose. "I don't want to use bleach either."

She finished trimming Molly's hair then, after using bobby pins to set some loose curls, she wrapped it all up in a hairnet. "I wish we had a hair dryer."

"Aren't they terribly expensive?"

"I saw a Bakelite hair dryer kit at Anderson's that was reasonably priced." She adjusted the hairnet. "Anyway, I promised Mam we'd put the roast in the oven. Why don't you get it started and stay in there for a while. The heat from the stove will help dry your hair. Meanwhile, I'll do my own."

With Molly gone, Colleen spent some time on her own hair then touched up her fingernail polish. She'd been wearing crimson lately, for Christmas. Perhaps Molly needed some color on her nails too. Before baby sister could protest, Colleen was painting her nails crimson as well.

"That's kind of pretty." Molly fluttered her red nails in the air.

"I thought it looked Christmassy." Colleen set her cosmetic case on the kitchen table. "Let's just stay in here since Mam's not around to complain about the mess. Plus, the light is good." She wanted to add that this room was also free of mirrors, which would prevent Molly from taking any sneak peeks and overreacting.

Because they still had lots of leftovers from dishes brought to them by friends and neighbors after news of Peter had spread, they each made themselves a plate, picking from it while Colleen continued to work on Molly.

"You're not overdoing it, are you?" Molly asked with concern while Colleen put some eye shadow on her eyelids.

"I'm using a very gentle touch," Colleen assured her. "I know you're not ready to look like me...yet."

"Yet?" Molly snickered. "I'll never look like you, Colleen. You're beautiful."

Colleen paused and looked at her little sister in wonder. "And you don't think you are beautiful too?"

Molly let out a stifled laugh. "No!"

Colleen just shook her head. Well, maybe it was good that Molly didn't know how pretty she was. Colleen wouldn't want it to go to her head.

By four o'clock, Colleen was done with Molly and standing her in front of their full length mirror. "Keep your eyes closed until I say 'open,'" she reminded her again. Colleen made some adjustments to the blue satin dress she'd loaned Molly for the evening. She'd had to tug up the bodice a bit and fluff out the full skirt, but the dress fit surprisingly well. Colleen hadn't realized they were so close to the same size. She used the brush to smooth Molly's hair, which was curling gently on her shoulders now. Molly really did look beautiful—so beautiful that Colleen felt a tinge of concern. Was it possible that Molly was prettier than Colleen? That would be hard to swallow. Already Colleen was feeling envious of Molly's nice, straight little nose. Colleen's had a little bump on the end of it. Probably why Dad thought she looked like Ginger Rogers.

"Come on," Molly begged. "Can I open my eyes?"

"Yes, yes. Open them." Colleen watched as Molly's eyes not only opened but opened wide.

"Oh, my goodness!" Her hand flew to her mouth. "Is that really me?"

Colleen grinned. "Yep, it is. Not bad, eh?"

"I look so old." Molly stepped closer to the mirror, inspecting herself closely.

"Yes, this isn't what I'd call an *everyday* look, Molly. I did try to use a lighter touch, but Christmas is a special occasion."

Molly turned to Colleen with misty eyes. "Thank you so much, Colleen. I didn't think I wanted to do this, but now that you did it, I'm glad." She hugged her.

"And you have to promise me you won't go to school looking like this." Colleen pushed a loose strand of hair back into place. "Otherwise Mam will skin me."

"No, of course not."

"Although just a touch of lipstick probably wouldn't hurt anything." Colleen checked out her own appearance now, ensuring every hair of her French twist was in place and shaking a trace of face powder off the full skirt of her black velvet gown. She'd made this dress for herself after seeing one like it in a Bette Davis movie last winter, but not too pleased with how it turned out, she'd never worn it before. Maybe it was just the severity of the color. "I wasn't sure how to dress for going out to the Conrad farm," she confessed. "Geoff's mother is, uh, rather conservative. I thought it might help if I was too. Although I've never really loved this gown."

"I wondered if that was why you chose it." Molly ran her hand over a three-quarter-length sleeve. "Although I do love this dress, Colleen. It's so sophisticated. If you ever decide you don't want it anymore, I hope you'll give it to me."

Colleen smiled as she adjusted a rhinestone earring. "I'll keep that in mind."

They were just clearing the beauty products from the kitchen table when the doorbell rang and, thinking it was too early for Geoff, Colleen asked Molly to get it.

"It's Geoff," Molly called out.

Colleen set down her cosmetic case and came out to greet him. As usual, Geoff was dressed stylishly, and the smile on his face showed that he approved of her too. "You girls look so beautiful," he told them. "Like you should be on the front of a fashion magazine."

Molly held up a finger. "That reminds me. I want to take a photograph of you two together. Do you mind?"

"Not at all." Colleen struck a pose.

"We should stand in front of the Christmas tree," Geoff suggested.

Molly frowned. "We don't have a tree this year."

"Mam didn't want one," Colleen told him.

"Understandable." He nodded. "If it's okay, I'll take a picture of you two girls as well."

Molly returned with the little Brownie camera that Peter had asked her to keep for him while he was gone. She carefully attached the flash then focused on the handsome couple and took a picture. Then Geoff took over the camera, and Molly and Colleen posed together.

"Don't let Hollywood get a hold of that photo," Geoff said as he handed the camera back to Molly.

"I still have about half a roll of film," Molly told them. "I'm eager to use it so I can get it developed." She let out a sad little sigh. "There are pictures of Peter on here before he left. From the day he took me to Golden Gate Park. And in his uniform."

"Everyone will want to see those photos," Colleen said as she pulled on her furry jacket. She nodded toward the kitchen. "Do you mind cleaning things up in there?"

"Not at all." Molly hugged her again. "Thanks."

"Merry Christmas." Colleen pulled on one of her long black

gloves, staring in wonder at her glamorous looking baby sister.

"Merry Christmas to you too," Molly told her. "To both of you and to Geoff's family."

"We'll see you later tonight," Colleen promised as Geoff opened the front door. "Hopefully around nine. But be sure and get a picture of Margaret and Brian when he gives her the ring."

Molly promised to do that as Colleen and Geoff went outside. And then Colleen paused on the stoop, suddenly feeling uneasy—almost as if something were wrong.

"What is it?" Geoff asked. "Did you forget something?"

"I, uh, it's just that..." She looked at him. "I...I don't know."

"What?"

She pursed her lips. "It's just that I felt so nearly happy just then—I enjoyed fixing Molly up like that. But now I feel guilty about it. I mean, in light of Peter...I shouldn't feel *happy*, should I?"

Geoff gathered her in his arms, holding her close. "I think you should feel however you want to feel, Colleen. And somehow, although I never knew your brother, I'm certain Peter would approve."

Colleen wasn't so sure, but she simply nodded. She wanted it to be true, but somehow she felt uncertain. She sometimes felt like she *owed* Peter something, although she couldn't explain what or why or how. She suspected her feelings were related to the fact she'd never felt like a "proper" sister—whatever that might be. But Margaret was so responsible, proving how dependable she was when she took over management of the store. Meanwhile, Bridget was the scholar. Peter had been so proud that she was about to earn her nurse's degree. And then, of course, there was Peter's favorite sister—young Molly with her heart of gold. In Peter's eyes, she could do no wrong.

Colleen had been the black sheep of the family for as long as she could remember. Peter had tried to counsel and redirect her a number of times, but her stubbornness always stopped him. Oh, she knew that her big brother had loved her, but she also knew she'd never lived up to his idealistic expectations. Perhaps that was why she felt she owed him something now.

Eighteen

Before long Geoff was driving them through the countryside with the radio, tuned to a jazz program, playing softly. The dusky sky, painted with lilac and gold, illuminated the fields and trees like a piece of living art. Everything about this moment felt so perfect, she wished it could last forever. Although at the speed they were traveling, it would soon be over.

As usual, Geoff drove fast. But the speed didn't bother her. In fact, she liked it, even found it exciting. Sometimes driving with Geoff felt like being in a movie. He had apologized once, explaining how pilots were notorious for driving overly fast. "Driving slow makes me want to nod off—and that could be dangerous. But speed keeps me alert and on my toes," he'd assured her. "Keeps my senses tuned in. Kind of like flying."

"I hope I get to fly with you someday," she said dreamily. "That would be so wonderful."

"I'm planning on it." Now he asked her about Brian proposing to Margaret, and she explained about ring shopping today, assuring him that Margaret's ring couldn't possibly outshine Colleen's, which made him laugh. And, once again, Colleen felt almost completely and perfectly happy—but once again it troubled her. She hoped Geoff was right...that Peter would approve. Deep inside, she felt he would. She hoped he would.

Geoff's family's farm looked sweet in the amber light as he parked in front of the big old house. Not for the first time, she thought it must've been a magical place to grow up in. It was no wonder that Geoff was such a special guy. How could he not be? Just being here felt good, and as they walked up to the house, she spied a tall Christmas tree through the front window. It all looked so perfect.

However, as they got closer to the house, Colleen was attacked by a set of nerves that made her stomach twist and turn. She wasn't used to being disliked by anyone. Even in high school, when there were girls who didn't like her or were jealous, Colleen usually managed to win them over with her "Irish charm" as Dad liked to call it. But, so far, her Irish charm had failed her when it came to Geoff's mother. Although his grandparents had warmed up a bit, Mrs. Conrad was as cold as her icy blue eyes. And Colleen was not looking forward to seeing her again.

"You okay?" Geoff asked as he reached for the doorknob.

She took in a deep breath, forcing a smile. "I hope so."

"Don't let her get to you." Geoff still hadn't opened the door.

"All right." She nodded firmly.

"You should know something, Colleen," he said quietly. "One of the many things that attracted me to you was your strong will. I felt you would be able to stand up to my mom. But I know it's not easy."

"Really?" She blinked at him. "You picked me because you thought I could—"

"I picked you because I fell in love," he said quickly. "But it helped cinch the deal to know you weren't a pushover."

She smiled. "Yes, I've never been accused of being a pushover."

"Hello?" Mrs. Conrad, dressed in a pale blue sweater set and gray wool skirt, opened the door. But with Geoff's hand still on the knob, he nearly toppled forward with the motion. "Oh, my." His mother stepped back. "Were you planning to join us? Or did you want to stand out on the porch all night?"

"Merry Christmas, Mother." He planted a kiss on her pale cheek.

"Merry Christmas, Mrs. Conrad," Colleen said brightly, forcing a stiff smile.

"Come in before the house gets cold." She opened the door fully, waiting for them to enter the living room.

"It looks so pretty in here," Colleen told her. "The fireplace and the tree and everything. Like a Christmas card."

"And it smells good too." Geoff was helping Colleen off with her coat. "Boy, am I hungry. Navy food takes some getting used to."

"Your grandmother has been helping the cook today." She waved them into the living room. "Please, make yourselves at home. I'll tell the folks you're here."

After his mother left, Geoff opened up the bar next to the fireplace. "She said make ourselves at home. Can I get you something?"

"Uh...I guess I'll have a cola," she said cautiously. Geoff was no fool—he knew that she imbibed occasionally when socializing. And it wasn't like Geoff was a heavy drinker, although she'd seen him enjoy a cold beer a time or two. But she didn't want to make the wrong impression on his family.

"Coming right up." He busied himself with the glasses and ice, humming "We Wish You a Merry Christmas" and eventually presenting her with a glass. "Here's looking at you." He winked as he lifted his glass then waited for her to take a sip.

It took a couple seconds for it to register that this was not straight cola. "*Geoff*," she said quietly. "What did you—"

"May help you to relax," he whispered just as the sound of footsteps came into the room.

"Merry Christmas," Geoff's grandmother announced as she and Mr. Conrad, followed by Geoff's mother, came into the living room. To Colleen's relief, his grandmother wore a festive green dress trimmed with sparkly beadwork and, after greetings were exchanged, she sat down next to Colleen. Meanwhile, Geoff played host at the bar, fixing mixed drinks for everyone.

Colleen turned her attention to the grandmother. "That emerald green looks very nice on you, Mrs. Conrad. It brings out your eyes."

"Please, don't call me Mrs. Conrad." She lowered her voice. "You'll be family soon. Just call me Grandma."

Colleen smiled. "Thank you."

"And you have my most sincere condolences for your brother," she said gently. "Geoff told us about it."

Geoff's grandfather and mother expressed similar sympathies and questioned Colleen a bit on how her family was doing. Although Colleen had told Geoff about her dad's illness, she'd asked him not to mention it to his family. It felt like it would simply be one more strike against her—at least where his mother was concerned.

"I was sorry I couldn't attend Peter's services," Geoff said as he handed his mother a drink. "But, like I told Colleen, I was there in spirit."

The room got quiet again, and Colleen wished for something clever to say, something to reroute the conversation into a pleasant arena.

Geoff's grandmother reached over to give Colleen's hand a warm squeeze. "You look so pretty tonight. Such a fashionable girl." She stroked a fold of Colleen's full skirt. "And I just love velvet. Such an elegant gown."

"I made it myself," Colleen quietly informed her.

"You *did?*" The older woman clasped her hands together. "Did you hear that, Ellen? Colleen sewed the gown she's wearing. Isn't it beautiful?"

"Yes, but with that low-cut neckline, I'm worried she might catch a chill," Mrs. Conrad said crisply.

"I'm warm enough." Colleen wanted to add that the only chill in the room was Geoff's mother but took a sip of her drink instead.

"As you can see, we're a close-knit family," his grandmother told Colleen. "Is your family like that?"

"Very much so." Colleen eagerly described how close she was to her sisters and how their house could get quite noisy at times.

"And grandparents? Aunts or uncles?"

"My grandfather on my mother's side passed away about five years ago, and my grandmother lives up in Oregon with my mother's sister, Aunt Kate, so we don't see them too much. My father's parents are still in Ireland. He's invited them to visit, but so far I haven't met them."

"So your father was an immigrant?"

"He came over as a young man, along with his best friend."

"For political reasons?" Mrs. Conrad asked.

"For a better life." Colleen repeated what she'd heard Dad and Mr. Hammond say for years. "Ireland was not a pleasant place to live."

To her relief, Geoff changed the subject by telling them about his pilot training in San Diego. He told a couple of interesting stories, explaining how the pilots got VIP treatment. "Much better than the sailors. It seems we're the top of the food chain." He chuckled. "But from what I hear that can change quickly. About half of the pilots in the program won't make the final cut."

"Won't make the final cut?" his grandfather asked. "Why?"

"Lots of reasons. And flying is just one piece of the pie. The academics are tough too." He told them about the geometry test he'd taken just yesterday. "I think I passed, but I plan to crack open some books before the next exam."

"Why does a flyer need geometry?" Colleen asked him.

"Really?" Mrs. Conrad gave Colleen a look of pure disdain. "Do you not understand that a pilot must be able to read maps and calculate locations, and that requires some basic geometry?"

Feeling as if she'd been slapped, Colleen didn't respond. Instead she sipped her drink.

"Most people aren't aware of the math requirements in the navy pilot program," Geoff said quickly. "Some of the pilots—and I mean experienced ones—have been caught off guard by how much math we're expected to do. And it's not just maps. We have to calculate and cross-calculate things like weight and thrust and speed and all sorts of stuff." He grinned. "I actually sort of like it."

"You've always been good at math," his grandmother said warmly. She turned to Colleen. "When he was a little boy, I made him count the eggs and the chickens and figure out the average amount of eggs per chicken per month." She chuckled. "And he did it." She looked at Geoff. "Do you remember?"

He just laughed. "Well, thanks for starting me out early."

The cook announced that dinner was ready, and they all stood. Mr. Conrad reached for his wife's hand, and Geoff reached for Colleen's. But his mother loudly cleared her throat. "Have you forgotten your manners, son?"

Geoff exchanged an uneasy glance with Colleen. "How about if I have a lady on each arm?" He winked at Colleen.

"But of course." She grinned back at him. Maybe it was the contents of her drink, but as they paraded to the dining room, she felt much less concerned about Mrs. Conrad.

"This is so beautiful." Colleen stared at the perfectly set dining room table. The tall white candlesticks glowed elegantly, and the china and crystal and silver all gleamed. It looked like something right out of a movie set—and nothing like the family meals at the Mulligan home.

"Well, this is a celebration," his grandmother said as her husband helped her into her chair. "Worthy of the good china and silver and all the trimmings."

"Yes, yes...Merry Christmas to everyone," Mrs. Conrad said stiffly as Geoff pulled her chair out for her.

"No, I meant this is a celebration for Geoff and Colleen's engagement."

"That's right," his grandfather agreed while Geoff helped Colleen into her chair. "Louise has even chilled a bottle of champagne to celebrate the occasion."

Seated directly across from Mrs. Conrad, Colleen couldn't miss the glint of disapproval in her eyes. She clearly did not want to celebrate her son's engagement. In fact, Colleen wryly wondered if she should be cautious about arsenic tonight. But the thought simply made her giggle.

"Is something amusing?" Mrs. Conrad asked her.

Colleen simply smiled. "No, no, not really."

After they were all seated, Mr. Conrad bowed his head to say a formal prayer, and then the cook, who was acting as their server, began to ladle out soup. Colleen wasn't greatly experienced at formal dining, but she felt confident that she knew enough not to embarrass herself. She also knew that if one waited long enough, one should be able to follow the hostess's lead. But discreetly.

Toward the end of their meal, which Colleen felt she was barely tasting—or perhaps it was simply a bit bland—Geoff picked up his butter knife and dinged it onto his crystal water glass. "I have an announcement," he said formally. Although they'd already been fairly quiet, they now became silent. Geoff picked up the bottle of champagne, which his grandfather had uncorked earlier, and refilled everyone's glasses. Even Colleen's, despite his mother's disapproval.

"Lift your glasses with me," he instructed. "Let's toast to my good news. Colleen has agreed to marry me at City Hall later this week and then we'll—"

"*What?*" His mother set her glass down so hard that Colleen was surprised the slender stem didn't shatter.

"We're going to get married," Geoff firmly told her. "That way she can go to San Diego with me and—"

"Have you lost your mind?" his mother demanded.

"Ellen," his grandmother said gently but firmly. "Remember, it *is* Christmas."

"I *don't* care." Ellen abruptly stood. "I will *not* permit this."

"Permit it?" Geoff challenged. "Don't forget, Mother, I am of age. I don't need anyone's permission to marry."

"But it is perfectly senseless. You barely know this girl and—"

"Please, sit down, Ellen," his grandmother interrupted.

"Yes," Mr. Conrad agreed. "Let's discuss this calmly."

"I don't see that there's anything to discuss," Geoff told him. "Unless it's to give your congratulations."

"Yes, of course," his grandfather said. "But I'm afraid I must support your mother on this, Geoff. This marriage feels sudden to me. Why are you in such a rush?"

Geoff looked from one to the next without speaking for a long moment. "Do you really want to know?"

"Of course," his grandfather declared.

"Colleen and I won't have much time together as it is. Even if we marry this week, there will be no time for a proper honeymoon.

We'll get set up in the officers' housing in San Diego. My training in Coronado will finish in about six weeks, and then I'll go—well, wherever the navy sees fit to send me. Probably the Pacific."

"You only train for six weeks?" Ellen's eyes grew wide. "Are you serious?"

"Six weeks in Coronado," he explained. "And that's because I already have my license and a good log of hours. Naturally, I'll continue my training—"

"What? In active duty?" she demanded.

"Mother." Geoff gave her a stern look. "Must you question everything?"

"You know I never wanted you to enlist, Geoff. And then to go in as a pilot?" She bristled. "Isn't it enough that I lost your father to war? Must I lose you too?"

"You're not going to lose me," he assured her. "And if I hadn't enlisted, I'd probably just be drafted anyway. Wouldn't you rather I have a say in what I do in the war effort?"

"But you could've asked for a desk job," she protested. "Being an only son of a deceased war veteran, they would've given you special consideration and—"

"I don't want special consideration, Mother. I want to fly!" He turned to Colleen. "And I want to marry this woman."

She forced an uneasy smile.

"Yes, so you have said." Ellen scowled darkly. "Have you never heard the old adage, 'marry in haste and repent at leisure'? What if you spend the rest of your life regretting—"

"The only thing I regret right now is bringing Colleen here." Now Geoff stood. "If you will excuse us—"

"No, no," his grandfather protested. "Don't end it like this, Geoff."

"It's Christmas," his grandmother said. "Please, don't go yet."

"Let's go into the living room and discuss this rationally." His grandfather stood.

As they went into the living room, Colleen glanced at the clock and wondered what her family was doing right now. She knew their holiday wouldn't be exactly merry, but she felt certain it would be better than this. Geoff's family's house might've *looked* like Christmas, but it did not *feel* like Christmas. Not to her. As they sat down in the living room, Colleen decided to grab this bull by the horns—even if this bull was really Geoff's mother.

"I'm curious, Mrs. Conrad. Why exactly are you so opposed to your son marrying me?"

Ellen looked caught off guard.

"Go ahead and tell me," Colleen urged her. "I can take it."

"Well, for starters you are young." She scowled. "Despite your indulging in the champagne tonight, you are barely more than a child. You are only eighteen."

"I was only eighteen when I married Edgar," his grandmother said gently.

"Yes, but that was long ago. It was acceptable then."

"My mother was only seventeen when she married my father," Colleen told them. "And they've been happily married all these years."

"Lucky them." Mrs. Conrad pointed at Geoff. "Do you know that he never even met his father? He was born after my husband died in battle."

"I'm sorry you lost your husband," Colleen told her. Then not knowing what more to say, she mentioned that her own dad had served in the war too. Not that it seemed to help.

"Another thing," Ellen said sharply to Colleen. "You've no intentions for any further education...not even secretarial school. Is that right?"

"That's true."

"Do you think a young woman can simply live off of her good looks?"

"Some of them do." Colleen smiled. "In Hollywood."

"It doesn't matter to me that Colleen has no interest in more education," Geoff declared. "I never found a girl in college that I wanted to marry."

"Something else troubles me." His mother narrowed her eyes. "You mentioned your brother's funeral service at *Old Saint Mary's*. Am I to assume that you are a Roman Catholic?"

"My family is Catholic," Colleen admitted. "I've been through catechism, but anyone who knows me wouldn't call me a *good* Catholic." She couldn't help but chuckle. "I haven't been to confession in ages."

"And you feel *that* is something to be proud of? Or that it's amusing?"

"I only feel that just because my family is Catholic doesn't mean I am Catholic. Good or bad. It's not as if someone is born into a religion. As for being Catholic, it is a choice. And the truth is I'm not sure what I believe. Oh, I believe in God. But beyond that, well, I honestly don't know."

"Do you know that Geoff is Lutheran?"

"Please, Mother." Geoff looked seriously troubled and Colleen knew he regretted bringing her here. "If you must know, I agree with Colleen. I may have gone to a Lutheran church as a child, but my faith is my own. I can be anything I like."

"Perhaps you'd like to be an atheist."

"Oh, Ellen." Mr. Conrad looked distraught.

Colleen was fed up. "There are a few other things you may be interested to know about me too." She stood now, pacing in front of the fireplace dramatically. "For one thing, I smoke cigarettes. My family hates that. But I do it anyway. Speaking of my family, we're Irish and quite loud. And although we own a grocery store, we are not wealthy. Not by any means." Colleen strode over to Geoff's mother for her final statement. "And my father was recently sent to a sanatorium with *tuberculosis*."

Geoff's mother leaned back with wide eyes, as if she was worried that she might catch something from Colleen.

"Don't worry. I've been tested. I'm not contagious." Colleen turned to Geoff. "I'd like to go home now."

"Good idea." He stood.

"Thank you for a very interesting evening." Colleen went over to Geoff's grandmother, taking her hand. "I have enjoyed getting to know you—and Mr. Conrad too." She smiled sadly at them. "I apologize for leaving early and wish you both a Merry Christmas."

To Colleen's relief, Geoff's mother said nothing as they grabbed their coats and exited the house. And it was a good thing, since Colleen was tired of biting her tongue. One more word from that woman and Colleen felt certain that she wouldn't be able to control herself. She would probably *speak in haste and repent at leisure*!

Nineteen

Margaret had wanted to keep the store open until the usual closing time, but her mother insisted it was time to shut down. "It's Christmas," Mam said wearily. "The Hammonds are coming over around six. We need to fix some things for supper."

"But Mrs. Hammond already sent most of the food over to our house," Margaret reminded her. "Molly said it's all there and that it looks good."

"Yes, but I had Molly put a roast in the oven. I need to check on that."

"There aren't any customers right now anyway," Bridget told Margaret. "Why not go ahead and lock up before some indecisive last minute shopper wanders in?"

"Fine." Margaret reluctantly tromped to the front of the store, locking the door. If she had her way, despite it being Christmas Eve, she would keep the store open until midnight. Because the last thing she wanted was to spend the evening with the Hammond family. And even though she didn't expect Brian to show his face tonight, it would still be difficult being around his family. One more word of sympathy about her and Brian's breakup and Margaret would probably scream bloody murder. As if it weren't painful enough losing her only brother, but she also had to be subjected to a broken heart. Well, it just seemed so unfair.

"I'm not feeling very well," Margaret quietly told her mother and Bridget as she drove them home. "I think I'll just spend the evening in my room, if you don't mind. Just in case I'm coming down with something. I wouldn't want to expose—"

"Come on, Margaret," Bridget leaned over the seat's back. "You're not sick and you know it. You're just broken up over Brian. You'll get over it more quickly if you just face it head on."

"Is that your professional medical opinion?"

"No, of course, not. It's my sisterly opinion."

"I'm inclined to agree with her," Mam said.

"And our Christmas gathering is thin enough already," Bridget added. "One less person will be noticed. Besides that..." She let out a sad sounding sigh. "This will be my last Christmas at home until... well, who knows. Anyway, I'd like to have as many of us there as possible. Including you, Margaret."

"And Colleen even promised to bring Geoff back with her later," Mam added. "So, please, don't hide out in your room." She reached over and patted Margaret's shoulder. "I understand you feel badly, but none of us are going to be feeling overly merry tonight."

"It'll probably be like a Christmas wake," Margaret said dourly. As she parked the car in back of the house, she imagined them all sitting around with gloomy faces. Why hadn't they just cancelled Christmas completely? But then, seeing Bridget getting out of the car, carrying the box of groceries up the steps, Margaret knew that she would have to put on her party face—if only for Bridget's sake. What if this really did turn out to be Bridget's last Christmas? The thought of this made Margaret feel slightly ill. What was happening to them? What had become of the merry Mulligans?

"Oh my goodness!" Mam exclaimed as they went in through the

back door into the kitchen. "Molly Irene Mulligan—is that really you?"

Margaret peered over her mother's shoulder in time to see Molly doing a little spin in the kitchen. Her hair had been cut and was becomingly styled. She had on a bit of makeup and was wearing Colleen's topaz blue gown.

"You look all grown-up." Bridget set the grocery box on the table.

"You really do." Margaret moved closer for a better look. "I accused you of looking like a six-year-old, but now you could probably pass for a twenty-six-year-old." The truth was, Margaret's baby sister looked more sophisticated than Margaret.

"Colleen told me to urge you both to dress up too, since she's bringing Geoff back here later. She wants him to see our family at our best."

Mam looked doubtful, but then she agreed. "I suppose we could make a bit more effort. After all, it *is* Christmas."

Margaret stared at her mother. She wasn't sure what was going on exactly, but for some reason her mother seemed to be making a turn around. Just yesterday, she'd seemed inconsolable, but today she'd made an effort, acting more like her old self. Perhaps it was simply for Christmas. Just the same, Margaret intended to lay low.

"We'll all take a few minutes to clean up and dress for dinner. And then I expect you girls to don your aprons and help me in the kitchen. Mrs. Hammond might be bringing most of the food tonight, but we still have work to do."

"I don't mind helping," Margaret said, "but I don't see the need to dress for—"

"Mary Margaret," Mam said firmly. "Please, don't argue with me."

Margaret suppressed the urge to carry on. But, really, wasn't it enough that she was willing to join them—must she dress up as well?

"Come on, Margaret." Molly grabbed her by the hand. "Since Colleen helped me, I will help you."

"Really?" Margaret frowned at her. "Since when did you become a fashion expert?"

"I don't know." Molly shrugged. "Since today I guess."

Margaret opened her closet, which was not nearly as glamorous as Colleen's, and just stared blankly at the contents.

"Here." Molly reached past her, extracting the pale green silk dress that Colleen had found on a markdown rack last summer. It had been far too big for Margaret, but Colleen had cut it down, altering it to fit perfectly. It was definitely Margaret's prettiest dress.

"It's a summer dress," Margaret protested as Molly held it up to her.

"Yes, but the house will probably get warm and stuffy tonight. Besides, you can put on a sweater if you need to." Molly shoved the dress toward her. "I'll go find some shoes in Colleen's closet. She won't mind."

As Margaret slipped into the dress, she wondered if looking prettier than usual might help her to feel more confident tonight. Colleen would probably think so.

"Here." Molly presented a pair of dark green high heels. "These will look nice. And you should wear your pearl earrings and pin up your hair. Colleen pinned hers up earlier. ."

Margaret paused to stare at Molly again. She wanted to ask where her baby sister had gone to and if she was ever coming back, but she didn't want to hurt Molly's feelings. Especially since she'd been supportive of Colleen's idea to make Molly look older in the first place. Just the same, she already missed Molly's pigtails, and it hurt to think what Peter would say if he could see her.

"You look beautiful," Molly told Margaret as she watched her put the last pins into her hair. "Do you know that I always wished I'd have red hair like you when I grew up?"

"You mean *auburn.*" Margaret turned to look at her. "Brian may be called redhead, but my hair is definitely auburn."

"Yes. *Auburn.* It's so pretty. And Dad is right. You do look like Maureen O'Hara. Even prettier, I think."

"And you are full of the blarney." Margaret hugged her. "But thank you."

Molly lifted the hem of the green silk skirt, letting it drift gracefully back down. "I love this dress," she told her. "And if you go to midnight Mass tonight, you should borrow Colleen's fur jacket to stay warm."

"Trust me, I will not be going to midnight Mass," Margaret assured her.

"You never know." Molly took her hand. "We better go help Mam."

Molly was eager for the Hammonds to arrive. She was so glad that Margaret hadn't refused to dress up tonight. And even though Margaret seemed fairly certain that Brian wouldn't join them for Christmas Eve, she still seemed to be on pins and needles. She even dropped a cookie tin when the doorbell rang.

"I'll get it." Molly ripped off her apron, hurrying for the front door. So far, she had kept the news of Brian's intentions completely to herself. No one suspected a thing. But she couldn't wait to see Margaret's face—after Brian popped the question. Hopefully he wouldn't wait too long.

"Welcome," she told the Hammonds, opening the door wide so all four could come inside before she quickly closed it to keep the indoor lights from shining outside.

"Who is this?" Mr. Hammond demanded as Molly took Mrs. Hammond's coat. "Do the Mulligans have another daughter that we've never met before? Do they keep this one locked in the basement?"

"Oh, Mr. Hammond." Molly smiled shyly. "You know it's me."

"You look so grown-up, Molly." Mrs. Hammond set her handbag on the hall tree bench. "I can hardly believe my eyes."

Molly quickly explained that Colleen was responsible for this change. But as she spoke, she felt Patrick staring at her—and his expression was odd...not particularly pleasant. But before he could say anything, the rest of the Mulligans emerged from the kitchen, greetings were exchanged, and Margaret, though clearly uncomfortable, was very composed and polite. There was pain in her eyes as she excused herself to the kitchen. She was obviously trying to avoid Brian.

Bridget took over playing host, inviting Mr. Hammond, Patrick, and Brian to sit in the front room—the way that Dad would do if he were here. Meanwhile, Molly followed Mrs. Hammond and Mam to the kitchen.

"Molly, you take that out to the front room." Mam pointed to the silver-plated tray that they'd filled with homemade appetizers. "And Margaret, you ask the fellows if they'd like some eggnog or something else to drink."

Following orders, Molly and Margaret returned to the front room. But before Margaret could take any drink orders, Brian asked to speak privately with her. "Can we go outside to—"

"I, uh, I don't know." Margaret frowned. "I need to get drinks for—"

"Here!" Molly had already set down the appetizer tray in order to grab Margaret's coat, which she was now thrusting at her. "I'll get their drinks for them, Margaret. You go ahead and go."

"But I—"

"Go on with you, Mary Margaret Mulligan." Molly gave her a firm shove. "See you later!"

Mr. Hammond was chuckling loudly as Molly retrieved the appetizer tray, setting it down on the coffee table and neatly laying out little paper Christmas napkins in a row beside it. Bridget, still in the dark about Brian's intentions, looked slightly bewildered. "What's going on here?"

"I guess I can tell you now." Molly stood up with a smile. "Brian is going to propose tonight."

"Are you serious?" Bridget's brown eyes grew wide.

Molly nodded eagerly, quickly explaining their ring shopping trip earlier in the day. "Isn't it wonderful news?"

"I guess so." Bridget looked uncertain.

"Now, I'll take your drink orders." Molly told them their choices and, as she was going to fetch their beverages, Patrick stood, offering to help her carry them back.

"I hardly recognized you tonight," he said as they went to the dining room where Mam had set up the drinks.

"Oh, this." Molly shrugged. "It was the only way to get Colleen to bring Geoff back here tonight."

"Do you like looking like—like that?" Patrick frowned down at her.

Molly frowned. "Like what?"

"You know, so grown-up. Molly, you're only a child."

She felt a strange rush of indignant anger. "I'm not a child, Patrick. I'll be sixteen in March. Colleen and Margaret were right. It's time for me to act my age."

"But you do act your age."

"Well, they wanted me to look my age too." She put her hands on her hips, locking eyes with him. "And the truth is, I kind of like it."

"I just don't understand what was wrong with your pigtails and—"

"You sound just like Peter," she exclaimed. "And as much as I love my brother and always will, I know that wouldn't have forced me to remain a baby forever. Everyone has to grow up eventually, Patrick. I'm sorry you don't like it." Then, feeling close to tears, she turned on her high heel and ran to her bedroom, slamming the door behind her. She did not want to cry—did not want to turn into a baby. But really, of all people, she hadn't expected Patrick to be so demeaning. Not when he'd always treated her like an equal before. Really—she'd thought they were friends. What was wrong with him?

Despite the cold, damp air, which would play havoc with her hairdo, Margaret felt her cheeks growing warm as she and Brian walked down the sidewalk. He'd already apologized to her for what happened in the coffee shop. And she'd already told him that she regretted the words she'd said as well. Now they were simply walking along, holding hands, and not speaking at all.

And, really, she didn't care if they never said another word all evening. She was simply glad that he was back in her life, glad that he was walking beside her, holding her hand. And even if he never wanted to get married—ever—she wasn't even sure that she cared.

"Margaret," he said quietly, stopping on a corner and turning her to face him. "I love you."

Her heart swelled with happiness. "I love you too, Brian. I feel like I've always loved you. Like I will go on loving you forever."

"Me too. I think these past few days were a good lesson to me. I discovered what it felt like to have you taken out of my life. And I

MELODY CARLSON

didn't like it. Not one bit."

"I hated it too," she confessed. "I felt dead inside."

"I know." He pulled her close to him, leaning down for a nice long kiss that sent shivers of happiness from her head to her toes. And then, to her total shock, Brian got down on one knee—right there on the damp sidewalk. He took her hand in his and, holding it between both of them, spoke. "Mary Margaret Mulligan, you will make me the happiest man on earth if you will agree become my wife. Will you marry me?"

"Oh, yes!" she cried out. "I will. I definitely will!"

He stood up and gathered her in his arms again, kissing her with even more passion than before. And then he reached into his coat pocket and pulled out a small package wrapped in shiny foil paper. "Merry Christmas, darling."

Margaret held the small box with both hands. "But I didn't get you anything," she said meekly.

"Oh, yes you did," he told her. "You gave me your word that you'll marry me. Now, hurry up and open it."

With trembling hands, she tore off the paper to see what looked like a jeweler's box. "Oh, Brian..." She was almost afraid to breathe as she opened the lid and there, even in the dim light coming from the moon behind the clouds, she could see the glimmer of a diamond. "An engagement ring? Oh, Brian! When did you do this? How did you—"

"Never mind that. Try it on."

She reverently removed the ring from the velvet lined box, studied it in the moonlight, then handed it to Brian. "You put it on my finger for me." She held out her left hand, waiting as he pushed the ring into place—and just like magic, it fit perfectly!

"Oh, Brian!" She tipped her face toward him and they kissed again—this time for what felt like several minutes. Margaret felt lightheaded as they walked, arm in arm, back to the house. It was so amazing...so wonderful. Margaret couldn't remember the last time she'd felt this happy. Perhaps she never had. Oh, certainly, there was still sadness in her life—things that couldn't be changed and that still needed to be accepted—but even in her dreams, she'd never imagined she would feel this happy again.

Twenty

Molly knew by Margaret's glowing face that Brian had done it. But when Margaret held up her hand, waving it around for everyone to see, they all let out a big cheer. And none more loudly than Molly.

"It looks beautiful on you," Molly said as she admired Margaret's ring.

"I'm so pleased for you," Mam told Margaret. "Your dad will be so happy to hear this news."

"Do you want me to tell him tomorrow?" Bridget asked. "Molly and I are taking him his Christmas present in the morning."

"Can I go too?" Margaret asked. "To tell Dad the good news."

Bridget frowned. "Only two of us are allowed to visit—and that's even stretching the rules a bit." She glanced at Molly. "And you made that lovely package for him, I'm sure you want to take—"

"Margaret can go in my place," Molly offered. "She should be the one to tell Dad her exciting news."

"You're a darling!" Margaret hugged Molly.

"I'll make sure Dad knows you're the one who put his Christmas package together," Bridget told Molly.

"But it's from all of us." Molly forced a cheerful smile. Then to hide her disappointment about not getting to see Dad tomorrow, she went to get her Brownie camera, putting a fresh bulb into the flash attachment. "I want to get a picture of the newly engaged couple," she told Margaret, posing them in front of the china hutch.

Everyone was in fairly good spirits as they sat down to their Christmas Eve supper. The table was loaded with tasty looking dishes but, although every chair was filled, Molly couldn't help but notice the spots where Dad and Peter would normally sit. And just thinking of them made her want to cry again. As the table suddenly got quiet, she realized she wasn't the only one to miss them.

Mam looked across the table with a serious expression. "Jack, would you please say grace for us tonight?"

Mr. Hammond nodded and, bowing his head, quietly said his usual blessing then added a couple of extra lines. "We thank Thee for all the wonderful years we had with our beloved Peter as we fondly remember him tonight. And we ask Thee to be with Riley and to help him back to the fullness of health." As he said *amen*, they all echoed, crossing themselves and looking up with misty eyes.

"Well, it's most definitely a different sort of Christmas this year," Mam declared. "But we still have much to be grateful for." She smiled at Brian and Margaret. "And much to look forward to in the upcoming year. Merry Christmas everyone!"

They echoed her sentiments and soon were passing the food around, commenting on how delicious it all looked and eventually eating. As usual, the volume increased as the meal progressed. Molly played the waitress, running various things back and forth from the kitchen, refilling dishes, and trying to accommodate everyone. She didn't mind being busy though... It helped to distract her from missing Dad and Peter.

"Now that I've broken the ice," Brian was saying to Patrick, "perhaps you should consider taking the plunge too." He grinned at Margaret. "I must say the water is fine."

"Oh, my, wouldn't that be grand," Mrs. Hammond gushed. "What a joy it would be for both my boys to get engaged at the same time." She nudged Bridget with an elbow. "What do you think of *that* idea, dear?"

"Mother," Patrick scolded gently. "You know better than playing matchmaker. Remember what happened the last time you tried that with Howard and Marsha."

The mood lightened as they all remembered the fiasco Mrs. Hammond had created when trying to bring a pair of Mr. Hammond's employees together. Both of them wound up quitting their jobs at the leather shop, Mr. Hammond had to scramble to replace them, and Mrs. Hammond promised to never play cupid again.

"One engaged son is plenty," Mr. Hammond told his wife. "Let's not rush our young people, Louise. They have plenty on their minds right now anyway."

"Yes, I suppose you're right." Mrs. Hammond turned back to Bridget. "When do you take your nurse exams, dear?"

Bridget explained about her boards and how she would probably be shipped off to boot camp shortly after finding out the results. "Well, if I pass my boards, that is."

"Of course you will pass," Margaret assured her.

"But boot camp?" Mrs. Hammond frowned. "Do they really send young women to *boot camp*?"

"The ANC calls it basic training," Bridget explained. "But my friend Virginia heard that it's a lot like boot camp. We'll dress in fatigues and do drills and calisthenics and a lot of running."

"You have to do all that to be a nurse?" Mrs. Hammond asked.

"I expect they want to be sure that we're physically fit before they assign us overseas. Being an army nurse isn't for the weak of heart—or body." Bridget smiled. "But I believe I'm up for the task."

They had just finished supper when Colleen and Geoff arrived. Although they'd already eaten their main meal, they were grateful to have dessert. "We left early," Colleen explained. "So we could be with everyone here." She nodded at Mrs. Hammond as she made room for another chair at the table. "Because I saw those pies you brought over this morning. It took real control not to cut into that pumpkin one at lunchtime."

Molly rose to clear the table, insisting that the rest of them stay put and continue visiting. "That will make it less crowded in the kitchen." She glanced at Colleen, who was still standing. "But could you get their pie orders for me? Then I'll serve everyone."

"You got it."

"And don't forget to turn on the coffee pot," Mam told Molly. "It's all ready to go."

Molly carried a stack of dishes into the kitchen, setting them next to the sink, then returned for a second load. It made her feel glad to see everyone cheerfully visiting together. Christmas was really turning out much better than she'd expected. Sure, it was different... but at least no one was crying. Even Mam seemed almost happy, except for the sadness in her eyes.

Molly was just setting out the dessert plates when Colleen came in listing off the pie orders. "Thanks," Molly told her. "Now you should go back and join the others."

"This is so much better than at Geoff's house." Colleen rolled her eyes. "They might have a big pretty tree and a fancy table, but honestly, it was like having Christmas at the morgue."

"Well, I'm glad you're here." Molly cut into the apple pie. "Did you see how pretty Margaret's ring looks on her?"

"Oh, I totally forgot to look." Colleen hurried back into the dining room, letting out an enthusiastic shriek as she congratulated the newly engaged couple. As Molly cut pieces of pie, carefully setting them on plates, she wondered if there was anything she could say to Patrick to repair the rift that seemed to have settled between them. She knew that his reaction to her appearance was probably very similar to how Peter would've reacted if he were here. Patrick was simply feeling protective, wanting to preserve her as the baby of the family. That only made it more disturbing.

Besides, Colleen and Margaret were probably right—it probably was time for Molly to grow up. Good grief, she would be sixteen soon. Some girls her age smoked and drank and went out with college boys. Not that Molly had any intention of acting like *that*. But some people did consider sixteen nearly grown-up. And it wasn't as if she could turn back the clock. If Patrick couldn't accept that she was no longer a little girl in pigtails...well, there wasn't much she could do about it. But it still made her sad to think that perhaps he wouldn't want to be her friend anymore. Did this mean he wouldn't want her to write to him while he served in the navy?

Colleen wasn't surprised that everyone in her family wanted to go to midnight Mass tonight, but she was a bit stunned when Geoff announced that he wanted to go as well. "Are you sure?" she quietly asked him. "After all, it's a Catholic church."

"A church is a church, isn't it?"

She frowned. "I, uh, I don't know."

"And it's part of your life," he pointed out. "And your family's life. I need to experience it for myself."

Although Colleen had been looking forward to having her family all gone and the house and Geoff to herself, she went for her coat. Before long they were all piling into cars and slowly, because of the blackout and the rain, parading down the street toward Old Saint Mary's.

The Hammonds had already invited Geoff to spend the night at their house and, to Colleen's relief, he'd agreed. That meant she'd get to spend the whole day with him tomorrow. And hopefully, they would not go back to the farm—or if he wanted to go, she'd simply make an excuse to decline. Not that she wanted to be away from him—even for a few hours.

As they went into the church, Colleen tried to coach Geoff on what to do, and fortunately he appeared fairly comfortable. But as they took their seats, her mind began to wander. She knew that the Church would only honor her marriage if Geoff converted to Catholicism. She really didn't want to force him to do that—especially when she felt uncertain of her own commitment to the Church. And yet she knew that, if she didn't get married in the Church and if Geoff didn't convert to Catholicism, her family—particularly her parents—would probably throw a fit.

Because of everything going on and Dad's illness, no one had really questioned Geoff's religion. They probably assumed that he was simply a "good Catholic boy." And, in fact, she might've even said something to suggest this to Mam early on. Not an outright lie exactly, but just a way of keeping an even keel, so to speak. Colleen hadn't wanted to rock the family boat—not when it was already on such rough seas. Or so she'd told herself.

Geoff reached for her hand, clasping it firmly in his and sending a warm rush throughout her. She really did love him. And she did want to marry him—but at the same time, she felt concerned. His mother was so adamantly opposed to everything. Primarily Colleen. What would it be like to be married to a man whose mother despised you? Colleen could usually win people over, and she felt that she'd made good headway with his grandparents, but Mrs. Conrad seemed impossible.

When it was time to pray, Colleen did something unexpected—she actually asked God to show her what was the right thing to do. And although she didn't really expect to hear a response or get an answer, it felt surprisingly good to just ask. Sort of like lifting a load off her shoulders.

After the service, Geoff dropped Mr. and Mrs. Hammond, who'd rode with them, at their house. "We'll leave the door unlocked," Mr. Hammond told Geoff as he climbed out of the backseat. "Just let yourself in after you take Colleen home."

"Thank you."

"I'll make up the sleeper sofa in the front room," Mrs. Hammond told him. "Make yourself at home."

He thanked them again, and now it was just Geoff and Colleen. "Want to go for a little ride?"

"Sure," she agreed.

"I doubt there's anything open tonight since it's Christmas Eve, but I don't feel sleepy yet."

"Me neither."

There were very few cars on the road, and eventually Geoff parked on Nob Hill. He slipped his arm around Colleen, snuggling her close to him and after a bit—and after the windows nicely steamed up—he stopped kissing her. "We have to get married as soon as possible," he said in a husky voice. "What do you think about December 26th as an anniversary date?"

"It's a little close to Christmas," she said. "I've always heard you should plan your wedding date so that it's well spaced from birthdays and holidays."

"Why's that?"

"So that it stands out—something to celebrate all on its own."

"If I had a longer leave, I'd suggest New Year's Eve, but that might be problematic too. I mean, when it comes to avoiding holidays." He reached over to touch her cheek. "Oh, Colleen, let's just do it. Let's get married as soon as we can."

She took in a deep breath. "You know...I actually prayed about this very thing in church tonight, Geoff."

"Do you want me to become a Catholic?" he asked eagerly. "Is that it? Because if it is, I'm willing. I'll convert if that's what it takes."

She smiled. "It's not that easy, Geoff. It takes time to convert. You have to take catechism classes and meet with the priest and all sorts of stuff."

"Oh."

"And that's not what's troubling me anyway. Like I told your mom, I'm not really a good Catholic myself. I only go to Mass to keep my family from complaining. And I never go to confession anymore. Hardly ever pray the rosary. Well, except when I prayed it for Peter." She sighed. "A lot of good that did."

"I'm sorry."

"The real problem for me... Well, you can probably guess what it is."

"My mother."

She just nodded, feeling a lump in her throat. "I've never felt so—so disliked before." That was putting it gently, since she actually felt despised.

"My mother would probably dislike any woman I brought home, Colleen. You shouldn't take it personally."

"How do I not?"

"Just ignore her. That's what I try to do. She's always been very overprotective of me. I know it's because of losing my dad so early on. And I understand that. But I've just gotten to the place where I let it roll right off me. Like water off a duck's back."

"But wouldn't it be awful to have her so opposed to me? To practically hate me? I know you love your mother, Geoff. How can you so easily dismiss her like that?"

"It's just the way it has to be. If it makes you feel any better, she was just like that when I decided to take flying lessons. She threw a fit and didn't speak to me for months. But she eventually got over it, and she'll get over this too."

Colleen wasn't so sure.

"I want you with me, Colleen. I want you to come to San Diego. I want to know that you're waiting for me while I'm overseas."

"I will be waiting for you, Geoff, whether we're married or not."

"I know, but I want—"

"There's one thing I have to agree with your mother about, Geoff."

"You're kidding! What?"

"This does feel awfully rushed to me too."

"But it's because of the war. That has changed everything for everyone, Colleen."

"I realize that. But I have to think about my family too, Geoff. They've been through so much already. Losing Peter. Dad's illness. Bridget going off to the army. If I run off and get married, well, it'll be just one more blow to them."

He didn't say anything.

"Don't get me wrong," she said quickly. "There's a part of me that doesn't care—a part of me that would throw caution to the wind, marry you, and go to San Diego. But then I have to think about what comes afterward. You'll be sent somewhere...far away. Do I just stay down in San Diego? With a bunch of strangers? Meanwhile my family is—"

"You could go back home as soon as I get shipped out. That'd be okay."

"But that even seems a little odd. Being married, but living at home."

"Then get an apartment."

"By myself?"

"Get a roommate. Maybe Margaret would—"

"I just wonder if we aren't in over our heads a little. Too much too soon. What is wrong with being engaged for a while...say, six months? You'll get to come home on leave sometimes, won't you?"

"I don't know. I hope so."

"Well, maybe if we gave it some time, maybe I could even win your mother over."

He let out a long sigh of disappointment.

"Imagine how it could be, Geoff. What if both your family and my family were completely onboard with our marriage, what if we had a wedding next summer that everyone could come to, and they could all get to know one another? Wouldn't that be wonderful?"

"I guess."

"Are you afraid you'll quit loving me after six months?"

"No, Colleen," he declared. "I will never quit loving you. Something happened that day we met on the street. It felt like something inside me clicked—like this is the girl for me. Like we are a perfect fit. Oh, it didn't make any sense because I didn't really know you, but the more we talked, the more we were together—I just knew it." He reached for her face with both hands, planting a firm kiss on her lips. "You want to know what bothers me more?"

"What?"

"That you will find someone else while I'm away."

"Oh, Geoff, that won't—"

"You don't know that, Colleen. You're a beautiful woman. You've even considered running down to Hollywood. What if you did that? What if some smooth-talking movie star—like Clark Gable or—"

"Clark Gable is too old for me."

"Or Dick Powell or James Stewart or—"

"Stop it." She started to laugh. "I love *you*, Geoffrey Edgar Conrad. Don't you know that by now?"

He hugged her. "I think I do, but I guess I still question if it's really true."

"But I want to wait six months," she said quietly. "And during that time, I will do everything I can to win over your mother."

"And if you don't?"

"Then I'll marry you even so. I promise!"

"I will hold you to that promise, Colleen." They sealed it with a kiss, and before long the windows steamed up all over again. But by the time Geoff was driving her home, Colleen felt confident that they'd made the right decision. Six months just felt better than this week. Perhaps God had heard her prayer after all.

Twenty-one

Some of Margaret's previous enthusiasm had evaporated by the time she and Bridget were driving home from the sanatorium. "Dad didn't look good," she told Bridget. "Did you notice how thin his face seemed?"

Bridget just nodded.

"And even though he was glad to hear about my engagement, he seemed so sad."

"Being confined in a sanatorium—away from your family and friends and home...well, that would make anyone sad, don't you think?"

Margaret sighed. Life had been so busy lately, she hadn't really given Dad or his health much thought. And seeing him like he was today filled her with gloom. "What are his chances of getting well?" she asked quietly.

"The truth?"

"Of course."

"Promise you won't tell Mam?"

"Okay." Suddenly Margaret wasn't sure she wanted to know the truth.

"He probably has about a fifty percent chance of recovering."

"Oh, dear..."

"So...maybe we could talk about something else?"

"Yes, yes, of course." Margaret thought for a moment. "So...do you feel ready for your board exam?"

Bridget shrugged. "I'm working on it. Some days I feel a little worried, but for the most part I think it'll go okay."

"Are you still excited about becoming an army nurse?"

Bridget nodded eagerly. "I can hardly wait, Margaret. I mean, I'm sad to leave the family behind. But I'm so ready for this. To travel, to help servicemen, to meet other medical professionals like me. It's going to be a whole new world."

"You're a lot braver than I am."

"I don't know. I think you're brave to want to get married. That would scare me to death."

"I couldn't believe what Brian said last night." Margaret shuddered. "Pestering Patrick to test the waters. Good grief. I don't know what he was thinking."

"He was probably thinking that he was glad to have proposed to you."

"I felt so sorry for Patrick and you. How embarrassing."

"Oh, it was okay."

"What if Patrick did propose to you? What would you say?"

Bridget waved a hand. "Don't worry, he won't."

"How do you know that?"

"We're just friends. We've always been just friends. Our parents always try to make it seem like more, but it's not."

"But what if it was?" Margaret pressed harder. "What if Patrick wanted it to be something more? Think about it, Bridget. Patrick would be quite a catch."

"All I can think about—at the moment—is what it will be like to be in the ANC. That's more than enough for me. But what about you, Margaret?"

"What do you mean?"

"Are you looking forward to being married?"

"Of course." Margaret stared down at her ring. "I can't wait."

"Have you thought about a date yet?"

"Not really. I mean, it would be nice if Dad was home, but you said that could be up to a year. I really don't want to wait a year."

"It's possible Dad could get better sooner. Some patients recover within six months, but it's not something you could count on."

"I always thought I wanted to get married in June. But now I'm not so sure."

"I'll probably be stationed overseas by then. I doubt I'd be able to come home that soon for the ceremony. For that matter, I wonder if Brian would be able to come home by then. I don't really know how getting leave works. I guess I should look into it."

"So Dad may still be sick and you may be overseas...and obviously Peter can't be there." Margaret let out a sad sigh. "It just doesn't feel like a very festive wedding to me."

"I guess you'll just have to make the best of it."

"Maybe Brian and I should get married right away," Margaret said suddenly. "If we planned a small ceremony before he gets shipped out, at least you'd still be here."

"Don't do it on my account."

"No, that's not what I mean. It's just that I *want* to marry him— and he wants to marry me. It feels like we've known it for years. What's the point in waiting?"

"I don't know. I guess that's something you'll have to discuss with Brian first."

"Don't worry, I will." But the wheels were already spinning in Margaret's head. She would see about reserving the church between now and New Year's. She had always dreamed of an evening wedding...with candlelight. Colleen could probably help her with a gown. Or perhaps a stylish suit. That would be more practical. Except that she'd always imagined going down the aisle in an elegant white gown. With her three sisters standing up with her. "You will be my maid of honor, won't you?" she said suddenly.

"If I'm here when you get married. Of course."

"Good. And Colleen and Molly can be bridesmaids. I want you all to wear blue."

"Sounds like you've got it all figured out."

"Well, it's something I've been thinking about for years."

By the time they got home, Margaret's mind was made up. Somehow she must talk Brian into getting married before he was expected to report for duty. She hurried into the house and found her mother removing a pie from the oven. "I have good news, Mam."

Her mother stood up with a hopeful expression. "Is your dad better?"

Margaret bit her lip. "I, uh, I really don't know. I mean, he was okay." She glanced at Molly, who was peeling potatoes. "And he loved the box. But my news is about something else."

"What is it?" Molly asked.

"I want to get married before Brian ships out in mid-January."

"That doesn't give you very much time." Mam frowned. "And you know that Geoff wants Colleen to marry him the day after Christmas—that's *tomorrow.*" She wiped her damp hands on the front of her apron. "Too much is happening. Too fast. It makes my head spin just to think about it."

"Then you're not happy for me?" Margaret frowned. "I thought you might enjoy a *real* wedding. Especially since Geoff wants Colleen to get married at City Hall."

"Colleen told me that she talked Geoff into waiting—six months," Molly said quietly. "I'm not sure if I was supposed to say anything though."

"Six months?" Margaret asked indignantly. "Colleen is having a June wedding?"

"Well, I don't know about that," Molly said quickly. "You should talk to her. But she and Geoff went for a drive."

"I was the one who was always going to have a June wedding," Margaret declared.

"Then why don't you wait until June?" Mam asked eagerly.

"Because it sounds like Colleen has already stolen that—"

"Colleen hasn't stolen anything," Molly protested. "She just felt it was wise to wait. After all, she's only known Geoff for a few weeks."

"Yes," Mam agreed. "I think Colleen is being quite prudent...for a change."

"Well." Margaret blew out a sigh. "Even more reason for Brian and me to get married before he ships out."

"What does Brian say?"

"I don't know. We haven't talked about a date yet." Feeling enthused again, she went on to tell them about her plans for an evening wedding, bridesmaids wearing blue, and all sorts of fun ideas. "Maybe you and Mrs. Hammond could make the wedding cake," she suggested to her mother.

"Shouldn't you be discussing all this with Brian?" Molly asked. "Before you make too many plans."

"Yes. I was just about to call him. But I wanted Mam to be in on this. A wedding is a family affair. At least, I want mine to be one."

"Well, you should discuss this with Brian—and the Hammonds too—and then we'll talk." Mam put the back of her hand to her forehead. "I think I need to go take a little rest. All this talk of weddings is making me tired."

"Do you feel okay?" Molly asked with worried eyes.

"Yes, yes. I'm fine. Just a bit weary." She pointed to the pile of potatoes. "Go ahead and put those on to cook, then mash them and place the bowl in the oven to stay warm until it's time to go to the Hammonds' at three. I'm going to put my feet up for a bit. And don't forget about the other pie," she called over her shoulder. "It needs about ten more minutes."

After Mam left, Margaret turned to Molly. "Do you think she's getting sick?"

"She said she was tired."

"But that's how Dad was...and then we learned it was TB."

"But Mam's been tested, Margaret. It was negative."

"Maybe she should get tested again." Margaret frowned. "Seeing all those people at the sanatorium, well, it was pretty scary. It's bad enough that Dad is there. But if Mam had to go—oh my, it would be just horrible."

Molly nodded grimly.

"And remember what Bridget said—if the doctor would've tested Dad earlier on, before the illness advanced, he would've had a better chance at a quick recovery."

"That's true. But there's not much we can do about this today. We should talk to Bridget—she's the medical expert of the family." Molly sighed as she picked up another potato.

Molly tried not to worry about Mam as she put the mashed potatoes into the mixing bowl. She knew Mam treasured the heavy McCoy bowl that had belonged to her mother . For that reason, Molly was always careful with it. She put some dabs of butter on top then covered it with foil and set it into the still-warm oven.

"Smells good in here," Bridget said as she came into the kitchen. "Any hot water for tea?"

"Right there." Molly pointed to the kettle. "Mam is resting right now, but we should be heading to the Hammonds' in about half an hour. Margaret was concerned about her."

"Concerned about what?"

"Well, Margaret might've been worked up after visiting the sanatorium. I can understand that. The place makes me uncomfortable too. But I'm willing to go—for Dad's sake."

"Yes, yes. But what's this about Mam?"

"Well, Mam was tired…and Margaret got worried that she might be getting sick. Like Dad. You know?"

Bridget's brow creased as she poured hot water into the teapot. "Maybe she should get tested again. Did she seem to have any other symptoms?"

"I don't really know what the symptoms are."

Bridget patted Molly on the head. "And you probably don't need to know. Seems to me you have plenty to think about these days."

Molly shook her head. "No, I should know about tuberculosis, Bridget. You'll be going away soon. Margaret is getting married. And Colleen, well, she doesn't usually like to think about serious things. At least, she didn't used to."

Bridget looked into Molly's eyes then nodded. "I think you're right. You should know. How about if I give you a medical booklet? You can read it now and keep it handy…just in case." She smiled. "Who knows, maybe you'll want to be a nurse too. You're certainly smart enough."

Molly considered this. "I don't know…."

"You wouldn't want to be a nurse?" Bridget looked surprised.

"Oh, I might want to...but there's something else I'd rather be."

"What?" Bridget filled a teacup.

Molly felt unsure. "Patrick is the only one I ever told this to. Because he never made fun of me."

Bridget's expression grew somber. "Meaning your sisters tease you too much."

Molly shrugged. "You're not as bad as Colleen and Margaret."

"Well, you don't have to tell me if you don't want to."

Molly considered how Bridget was soon going to war and instantly knew she could trust her. "I want to be a writer. My teachers tell me that I have real talent, but I'm almost afraid to believe them."

"You better believe them." Bridget took a sip of tea. "And I'm looking forward to some really good letters from you when I'm overseas."

"I already promised you I'd write," Molly reminded her. "I plan to keep that promise."

"Good. And if you read the booklet I give you, maybe you'll be well enough informed that you can share medical news about Mam or Dad."

Molly was about to assure her that she would, but a knock on the back door stopped her. "I'll get it." She hurried back to see that it was Patrick.

"My mother sent me over to pick up the foods you ladies were bringing over to our house. My car's out back." He seemed to be studying her with interest. "I'm relieved to see you look more like the real Molly Mulligan today." He pointed to her hair. "Although I still miss the pigtails. Why did you cut your hair?"

"Colleen cut it."

"But *why?*"

"Because I made a deal with her," she said with exasperation.

"Remember I told you, it was my way to get her to spend Christmas Eve with—"

"Yes, yes, I remember that. But I still think it was a mistake."

"Why's that?" Bridget asked him with interest.

Patrick had a lopsided grin. "I suppose I just wanted our Molly to stay a little girl forever."

"Well, I think Molly's hair looks nice like that." Bridget touched her own short brown curls. "Busy modern women don't have time for long tresses." She winked at Molly. "Right, sis?"

Molly just nodded.

"Call me old-fashioned then." Patrick shrugged then sniffed at the apple pie on the counter.

"Poor Pat." Bridget playfully poked him in the ribs. "We all have to grow up eventually. Even Molly. You know she'll be sixteen in March."

"Don't remind me." Patrick looked around the kitchen. "So, do you have some things ready for me to take over? My car's still running."

"Yes." Molly pointed to the dishtowel-lined wooden box on the table. "Mam said put the pies in that." As he loaded the pies, she used potholders to remove the McCoy bowl from the oven. "Be really careful with this bowl." She wrapped it in more dishtowels. "On second thought, I'll ride with you and carry this in my lap—to make sure it gets there safely. Otherwise Mam will be upset."

He pointed to her. "Are you ready to go like that? Or did you need to change into another one of your big sister's party dresses?"

She smirked at him as she untied her apron. She'd dressed simply today. Just her navy blue sweater set and a red and blue plaid skirt. "I'm fine like this."

"You got that right." He picked up the box of pies.

They soon had everything loaded in his car, and Molly, in the front seat with the hot bowl wrapped in a towel sitting in her lap, had to chuckle. "What a great way to stay warm in winter. Carry a bowl of hot mashed potatoes wherever you go."

"How about we take the long way home?"

"The long way?"

"I heard that it's good luck to drive over the Golden Gate Bridge on Christmas Day."

"Really? I've never heard that before."

"Well, I figure that since I'm shipping out soon, I should gather all the good luck I can before then."

"For sure. Let's do it."

"And that'll give me time to tell you something."

"What?"

"I want to apologize. I was very rude to you last night. And I really am sorry about it. I don't know why I got so mad to see you dressed up like Colleen."

"It's okay. It just reminded me of Peter. He would've acted exactly the same way."

"Even so,,,he's your brother. He had a right to act like that. I don't."

"But you're like a brother, Patrick. I don't mind if you treat me like a sister. Peter would approve."

"I know. But I still don't want to act rude. That's wrong. And I know it hurt it your feelings."

She felt a clutch in her chest, remembering how she'd been close to tears last night. "It did hurt. You know what I was most worried about?"

"What?"

"I was afraid we weren't going to be friends anymore and that I wouldn't get to write to you when you're overseas."

"Well, that would be a huge mistake. We will always be friends, Molly. And I would be very honored to get letters from you."

She sighed in relief and, with her hands snuggled into the towels wrapped around the McCoy bowl, she felt the warmth running all through her. *Patrick was still her friend!*

Twenty-two

M olly knew better than to voice her opinion out loud, but one week seemed too little time to plan a wedding—at least, the kind of wedding Margaret hoped for. "I think you had the right idea," she confided to Colleen on the morning of Margaret's wedding. "Just go to City Hall and get it over with."

Colleen laughed as she pinned the hem into Molly's bridesmaid dress. Despite keeping the designs simple and having some girl-friends helping out with the sewing, Molly's dress was still not quite finished. And right now, Mam was adjusting the fit on Margaret's store-bought gown. Fortunately, Colleen had found a marked-down wedding dress at City of Paris. A gown that Margaret felt was perfect and only needed minor fitting alterations.

Meanwhile, Mrs. Hammond had insisted on making a three-lay-ered wedding cake with lemon custard filling. Her sister-in-law Gloria, the owner of a downtown florist shop, was handling all the flower arrangements, including a family discount for the Mulligans. According to Margaret, orchids would decorate the church "to honor Peter." Margaret had explained how the Hawaiian blooms and other imported goods could soon be shorted on the mainland due to the war.

"I just hope nothing goes wrong tonight," Colleen mumbled

with pins between her lips. "Everything has been such a rush. And Margaret's always had such big dreams for her big day."

"And a June wedding." Molly turned a half-step as Colleen stuck in another pin.

"And it's ironic that I'm the one getting the June wedding. Especially since I probably would've been fine with a City Hall wedding."

"Patrick said that Brian wanted to wait until June," Molly confided to Colleen. "But Margaret insisted."

"As we knew she would."

"Why is she is such a hurry?" Molly turned again.

"The truth?"

"What do you mean?"

"You know what a worrywart our dear Margaret can be." Colleen lowered her voice. "She's probably terribly concerned that Brian will get injured...or even killed. She wanted to be sure they got married first. Just in case."

"Oh, Colleen, that's so sad."

"Sad but true. And to be honest, Geoff has shared similar thoughts with me. I finally decided that I'm doing him a big favor by making him wait."

"Why's that?"

"He'll have to keep himself alive—in order to marry me." Colleen chuckled like this was a good joke.

But Molly didn't think it was funny. Still, she said nothing, just turned again. This war was serious business—and they all knew it. Yet they couldn't go around with long faces forever. But still, to laugh about dying in the war...well, that just felt wrong.

"Colleen?" Mam called out as she entered their bedroom. "We need your opinion. I say it's a perfect fit, but Margaret thinks it should be tighter."

"I want my waist to look like Scarlett O'Hara."

"That is perfectly ridiculous," Mam declared. "You may faint at the altar."

Molly turned so that she could see Margaret. The creamy white satin-and-lace gown was perfectly elegant. "Oh, my!" She gasped. "You look so beautiful, Margaret. Like a princess. Or a queen."

Colleen walked all around Margaret, checking on the fit and the hemline and sleeve length, finally nodding with approval. "It looks perfect. And that bodice is like a glove."

"What did I tell you?" Mam said to Margaret, but the bride still seemed uncertain.

"It really is gorgeous, Margaret. Don't you like it?" Molly asked.

Margaret sighed. "Yes, yes. I love it. I just want everything to be flawless. And I worry that I've pushed this wedding so hard and so fast that everything may go to pieces at the actual ceremony." She fingered a seam of Molly's gown. "What if your dress falls apart?"

Molly smiled. "Nothing will fall apart. In fact I was just thinking how everything has been falling very neatly into place."

"Hopefully it will continue." Margaret checked her image in their mirror. "Because I want to make this a perfect memory. Something I can hold onto forever."

Molly thought about what Colleen had said just moments ago—her suspicions that Margaret was fretting that Brian might be killed on the battlefield. And, really, who could blame her? After all, he was going into the army. Weren't soldiers usually in the middle of the battles?

"It's going to be a beautiful wedding," Mam reassured Margaret. "I still can't believe you pulled it all together in less than a week. But then, you've always been the organized one."

"I owe a big thanks to all of you." Margaret held out her arms as

Mam unzipped the side of her dress. "If you all hadn't helped out so much, it never would've happened."

"Well, there's still a lot on my list for today," Mam carefully lifted the dress off of Margaret. "We all have much to do. So I better get back to it."

"I promised Bridget that I'd get to the store by ten," Molly told Colleen. "But I'll take my dress with me and work on the hem there."

"I wish we'd just closed the store today." Mam carried the gown like a baby toward the door. "One day...what would it matter?"

"That would've been a mistake," Margaret insisted, though Mam had disappeared. "New Year's Eve is tomorrow. People will be shopping for celebrations today, and some late deliveries came yesterday and still need to be put away. Bridget and Molly will have their hands full, but they can handle it—and close early. Plus, I scheduled Jimmy for full days until school starts up again."

"I probably should've gone in to the store today," Colleen said. "But it's Geoff's last day of leave...and then he gets sent somewhere in the Pacific. He can't even tell me where exactly. Anyway, I promised to go out to his farm again." She rolled her eyes. "Not that I'm looking forward to it."

"I wish you'd invited his family to my wedding," Margaret said. "I'd like to meet the Conrads."

"No, you would *not*," Colleen assured her. "Oh, his grandparents, maybe. But not the Wicked Witch of the West."

Margaret laughed. "What a name for your future mother-in-law."

"Tell me about it. Mam scolds me whenever she hears me say it. She thinks I should respect Mrs. Conrad. I say, wait until you meet her yourself!"

"It's hard to imagine anyone being that horrible," Molly told her as Colleen put in the final pin. "Are you sure you're not just being dramatic?"

"I wish I was being dramatic." Colleen stood up, placing her hands on her hips. "Unfortunately, I'm not." She turned to Margaret, who was still standing by the door in her slip. "Do you know how lucky you are to get Mrs. Hammond for a mother-in-law?"

"Maybe you should've married Patrick," Margaret teased.

Colleen rolled her eyes. "Tell that to Bridget."

"I remember a movie," Molly said a bit dreamily, "where the best man and the maid of honor looked at each other during the wedding ceremony and fell in love. Maybe that'll happen with Bridget and Patrick too."

"That'd be wonderful." Margaret smiled. "I told them that they are expected to start the second dance at the reception. Maybe that'll help spark some romance with them."

Molly almost admitted her plan to write letters to both Patrick and Bridget—acting as their connection while they were both overseas. It wasn't that she saw herself as a matchmaker exactly, but perhaps she could do some gently nudging and hinting.

New Year's Eve day passed incredibly fast for Margaret. And yet, when it was time to go to Old Saint Mary's, she felt ready. Geoff, whose leave ended tomorrow, insisted on playing chauffeur to all the Mulligan girls, picking them up at six in order to give them time to dress for the seven o'clock ceremony. The Hammonds would pick up Mam later.

"Are you nervous?" Molly asked Margaret.

She nodded. "I guess so."

"Do you think Mrs. Hammond and her sister-in-law finished decorating the church by now?" Colleen asked from the front seat.

"I'm sure they must've." Margaret tried to imagine what the sanctuary would look like with the orchids, ivy garlands, lit white taper candles. It would be so beautiful. But more than this, Margaret was thinking about Brian, imagining how handsome he would look in a tuxedo. Would his face light up when he saw her coming down the candlelit aisle? Or would he still have that caught-in-the-headlights expression he'd been wearing lately? As if he'd been trapped by her with no say whatsoever in the recent turn of events. But she felt certain that, once it was all over and once they were all by themselves on their honeymoon, he would finally appreciate her decision not to wait.

"I want to thank you again, Geoff." She put a hand on his shoulder. "For offering us your family's cabin in the mountains. It's such a generous gift."

"You're very welcome to it, Margaret. And Brian has already thanked me again and again."

Margaret knew that part of Brian's worries had been related to finances. As a college student with a part-time job in a department store, it wasn't as if he had deep pockets. Geoff's offer of his grandparents' mountain cabin had felt like a true Godsend.

"It's been wonderful how well everything has worked out," Margaret said quietly. "As if it really is meant to be."

"Of course it's meant to be," Molly assured her. "You and Brian have been in love for as long as I can remember. It's about time you two got married."

Margaret felt a bit uneasy as she nodded. She hoped Molly was right. But the truth was, she sometimes questioned it herself. What if she had pushed Brian too hard? What if they were doing this too fast? Or what if it was wrong not having Dad here to give her away? Would guests think it strange that her soon-to-be father-in-law was walking her down the aisle?

Before she could answer any of these questions, Geoff was letting them out in front of the church, and suddenly they were gathering up all their gowns and shoes and miscellaneous wedding paraphernalia and hurrying into Old Saint Mary's.

Molly had never been in a wedding before and being a bridesmaid was an assignment she took seriously. She tried to make herself helpful in every way possible, but as Colleen found herself making a last-minute adjustment to Bridget's gown, Molly positioned herself right next to Margaret, making it her mission to reassure her sister that this really was going to be the happiest day of her life.

"I don't know what's wrong with me," Margaret said in a hushed tone. "I was the one who wanted to do this before Brian left for the war. And now...well, I'm just not sure anymore."

"Do you *love* Brian?" Molly quietly asked.

"Of course, I do. You know I do."

"Then what else is there to question?"

Margaret let out a long sigh. "I know you're right. It's just that so much has happened lately... I feel so unsettled right now. As if something is wrong. Something is missing. Does that even make sense?"

"Something—rather someone—is missing. *Two* someones." Molly straightened a wrinkle in Margaret's veil. "I'm sure we all can feel it. But there's nothing we can do about it. And feeling bad isn't going to help."

"But how do I stop feeling bad?" Margaret looked close to tears now.

Molly glanced over to where Colleen was furiously repairing

a separated seam on Bridget's dress, suddenly realizing it was up to her to help Margaret. "Patrick told me something," Molly began slowly, trying to remember how Patrick had put this. "He told me that Peter would want us all to be happy. And that if we are unhappy—because of losing him—then it would be like the enemy had won. It would be like giving the Japanese the victory—not only over destroying Peter's ship, but destroying his family as well. The way we honor Peter is to live our lives with strength and joy. So imagine that Peter is watching us tonight—imagine the joy he'll feel if he sees you having the happiest day of your life. There's no better way to honor him."

Margaret's eyes seemed to flicker with hope. "That actually makes sense." She hugged her. "For the baby of the family, you're a smart girl."

Molly laughed. "I'm just a parrot, repeating what Patrick told me."

Now Mam and Grandma Margaret and Aunt Kate were coming in to check on them, taking turns to ooh and ah over the gowns and the flowers, and then Mam grasped Margaret's hand. "I just spoke to your Dad, Margaret. Of course, he wishes he could be here, but he sends you his love. And this." She dropped an old Irish penny in Margaret's hand. "For your shoe."

"Yes!" Margaret exclaimed. "Of course."

"Your dad brought that over from Ireland with him." She kissed Margaret's cheek. "And that is from him too." She kissed her other cheek. "And that one is from me."

"I hear the organ music playing the beginning of 'Here Comes the Bride,'" Grandmother Margaret said. "We better let them seat us now, Mary."

And just like that, it was time to start. They lined up in the vestibule, watching as their relatives and Mrs. Hammond were seated and then Molly, being the youngest and least of the bridesmaids, took the arm of Brian's friend Howard and slowly strolled down the aisle.

In Molly's opinion, the wedding was the best ever! Not that she'd been to many. But this one felt purely magical. She'd never seen Old Saint Mary's looking so elegant. Even better than Christmas Eve midnight Mass, since tonight there were flowers and greens along with the glimmering candles. Colleen and Bridget, in their matching blue gowns, were as pretty as film stars. Molly had never seen Margaret look so beautiful, her expression one of perfect serenity as Mr. Hammond walked her down the aisle. She felt that her little pep talk had truly worked.

But it was Brian's face that Molly would remember always. It was as if he completely lit up when he laid eyes on his beloved bride. And in that amazing instant, Molly knew that she wanted to see that exact same look someday. She hoped that the man she would one day marry—many, many years from now—would look at her just like that!

Twenty-three

Colleen was trying not to feel sorry for herself on New Year's Eve. But it did seem wrong that Geoff had to ship out to San Diego today. Of course, he'd explained that was simply when the ship was scheduled. "Maybe our superiors are worried we'll get into some kind of trouble on New Year's Eve," he'd joked as she saw him off. Her one consolation was that his mother and grandparents had said their good-byes at home. As a result, she and Geoff had been free to openly express their affection toward each other. And when a photographer from the *Chronicle* asked to take their photo, they had cooperated—even hamming it up some.

So when Colleen saw their picture on the second page of the newspaper the next morning, she wasn't even that surprised. Naturally, she cut it out and taped it to the side of the mirror of her vanity table. And then she cut another one out of a newspaper at the store, which she planned to send to Geoff—along with a letter that she had told herself she'd write today…but hadn't gotten around to doing yet. She didn't have a good excuse, except that she wasn't much of a writer. And she was not in a good mood.

Her mood this evening was partly due to missing Geoff. But besides that—and she didn't plan to admit this to anyone—she was out of sorts because she knew her friends were out on the town

celebrating New Year—meanwhile, she was stuck at home. Mam
had already gone to bed. Bridget had her nose stuck in a textbook.
And Colleen was playing cribbage with Molly—and losing. Happy
New Year.

"Do you think Brian and Margaret are having a good time on
their honeymoon?" Molly asked absently.

Colleen couldn't help but roll her eyes. "I'm sure they're having
the time of their lives."

"Sounds like sour grapes," Bridget said from where she was curled
up on the sofa with one of her nursing books.

"It's not sour grapes," Colleen retorted. "I'm just bored, that's all."

"Do you regret not marrying Geoff?" Molly asked. "I mean, you
could be down in San Diego right now. That could be exciting."

"From what I've heard, San Diego is nothing special. Just a hole
in the wall naval base. That town doesn't have nearly as much going
on as San Francisco. Or Los Angeles. I wouldn't mind being stationed
down there. I may even get discovered and wind up being a movie
star." She laughed, knowing how unlikely that would be. "But I don't
think LA even has a naval—" She stopped as the doorbell rang. "I'll
get it," she offered, hurrying to answer it before it rang again since
Mam had gone to bed early tonight.

"Patrick." Colleen smiled, opening the door wide. "Come in."
She tugged him inside, quickly shutting the door to prevent light
from streaming out. "What are you doing out by yourself on New
Year's Eve?"

"I was out taking a walk, and I got an idea. I thought I may be
able to find someone here to go to a movie with me."

Colleen glanced at Bridget, who was closing her textbook. "I bet
Bridget would like to go," she told him. "She's had her nose in a book
all day. Her mind probably need a break."

Bridget stood up, stretching her shoulders. "I agree. I do need a break."

"Great." Patrick nodded at Molly. "How about you, Molly? Wanna come too?"

Molly looked about to decline, but before she could answer, Colleen spoke up. "What about me?" Colleen asked. "I'm so bored I could scream. Am I invited too?"

Patrick laughed. "You sure are. I'd love to take three Mulligan girls to the movie. Your mom too, if she wants."

Molly explained that Mam had gone to bed. "I think the wedding wore her out." She lowered her voice. "And she's probably missing Dad."

"I'll write her a note," Bridget offered, "in case she gets up and wonders where we've run off to."

Before long, they were bundled into their coats and heading toward the city center. Sure, it wasn't very glamorous sitting in the backseat with Molly, but it was preferable to being stuck at home. Molly had asked Colleen if she regretted not having married Geoff— like he'd wanted—and although she acted as if she had no regrets, Colleen was not so sure. What if she'd made a mistake?

Yet it had seemed the right choice at the time. And Geoff's mother was certainly relieved. Not that she'd given Colleen any credit for the decision. Colleen had almost wanted to change her mind when she'd seen how Mrs. Conrad had looked so victorious. Like she had the upper hand. Like Geoff wouldn't have gladly eloped with Colleen if given the chance. Perhaps she had made the wrong choice after all. But it was too late now.

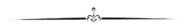

As they got their seats in the theater, Bridget wasn't sure if she was glad to have her sisters along or not. On one hand, it took the pressure off her—so that it didn't feel like a real date. Although both Colleen and Molly seemed determined to pair her off with Patrick. First, they'd made sure she'd ridden in the front seat and just now, they were determined that she sit beside him in the theater. Not that she minded. After all, it was only Patrick. It was like being with her brother. Wasn't it?

But as the lights went down, Bridget wondered how it would actually feel to be on a real date with her old friend. Her experience with dating was severely limited. In fact, she'd only had one beau in her entire life—not that she could really call Rolland Moore a boyfriend, even though he had seemed to like her. He'd taken her to senior prom, as well as to the movies a couple of times. But other than a quick good night kiss, the relationship had felt rather unromantic to her. Nothing like what she expected from a real romance. Certainly not like the ones she'd seen in the movies. Although she hoped tonight's films weren't romantic. That might be uncomfortable.

Fortunately, the first feature turned out to be a screwball comedy with Carole Lombard and Robert Montgomery. Entertainingly lighthearted. But before the next movie started, a newsreel began to roll, with actual footage of the destruction and devastation from Pearl Harbor playing across the screen. Bridget felt like playing the child by closing her eyes and covering her ears to block out all the details. Yet she knew this was not how an army nurse should act. And so, feeling stunned and shocked, she watched and listened while the horrible events of that unforgettable day played across the silver screen.

It wasn't until the newsreel wound down with the narrator quoting President Roosevelt, saying that "this day would live in infamy" and that vengeance would soon be wrought, that Bridget realized that both Colleen and Molly had exited the theater. With a lump in her throat, she knew she needed to join them. "Excuse me," she whispered to Patrick. "I need to go." As she hurried down the aisle and into the lobby, she realized that Patrick had followed her. And there, by the popcorn machine, she found Colleen and Molly. Colleen was visibly upset, but Molly was sobbing uncontrollably.

The four of them huddled together, hugging and talking and trying to console each other. And they were not alone in their shocked sorrow. A few others had left the theater as well.

"That's enough for me," Colleen announced. "I'd rather be home playing cribbage right now."

"Me too." Molly sniffed. "I don't even mind walking."

"No, we'll all go home," Patrick told them. "I don't want to see another movie anyway. Besides, it looks like the next one is a horror film."

And so, after only one movie, they all went home and played canasta with the radio tuned to an upbeat musical program. Colleen and Molly even made popcorn. By the time midnight rolled around, they were all in much better spirits and everyone hugged as they all said, "Happy New Year!"

Bridget was glad to say good-bye to 1941. In so many ways the past year seemed so full of sadness and pain. Despite the war and the challenges she knew would be ahead, she felt 1942 would have to be an improvement. One could only hope.

As badly as Molly wanted Bridget to go down to the wharf to see Patrick off, she knew it was impossible. "I just don't see why your board exams got scheduled on the exact same day that Patrick ships out." Molly paused from scrubbing scorched oatmeal from the bottom of the saucepan. "It's just not fair."

"It wasn't as if the Board of Registered Nursing knew Patrick was shipping out today," Bridget told Molly as she pulled on her coat.

"I know, but it's just too bad." Molly rinsed the pan, setting it in the drainer to dry.

"At least you and Mam will be there to see him off, Molly." Margaret reached for her handbag. "I'd go too if I didn't need to be at the store. I'm still trying to catch up after being gone on our honeymoon." She sighed sadly. "Besides that, I'm not sure I could keep it together. I only told Brian good-bye a few days ago—and seeing all those young men in uniform, well, it tugs at your heart strings. Be sure to take a fresh hanky with you."

"I *love* seeing the boys in their uniforms." Colleen put on her hat. "If Margaret didn't need me so badly at the store, I'd be happy to go to the dock with you."

"And I'd be happy to let you," Margaret told her. "But I have to work on the books, and you need to receive the shipment that's supposed to arrive this morning."

"And I'll be there to help out this afternoon," Mam reminded them.

Colleen patted Molly's hair, which she'd help to style this morning. "So you and Mam will have to give Patrick our best wishes."

"I'm glad I get to go." Molly removed her apron. "Not just because I get to miss half a day of school either. I'm going to take my camera and get some pictures."

Mam looked more closely at Molly now. "Don't you look smart. Is that Colleen's suit?" She fingered the black velveteen collar of the tweed jacket.

"I made her wear it," Colleen told Mam. "I thought she should look stylish since she's there to represent our family."

"I hate to rush you," Bridget said to Margaret. "But I don't want to be late for my exams."

"Yes, yes." Margaret jingled her car keys. "Let's go."

"Good luck with your exam." Mam kissed Bridget's cheek.

"Yes," Molly agreed. "I'm sure you'll ace it. But good luck just the same."

They all said good-bye then the kitchen quieted. "There's a little coffee left," Molly told Mam. "Want me to pour you a cup?"

"Thank you." Mam sat down at the kitchen table.

Molly fixed it with sugar and cream just like Mam liked it. Then she poured the last of it into another cup, adding milk until it was an almond color.

"Coffee milk?" Mam asked.

Molly nodded as she sat across from her. "Like Dad used to make for me."

Mam sighed. "How I miss him."

"Yeah...so do I."

"And Peter." Mam pulled a handkerchief out of the cuff of her dress, dabbing at a stray tear. "When Margaret talked about the boys in their uniforms...well, it reminded me of when we saw Peter off at the docks. And how that was the last time we saw him."

"Will you be okay seeing Patrick off today?" Molly asked quietly.

"Yes...yes...but I feel a little teary just now."

Molly felt a lump in her own throat as she looked at the kitchen clock. "I wanted to go to Anderson's this morning," she told Mam. "But they don't open until nine."

Mam frowned. "But the Hammonds are picking us up at nine thirty."

"I know. But I thought maybe they could swing by Anderson's and pick me up there. My developed photographs are supposed to be ready this morning. I wanted to give some pictures to Patrick to take with him."

"Oh, yes, that would be nice. I'm sure the Hammonds won't mind picking you up."

"And I have some pictures of Peter," Molly told her. "In his uniform."

Mam's eyes lit up. "In his uniform?"

"Yes. And some pictures of Dad too. And pictures at Christmastime and Margaret's wedding."

"I can't wait to see them, Molly."

"I just hope they turn out."

"Why wouldn't they?"

"I'm afraid I may've done something wrong," Molly admitted. "Peter taught me how to use his camera before he left, but I've never seen a developed photograph yet. I mean, one that I took myself."

Mam looked at the clock. "It takes about half an hour to walk to Anderson's. You should probably leave in about ten minutes. To give yourself plenty of time."

Molly nodded as she finished her coffee milk. "Yes, that's what I was thinking too." She stood. "I'll get ready to go."

Molly took her time as she walked toward town. It was a beautiful morning, with not the slightest breeze, and the sun shone brightly down. Perfect for a nice stroll, although it did feel a bit odd to be on the street right now while her friends were sitting in classrooms. Almost as if she was someone else—not young Molly Mulligan, the baby of the family. Dressed in Colleen's tweed suit, with her camera case over her shoulder, she felt older too. She imagined she was grown-up and on her way to work. Perhaps she was working at the newspaper... Would she be a writer or a photographer? Was it possible to do both? She wondered what it would be like to be an adult and have the freedom to come and go as she pleased.

When she got to Anderson's Drug Store, the storekeeper was just unlocking the front door. She explained to the young woman that she'd come to pick up her developed photographs and was pleased to discover that they were there. She paid for them but felt nervous as she carried the package over to the soda fountain. What if the photos didn't turn out right? She would be so disappointed. She sat on a stool then carefully opened the thick envelope, sliding the black and white photographs onto the counter—and staring in wonder.

There was a great picture of a smiling Peter, dressed in cords and a sweater, standing on the steps at the Golden Gate Park. And another one with both her and Peter at the Japanese Tea Garden. She'd forgotten all about how they'd asked a gentleman to take that one for them. There was even a picture of Peter and Patrick in front of the Hammond's house. Peter was in his white navy uniform, but Patrick was wearing his sailor hat, and the two of them were happily grinning. And there were several more shots of Peter in uniform. One at home with Mam and Dad. One with Peter and his four sisters. And three different photos Molly had taken down at the docks in front of the USS *Arizona* on the day he shipped out. In two of the photos, he was smiling. But in one photo he looked very somber... almost as if he knew something.

Molly felt the lump in her throat again and was afraid she was about to burst into tears. "Oh, Peter," she whispered as she stared at the image. Her chest hurt, and it felt difficult to breathe.

"Do you want to order anything?" the storekeeper asked from behind the counter.

"Oh, uh, no thanks." Molly looked up in surprise, suddenly remembering where she was. "I just wanted to sit here a moment. Do you mind?"

"Of course not. Did your photographs turn out okay?" she asked with interest.

Molly nodded, holding up a picture of Peter in uniform. "This is my brother."

The young woman's eyes lit up. "Ooh, he's good looking. I wouldn't mind meeting him. Does he ever go to the USO dances downtown?"

"He was in Pearl Harbor," Molly said in a husky voice. "On the *Arizona*."

The woman's eyes grew wide. "Oh, my. Did he...was he...?"

"He didn't survive." Molly blinked back tears.

"Oh, dear." The woman pulled a couple of paper napkins out of the chrome container and, handing them to Molly, she came around to the other side and put an arm around her shoulders. "I'm so sorry. But I'm sure you must be proud of him. A young man giving his life for his country. He is a hero."

Molly just nodded, using the napkins to blot the tears now streaming down her cheeks. "I know I need to be strong. I need to honor his memory by not giving into sadness. But it's so hard sometimes." She laid down the somber photo and took a deep breath.

"I'm sure it is." The woman picked up the photo of Peter and Patrick. "Did you take these pictures yourself?"

"Most of them."

"It looks like you're a good photographer."

"Thanks," she muttered as she wiped her nose.

"Mind if I look?"

"Not at all."

Molly watched as the woman flipped through the photos, commenting on the various shots taken at Christmastime and Margaret's wedding and a sweet one of Mam and Dad before he went to the sanatorium. "You really are an excellent photographer," she said as she neatly stacked the pictures. "You must be experienced. Whenever I take a photograph, I manage to ruin it. I cut off heads and never get things centered. Or else the lighting is all wrong."

"The photos did turn out good, didn't they?" Molly stared at the photo on top. The one of Peter and Patrick. "Do you happen to have a spare envelope?" She pointed at Patrick, quickly explaining how he was shipping out today, and how she wanted to give him some photos to take. "Then I'll have to get more made from the negatives."

"Sure. I can get you an envelope." The woman went behind the counter, quickly returning with an oversized white envelope. "Will this work?"

"Thank you!" Molly slid several shots into the envelope. "I think it'll be nice for him to have these."

"Aren't you glad you took those photos," the woman said. "I mean before, well, you know. It must be nice to have those images to remember your brother."

"Yes. And I'm sure my family will enjoy them too." But as she slid them back into the envelope, she thought perhaps she should hold back the somber photo of Peter. That one might be hard for them to look at.

The bell on the door jingled, and Molly turned to see a tall hand-some sailor entering the store. With the sunlight shining brightly behind him, it was hard to see his face. But as he got closer, she recognized him. "Patrick!" she exclaimed happily. "Look at you."

He grinned, then gave a salute. "And look at you. So grown-up looking."

She held up the white envelope. "I have something for you—but do we need to go?" She glanced at the clock above the soda fountain, relieved to see it was only ten minutes past nine.

"We have time." He sat down on the stool next to her. "How about a soda?"

"It's kind of early."

"But just for old time's sake?" he asked hopefully. "I know how much you love a chocolate soda. Come on."

She laughed. "That sounds wonderful."

So while the woman fixed their chocolate sodas, Molly gave him the white envelope. "These are for you to take with you. I mean, if you want to."

He slowly went through the photos, commenting on how good they were. "I love these, Molly. Thank you so much." He pointed to her other envelope. "Do you have more in there?" One by one, she showed him the other photos, but slipped the somber one of Peter to the bottom of the pile to keep Patrick from seeing it.

"What's that one?" he asked as their sodas were set down.

"Nothing." She slipped the photos back into her envelope. "It didn't turn out right." She picked up her soda, holding it up like a toast. "Here's to you, Patrick. Or should I say, Second Lieutenant Hammond."

"I hope I'm always just Patrick to you, Molly." He held up his soda glass. "Here's to friends. Let's always be friends."

"Yes," she agreed, clicking her glass against his. "Always friends."

As she sipped her soda, Molly studied Patrick in his sailor uniform. For some reason the uniform made him seem younger—or maybe it was simply that he seemed more vulnerable. She noticed her camera case and knew what she needed to do.

She set down her soda and got out her camera. "Do you mind?" she asked as she pointed the lens toward him.

He grinned. "Go for it."

She took a couple of shots from two different angles and then the storekeeper offered to take a picture of both of them. Molly gladly agreed. "I'll try not to chop your heads off," she said as she held the camera up on the other side of the counter.

"My brother told me that it helps to steady the camera if you slowly exhale as you gently squeeze the button. You might try that."

"There," the storekeeper said as she handed the camera back to Molly. "Hopefully it'll turn out."

"Thanks. I'm sure it will."

As Molly put her camera away, she could feel Patrick watching her, but when she turned back, he looked away. And that's when she noticed the solemn expression in his eyes. Similar to the somber expression in the photo she'd taken of Peter in front of the *Arizona*. Was it happening again? Was this the last day that she would see Patrick? After all, that's how it had been with her brother. She felt a clutch in her chest. She didn't know if her heart could take that much sorrow again. And she wondered... Which was harder—to be the one going overseas...or the one staying home?

Twenty-four

B ridget was tired but satisfied as she and Virginia hopped on a cable car after finishing their board exams. She felt she'd done her best and suspected that was good enough to earn her registered nursing degree. Virginia did not seem quite as confident.

"Stop worrying about it," Bridget told Virginia as the cable car took them down Powell Street. Their plan was to celebrate with an early dinner in China Town—although Virginia's mood was slightly less than celebratory.

"What if I failed?" Virginia said glumly.

"Then you'll take it again. And you'll study harder beforehand."

"But you'll be off with the ANC without me." Virginia pouted. "And it was my idea in the first place."

Bridget suppressed the urge to laugh at her friend's rationale. "I'm sure you passed," she told her. "I've quizzed you on nearly everything that was on that test, Virginia. You knew the information. You must've passed it."

"You really think so?"

"I'm almost certain of it." Bridget smiled. "And if you promise to stop worrying about it, I'll treat you to dinner."

Virginia's eyes lit up. "It's a deal."

The cable car was soon at the edge of China Town, and before long they were seated at a popular Chinese restaurant which, due to the early hour, was not very busy.

"Just think"—Bridget poured some jasmine tea—"one month from now, we'll probably be in basic training."

"You mean *boot camp.*" Virginia grinned. "Think you can handle it, *Mulligan?*"

"I hope I can." Bridget grimaced. "But I remember Peter talking about his time in navy boot camp, right before he shipped out. He made it sound pretty grueling. Besides the fact that they got pulled out of bed in the middle of the night, he said there were days when he felt like his legs were going to fall off from all the running they did."

"But you're an athletic girl," Virginia reminded her. "You went out for all the sports in high school."

"I haven't been very athletic these past few years. Most of my energy has been focused on nursing school."

"That's true. Same thing with me."

"Maybe we should use the next couple of weeks to get ourselves into better physical shape," Bridget suggested. "That way we won't feel so terrible in boot camp."

"Good idea." Virginia frowned. "Well, that is, if I passed my exam."

"Remember our deal? Besides, you can get in good shape whether or not you passed, Virginia. But I'm sure you did." Even as she said this, Bridget questioned the idea herself. What if her friend failed her exam? Was Bridget really ready to go to ANC boot camp and then overseas without Virginia by her side? Because the truth was, it *had* been Virginia who'd pushed this crazy idea at the beginning. The main reason Bridget had felt willing to take on such a challenge was simply because of Virginia's confidence. But if her best friend stayed behind, would Bridget regret going forward alone?

"Now you look worried," Virginia said. "Sure you passed your exam?"

Bridget rolled her eyes and then, trying to think of something else to talk about, she informed Virginia about Patrick shipping out today. "I feel bad that I didn't get to see him off at the boat."

"I know you're good friends with Patrick, but is there more to it than that?"

Bridget shrugged. "Sometimes I wonder...but then it just doesn't seem to click into place."

"Well, it'll be more fun to be nurses if we're not tied down to anyone." Virginia's face lit up. "Imagine it, Bridget, all those wonderful men in their uniforms. We'll have the pick of the bunch."

Bridget laughed. "Really, Virginia. One might think your only interest in the ANC was to find yourself a man."

"Not just any man." Virginia chuckled. "I want an officer and a gentleman. Hopefully someone from a wealthy family—and as handsome as Clark Gable."

"Goodness, you don't ask for much, do you?"

Virginia's face clouded. "Well, just that I passed my exam."

Molly clipped the front page story from the *Chronicle*, skimming the article as she pasted it into the notebook she was keeping for her current events class. "Did you hear this, Mam?"

"What's that?" Mam turned from the pot of soup she was stirring.

"German U-boats were spotted on the East Coast yesterday."

"Which coast, where?"

"Our East Coast. Here in America."

Mam shook her head. "They seem to be coming at us from every direction."

Molly checked the clock to see that it was getting close to seven.

"Shouldn't Margaret and Colleen and Bridget be home by now?"

Mam frowned as she put the lid back on the soup pot. "Yes. I hope they haven't had car trouble again. With your dad and Peter gone, we're a helpless bunch when it comes to fixing anything."

"Maybe I should take auto mechanics class for my elective next term."

"Auto mechanics class for *girls*?" Mam scowled. "That doesn't sound right to me."

"But if I learned to fix our car, we could keep it running until Dad gets home."

"I'm sure your school won't let girls take a mechanics class, Molly. That's a man's world."

Molly wasn't so sure. In fact, she intended to find out. "How hard could it be to change the oil? Or a tire? Shouldn't we know how to do those things? With so many men heading off to war these days, shouldn't girls learn how to keep things running while the guys are gone?"

"Men have been going off to war for centuries, but that doesn't mean a girl should become an automobile mechanic."

"They didn't have cars in previous centuries," Molly pointed out, and before Mam could respond, Colleen burst into the kitchen.

"The car broke down by Union Square," she announced breathlessly. "Margaret is with it now. Bridget stopped by the Hammonds to ask Mr. Hammond to help with it." She threw her coat onto a kitchen chair. "And I'm starving." She peeked into the soup kettle. "Chicken and rice. Looks good, Mam."

"Go ahead and eat, Colleen. You too, Molly. Sounds like we won't be—" Mam's voice cracked with emotion. "Sitting down to supper together after all."

"It's okay, Mam." Molly put a hand on her shoulder.

"No. It's not okay. Nothing ever seems to go right anymore. Not for long, anyway. And now the car breaking down—well, I just get so tired of—"

"Sit down, Mam," Colleen insisted. "Have some soup and—"

"I don't want any soup!" Mam yelled. "I just want everything to go back to how it used to be!"

"You're worn out," Molly said gently. "Why don't you go lie down for a while? You can have your soup later." She led her out of the kitchen and into her bedroom. "Just rest for now, Mam. We can handle things."

Mam mumbled a quiet "thank you" as Molly closed her door. Poor Mam. She tried to be strong, but just beneath the surface she seemed fragile...maybe even broken. And with so much coming at them these last couple of months, why wouldn't she be? Plus, Molly knew Mam missed Dad. Probably much more than they could guess.

"Is she okay?" Colleen looked up from her bowl of soup.

"I don't know." Molly ladled out a bowl of soup then sat down. "Sometimes she seems just fine. And other times it seems like she's barely holding together."

"Yeah, I've noticed."

"I try to help out," Molly said sadly. "But I guess I should do more."

"Maybe we all can do more. At least Mam doesn't have to work at the store right now. But that could all change when Bridget leaves."

"I can work every day after school," Molly offered. "If that helps."

"Everything helps." Colleen checked her watch. "I was planning on going to the USO tonight. Will you be okay with Mam?"

"Why are you going to the USO?" Molly demanded.

"Because I want to." Colleen set her bowl in the sink.

"But you're engaged—"

"Yes, Molly, I know that." Colleen held her left hand up like proof. "But it's a Friday night, and I'm still a living, breathing young woman who needs to go out and have a good time occasionally. I like to dance. And there are plenty of servicemen in this town who like to dance too."

"But what about Geoff?"

"If Geoff is somewhere that has a USO, I hope that some pretty girl will dance with him too."

"Really? You don't worry some pretty girl may steal his heart?"

Colleen just laughed.

"It just seems wrong." Molly exhaled loudly. "If I was engaged to a serviceman, you would not find me dancing with strange men at the USO."

"I don't dance with *strange* men. I only dance with *nice* men." Colleen plucked a cookie from the cookie jar. "Later, sis."

Molly knew it was pointless to argue with Colleen. She would only dig in her heels deeper. Still, Molly felt badly for Geoff. She wondered if he would be as understanding as Colleen seemed to think. She also wondered if Colleen had written to him yet. The last time Molly asked, Colleen had been evasive—which insinuated *no*. But Geoff had been gone more than two weeks now, and he'd already sent a letter to Colleen. Wouldn't he wonder why his fiancée wasn't writing to him?

"Hello?" Bridget called out as she came in through the front door. "Anyone home?"

Molly hurried out to shush her, explaining that Mam was having a bad night and needed to rest.

"Is she sick?" Bridget reached for the small stack of mail.

"Not really. Just tired and sad, I think."

"The Registered Nursing Board." Bridget held up the long white envelope with a serious expression. "My exam results."

"Open it," Molly insisted.

Bridget waved the envelope back and forth with a frown. "What if it's bad news?"

"It's not," Molly said. "You know it's not." Even so, Molly waited on pins and needles as Bridget picked up the ivory letter opener and slowly slit the envelope open, then, as if she had all the time in the world, she extracted the letter and carefully opened it. "Come on," Molly urged. "What does it say?"

"Just that I passed." Bridget grinned. "With high marks too."

Molly slapped her on the back. "Congratulations, Nurse Mulligan."

"I have to call Virginia and see if hers came."

Molly went back to the kitchen with mixed feelings. Of course, she was happy for Bridget. But this meant that Bridget would soon be gone. Just one more link of the Mulligan family chain that was being broken. No wonder Mam was upset tonight. She'd probably seen Bridget's letter and felt the same way.

Twenty-five

By early February, everyone had been touched by the war. Margaret sometimes felt that the Mulligans had gotten far more than their fair share of wartime suffering. To have lost Peter—even before the war was officially begun—was bad enough. But now Bridget was in boot camp, which sounded grueling to Margaret. She couldn't imagine dressing in men's army fatigues and crawling in the mud. And yet, according to Molly, who'd just gotten a letter from her eldest sister, that was exactly what Bridget was doing. She had been a bit reserved when it was time to go because she wouldn't have her good friend along with her. Virginia had failed her board exam, and poor Bridget was on her own.

Brian was still in Camp Roberts and, according to his most recent letter, he didn't like his basic training any better than Bridget seemed to like hers. Margaret wondered why the armed forces were so intent on torturing their new enlisted folks.

She looked up from the order form she was working on as the bell on the door jingled. "Hello, Mrs. Jones," she called out, trying to sound friendlier than she felt. Mrs. Jones was not her favorite customer.

"Good morning, Margaret." She came over to the counter, glancing around in her usual busybody way and, spying an unopened

V-mail letter on the counter, her brows shot up. "News from your husband?"

"That's Colleen's," Margaret said without looking up. "From her beau. She hasn't seen it yet."

"Oh, yes, he's the navy pilot, isn't he?"

"That's right." Margaret checked a box on the form.

"And where is he stationed?"

"I'm not sure." Margaret chewed on the end of the pencil. "You know they don't like to say." Of course, she was fairly certain that Geoff had just been stationed somewhere in the South Pacific. Although Colleen couldn't say for sure because any clues about real locations had been blacked out of Geoff's last letter. But based on his description of palm trees, sandy beaches, and tropical weather, Colleen had suspected he was on an island somewhere. And lately she'd been complaining about not having married him so she could be on an island too. Margaret seriously doubted that any wives—not even officer's—would be allowed in what was probably a battle zone.

"And what about your husband, Margaret? What do you hear from him?"

Margaret looked up. She wanted to ask Mrs. Jones if she'd come for groceries or for gossip, but she knew that would be rude. It was one thing for the customer to be rude to the storekeeper. But have mercy if it was the other way around.

"I got a letter from Brian just yesterday," Margaret said. "He's still at Camp Roberts. Doing basic training. He said they usually do it for six weeks."

"Well, I heard that six weeks is getting cut shorter in many places."

Margaret looked at her with interest. "Really? Where did you hear that?"

"I don't recall. But I did read in the newspaper that our army troops are starting to arrive in Great Britain. And isn't Brian in the army?"

Margaret nodded.

"Then that's probably where your man will be sent. Next it will be the European front. And I hear the fighting is going to be intense over there. Hitler's Nazis are ruthless."

"Hello?" Colleen called out as she came through from the back-room. "I have our lunch." She paused to look at Mrs. Jones.

"You got a V-mail letter," Mrs. Jones informed her. "From your beau."

Colleen just nodded, setting the bag on the counter.

"And what about that sister of yours?" Mrs. Jones continued. "Where is she these days?"

"Not far from here," Colleen said lightly. "Training."

"And getting shots." Margaret peeked into the brown bag.

"Getting shot?" Mrs. Jones looked horrified.

"No, medical shots—inoculations," Margaret explained. "For typhoid and yellow fever and cholera and so on."

"Oh, my. Poor thing. I hope she doesn't catch one of those horrid tropical diseases—you know the kind that there are no shots for and no—"

"Excuse me," Colleen interrupted. "Margaret, I really need to talk to you about that meat shipment that just came in. Can you help me in the backroom?"

Margaret eagerly stood, even though she knew there was no new meat shipment today. "Coming."

"Good grief," Colleen whispered as they left. "Why do you put up with her?"

"What can I do?"

"Make an excuse to leave."

Margaret shrugged. "But I still have to ring up her purchases."

"Yes, a head of lettuce that she'll tell you is wilted and a dinted can of tomatoes that she probably dropped on purpose in order to ask for a discount. The store may go broke without the tightwad's business."

Colleen frowned. "Darn. I wish I'd grabbed Geoff's V-mail and our lunch bag." She went over to the door to peer out and then, squatting like a duck, she waddled over, staying below the counter, and snatched the bag and the letter, waddling back and looking so silly that Margaret couldn't help but laugh. Colleen might not be the best at customer service, but she could be pretty funny at times.

They had just sat down to eat their sandwiches from the deli when Mrs. Jones called out. "Margaret Mulligan, where do you keep the sugar?"

"I'll be back," Margaret said as she went out. "How much sugar do you want?"

Mrs. Jones frowned. "Well, as much as I can have."

"According to the OPA, that would—"

"What is the OPA?"

Margaret was surprised that the know-it-all didn't know about the OPA. "The Office of Price Administration. I'm sure you read about the Emergency Price Control Act in the newspaper last week. The government granted the OPA the right to ration food to discourage hoarding. Sugar is on the list, so I can only sell you eight ounces."

"Well, then don't just stand there, measure me out eight ounces," she demanded in a demeaning tone.

"I've already done that." Margaret reached below the counter, producing a small brown bag marked *sugar, 8 oz.* and setting it on the counter.

"How do I know it's really eight ounces?"

"Weigh it for yourself." Margaret forced a smile. "Anything else?"

"Not right now." She glanced around. "What if I come in tomorrow? Can I buy another little bag of sugar?"

Margaret looked evenly at her. "Mrs. Jones, don't you believe that *every* citizen—not just those with loved one ones being sent overseas—should do their part to defend our country and win this war?"

"Well, of course. But I don't see how a silly bag of sugar—"

"If our government is considering rationing numerous items, not just automobiles like the WPB is currently doing, don't you think they have a good reason for doing so?"

"I can understand the need for metal—to make planes and ships and bullets. But sugar?"

Margaret took in a deep breath, praying for patience. "Will there be anything else today, Mrs. Jones?"

"No, thank you!"

As she rang up the few purchases, Margaret thought about the little speech she'd just given Mrs. Jones. Right now, Bridget and Brian and Patrick were being "tortured" in boot camp. If this was Margaret's "war effort"—to be a storekeeper who upheld the laws for the WPB and the OPA and deal with greedy, thoughtless customers, she really didn't have much to complain about. Did she?

Molly had just finished addressing the envelope when Colleen and Margaret came into the kitchen. "Mam left your supper in the oven," she told them.

"Writing another letter to Patrick?" Colleen said in a teasing tone.

"And to Bridget." Molly held up the two V-mail letters. "These were in today's mail, and I just wanted to answer them."

"What does Bridget say?" Margaret asked she carried her hot

plate of food to the kitchen table.

"She wrote most of the letter before they shipped out," Molly explained. "But it must've been sent from wherever she's stationed. She didn't know where they were headed, except that it was in the Pacific. And she added a couple sentences at the end, saying that it was hot and humid and the mosquitoes were terrible."

"That sounds like the Pacific," Colleen said glumly. "I thought it would be fun to be there until Geoff wrote to me about seeing giant, hairy spiders. As big as his hand." She shuddered as she sat down. "And snakes too."

"Bridget said there's lots of mud." Molly held the letter out to Margaret. "Go ahead and read it if you want."

While Margaret read Bridget's letter aloud, Molly started to run water in the sink to wash the dishes she and Mam had used earlier. "Why were you so late coming home tonight?" she asked them as she added soap flakes.

"I had a job interview," Colleen told her.

"A job interview?" Molly turned to look at her. "But you work at the store."

"I've been working at the store. But Barbara Hanley just took a job at the airplane factory. She told me they're still hiring and that the pay was really good."

"Colleen will make three times what we'll pay someone else to work in the store to replace her." Margaret set Bridget's letter down with a long sigh. "As hard as it will be to lose her, it's probably a good choice."

"Mam said she'll start working some," Colleen said cheerfully. "And when summer comes, Molly, you and Jimmy can pick up some hours too. Right, Margaret?"

Margaret just nodded, slowly picking up her fork.

"But do you *really* want to work in an airplane factory?" Molly stared at Colleen in wonder. She couldn't imagine her glamorous sister using tools and getting dirty. "I mean, I just started taking automobile mechanics at school." She held up her hands to show them the dark grease still wedged beneath her fingernails after working on a carburetor today. "It's not for everyone."

Colleen looked slightly concerned. "Good grief, Molly, you better get those hands into that dishwater and soak that grime off."

Molly laughed. "Yes, doing dishes—the working girl's manicure."

"What did Patrick have to say in his letter?" Margaret asked in a weary voice. "Brian hasn't heard from him, and I promised to catch him up in my next letter."

"Go ahead and read it," Molly said as she washed a water glass. "It's not as if it's private."

"Sounds like he's in the Pacific too," Margaret said after a bit. "So Brian's the only one on the European front."

"The only one for right now," Colleen said. "According to Geoff, that can change. Well, at least for pilots. I guess they move around more than soldiers."

"Have you been keeping up with your correspondence with Geoff?" Molly asked as she scrubbed a plate.

"Not as well as you do with Patrick and Bridget," Colleen said glumly. "But I've told him it's only because my life is so boring. I don't have anything to write about."

"Why don't you write him about your evenings at the USO?" Molly said in a slightly teasing tone. She still didn't approve of Colleen's night life. Not that she went out every night, but she did go out several times a week.

"As a matter of fact, I did mention the USO in my last letter. I told Geoff I'd been there for the Valentine's Day dance and how

I danced with a pimply faced soldier boy about to ship out to the European front. And that while the band played 'Just the Thought of You,' I imagined I was dancing with him instead. I think it was actually a rather nice letter."

"How very romantic," Margaret said with a trace of sarcasm.

"Well, maybe you'll have more to write about with your new job," Molly said. "Just think of it—you'll be helping to make planes, and in the meantime Geoff is over there flying them."

"Hmm...very interesting."

"Maybe I can take a picture of you," Molly suggested, "dressed up in your mechanical clothes. You can send it to Geoff."

"That would be funny." Colleen chuckled. "Give him something to show off to his flying buddies. I wonder what a girl wears to be an airplane mechanic. I forgot to ask Barbara about that."

"We have to wear coveralls in my mechanics class at school. We put them on right over our dresses."

"Are there many girls in your mechanics class?" Margaret set Patrick's letter down.

"Just Carol Myers and me."

"Nice odds," Colleen teased.

"What do you mean?" Molly rinsed the plate.

"You know, having all those boys to just two girls. What is that, about ten to one?"

"Kind of like being at the USO club?" Molly teased back.

For a while, no one spoke, just the quiet music playing on the kitchen radio, with Molly humming along as she washed a saucepan.

"So Molly..." Colleen began slowly. "Margaret and I were talking on our way home. It's your birthday on Saturday. And we'd like to take you out to celebrate."

"Really?" Molly set the dripping saucepan on the stove and turned to look at her sisters.

Colleen nodded. "Yep. You'll be sixteen, and we think you're ready to go out with the big girls. You'll have to dress up though. You interested?"

"Yes!" Molly said eagerly. "That sounds fun."

"Then it's a date." Colleen glanced at Margaret, who was very quiet. "Right?"

Margaret barely nodded, her eyes focused on her untouched plate. "I guess so."

"Are you okay?" Molly noticed that Margaret looked pale. "Is something wrong? Did you hear some news about Brian or something?"

"No, nothing like that." Margaret pushed the plate of food away.

"What's wrong then?" Molly came over to look more closely at her.

"I don't know." Margaret slowly stood, grasping the edge of the table for support.

"She's been off her feed today," Colleen told Molly. "Acting kind of puny."

"Maybe you should lie down," Molly suggested as she took Margaret by the arm. "Do you think you could eat soup? I could warm up some—"

"No, no...I don't want anything right now. Just to lie down."

Molly continued walking her to her room, making sure she got to her bed. "Is there anything I can get you?" she asked uneasily.

"No. Just turn off the light on your way out. I'll have a rest and eat something later."

Molly turned off the light and quietly closed the door, but as she walked through the front room, she felt like she'd swallowed a rock. Bridget had given Molly an informational booklet about tuberculosis, asking her to keep an eye on the family...just in case.

"Colleen," Molly said urgently as she returned to the kitchen. "Do you think Margaret has TB?"

Colleen looked up from reading Bridget's letter. "I, uh, I don't know."

"The way she looks, the way she's acting—it reminds me of Dad."

"But she got tested, like the rest of us, and it was negative."

"Yes, but Bridget warned we may need to be tested again. Especially since we visited Dad after getting the telegram about Peter. And then Margaret went again with Bridget to tell Dad about her engagement. Remember?"

Colleen slowly nodded. "I thought maybe she was just down in the dumps today because she's not real happy about me working at the airplane factory. But maybe she's actually sick."

"I've read about TB," Molly explained. "There's an incubation period—that's the amount of time between when a person gets exposed to the disease and when it becomes active. When it's active is when they begin to get sick. And when they begin to be contagious."

"Wow, you've really studied this, Molly. I'm impressed."

"Thanks. But anyway, the incubation period can be anywhere from two to twelve weeks."

"So Margaret was at the sanatorium at the end of December and this is the first week of March." Colleen started counting on her fingers. "That means, and possibly exposed to TB, about nine or ten weeks ago?" She frowned. "What should we do?"

Molly considered this. "I don't think we should tell Mam. Not yet anyway. She's still not handling things too well."

"At least Bridget got Mam retested for TB before she left—and that was negative."

Molly bit her lip. "She may need to be retested though. Until we've all made it past the twelve week period—testing negative—you never know for sure. Maybe we should all get retested."

Colleen let out a groan. "I hate stupid TB. And I hate stupid war. Why can't we just live ordinary lives?"

Molly had no answer to that question, but when she went to bed that night, she said a special prayer for Margaret, begging God not to let her be sick with tuberculosis. And then, just to add extra oomph to her prayer, she got out her rosary and prayed five Hail Marys.

Twenty-six

Margaret appeared to be back to her normal self the next morning, pleasantly humming to the radio as she drove them to work.

"Molly was very concerned about you last night." Colleen glanced at her sister, trying to gauge whether or not she was seriously ill.

"Poor Molly. She's such a tender-heart."

"Yes...but she made a suggestion," Colleen said cautiously. "She thought maybe you should get retested for tuberculosis."

"*Tuberculosis?* Are you kidding?" Margaret turned off the radio, looking at Colleen with a horrified expression.

"Bridget gave Molly some reading material, and she'd been studying up on it and, well, you were around Dad at Christmastime and Molly thought that—"

"Well, Molly doesn't need to be worried," Margaret declared. "I'm perfectly fine."

"Good." Colleen hoped she was right. Because if Margaret really was sick, besides being just plain terrible, it would be terribly inconvenient. For starters, Colleen wouldn't be able to accept the position at the airplane factory because her family would probably need her to take over managing the store. "You're sure about that?"

"Of course."

Colleen wondered how she could be so certain. "So, anyway...I'm supposed to start work at the factory on Monday. Do you think you can hire someone by then?"

"I guess I'll have to," Margaret said crisply.

"And you really don't mind me leaving?"

"Of course, I mind, Colleen. But I understand. It's a great opportunity for you." Margaret slowed the car down to a crawl, carefully turning into the alley behind the store.

Colleen wanted to tease her like she usually did, saying that she drove like a little old lady. Instead, she reminded her of yesterday's promise. "Like I said, I'll contribute to the household fund with my extra earnings. So it really will be a win-win for everyone."

Margaret said nothing as she parked in her usual spot. She turned off the ignition, removed the key, then turned to look at Colleen. "I'm pretty sure that I know what's wrong with me—I mean, why I've been sickish lately."

Colleen felt uneasy. "What is it?"

Margaret's smile was crooked. "I think—I really do think that I'm expecting a baby!"

"Are you serious?"

Margaret nodded eagerly. "I'm pretty sure that's what it is." She described some of her symptoms.

"But you haven't been to the doctor, have you?"

"Not yet. But I got to thinking about it. And last night, I did some reading in one of Bridget's old nursing books. I did the math...and, Colleen, it makes sense." Her eyes got bigger. "If I'm right about this, and if I really am pregnant, the baby should be due around October."

"Oh, Margaret! That's wonderful." Colleen reached over to hug her. "I'm so happy for you. Did you say anything to Mam yet?"

"No. I want to see a doctor first—just to be totally sure. I'd hate to get Mam's hopes up and find out I'm wrong. I just don't know how much more disappointment she can take."

"Good idea."

"I can hardly believe it, Colleen." Margaret giggled as they got out of the car. "I'm going to be a mommy."

"And I'll be an aunt," Colleen said happily. "This is so exciting."

"But please, don't tell anyone." Margaret unlocked the back door.

"Mum's the word." Colleen frowned. "Although Molly is going to ask me if I got you to agree to a TB test. She was terribly worried about you."

"We can probably trust Molly," Margaret admitted as they went inside. "Especially considering how she kept the secret when Brian was going to propose. That was impressive. In a lot of ways, Molly is old for her age."

"And she's almost sixteen," Colleen reminded her.

"So, anyway, I plan to call the doctor as soon as the office opens." Margaret turned on the lights. "And I read that it helps to eat saltine crackers for morning sickness. Although my nausea doesn't seem to come on until later in the day. But I read that can happen too. They just call it morning sickness because that's more common. And it sounds like it will be gone by the end of this month."

"You seem to know a lot about being pregnant."

"Thanks to Bridget's nursing book."

"Won't Bridgie be excited to hear this news!" Colleen put her handbag beneath the counter. "And—oh, my goodness—Brian is going to be a dad! When will you tell him?"

"I'll tell everyone and anyone—even cranky old Mrs. Jones—as soon as I know for sure and for certain."

Colleen frowned. "Oh, dear! How can I leave you for the airplane factory job now? I'll have to tell them I can't—"

"No." Margaret grasped Colleen's hand. "I thought about it last night. It's even more important now, Colleen. You need to have a good job that brings in a good income. Think about it. With your help, we may have to hire two people to work here. I mean, when I'm unable to work. And if you're making more money, it will help to cover that extra expense."

"Okay." Colleen reached for a box cutter to open a cardboard carton of canned tomatoes. "And if for some reason you need me to come back here, I can just quit at the airplane factory. Good grief, it's not as if I'm signing on for life." As she removed the cans, she thought about Geoff and the promise she'd made to him—now *that* was signing on for life. But she wasn't even nineteen yet... Was she really old enough to commit to something like that? As much as she loved him, she sometimes wondered if a flibbertigibbet, like her, really had the right stuff to be a dependable wife.

Molly was still feeling worried about Margaret the next day. So much so that she nearly slipped by mentioning her concerns to Mam. "I just want to go help out," she told her mother after school. "You know how Fridays can be busy."

"Yes, but Jimmy will be there by now," Mam pointed out.

"I know. But he'll probably be making deliveries. I'm sure Margaret and Colleen wouldn't mind some extra help. Unless you need me around here."

Mam sighed. "You're right. You should go help your sisters. I'd go myself, but I may be more useful in the kitchen. Those girls are usually hungry after work."

"And it looks like you're making chicken and dumplings tonight."

Molly smacked her lips. "That's my favorite."

"I know. Since you girls are going out tomorrow night, I decided we'll celebrate your birthday here tonight." Mam's smile looked forced. "How does that sound?"

"Perfect!" Molly hugged Mam. "And I'll let Margaret know that we have to leave work on time today."

"Thank you. I think I'll invite the Hammonds too."

On her way to town, Molly dropped Bridget's letter at the post office. Her goal had been to write both Patrick and Bridget weekly. And so far, she'd accomplished it. But to keep better track, she'd decided to write them on separate days. Now Patrick's letter went out on Mondays and Bridget's was posted on Fridays. And even though they didn't write to her as often—she knew they were busy—she felt it was her patriotic duty to faithfully write to them. As well as to send them photos. She planned to keep it up throughout the war, which she hoped wouldn't last forever. Besides that, she was trying to write to Dad every week too, as well as to send him photographs. Three letters a week along with her usual homework was a lot of writing. But at least she enjoyed it. And once Dad got well and the war wrapped up, her letter writing would slow down significantly.

Although based on a report she'd written for her current events class this week—after studying news stories from the past couple of years and making a very long list of all the countries that had been invaded and occupied—she suspected this war might take quite awhile. In fact, she'd felt rather dismayed after finishing her report. *Would the allies even be able to win this war?* And what would happen to the world if they didn't defeat the Axis? These were serious troubling questions that, for the most part, she kept to herself.

In the past she could talk to Peter about things like this. For some reason he was never terribly bothered by unsettling subjects.

The same with Patrick. If he were around, Molly knew he'd be willing to discuss these concerns with her. Or even Bridget. And Dad would be willing to talk about the war, especially since he'd already served. But he wasn't around. As it was, Molly sometimes felt a bit lonely within her own family—a family that seemed to get smaller all the time.

Molly had considered taking her worries to Mam but instantly knew that would be a mistake. Sometimes it felt like Mam was already hanging by a slender thread. And talking to Margaret when she was so fretful about Brian, constantly worried that he might not make it back in one piece—not to mention Molly's concerns about Margaret having TB...

And even though Molly could easily get Colleen to talk about certain "taboo" topics—like dating boys and smoking cigarettes and even drinking—she usually clammed up when war was mentioned. Molly wasn't sure if it was because of her concerns for Geoff or simply because Colleen was like that proverbial ostrich with her head in the sand.

Molly pushed open the front door to the store to see there were several customers shopping. Margaret was at the cash register, and Colleen was behind the meat counter. Molly called out a hello as she went for an apron.

"Can you put this order together?" Margaret handed Molly a slip of paper. "Jimmy will be back for it any minute."

"Sure." Molly smiled.

"Thanks for coming in," Margaret said. "I was just about to call Mam to send in help."

As Molly started to fill the first box, she told Margaret about dinner. "So we're supposed to not be late." Margaret promised to close the store on time as she started to ring up the next customer.

Molly continued gathering items to put in the box, only pausing long enough to answer the telephone and write down another order.

"It's a good thing I came," Molly called to Margaret as she carried the filled box to the backroom, where Jimmy was just coming in through the back door.

"I've got this almost ready to go." She set the box down on the work table, going over the list once more just to be sure she hadn't missed anything. As he came over to stand beside her, she noticed his cheeks were flushed. "You must've had a hard ride," she said as she wedged the five pound bag of flour more solidly into the corner.

"Not really." Jimmy gave her what seemed a self-conscious grin. "I was just thinking, Molly, you almost look like a grown-up these days."

Molly stood up straighter. "Well, I'm almost sixteen."

"I know. Colleen told me that awhile back. But for some reason I used to think you were just a kid."

"Because I used to be a kid." She adjusted the cans in the bottom of the box, balancing the weight out so it would ride better on the back of his bicycle.

"Well, gee, I was wondering, Molly. Do you ever wanna go to the picture show with me? There's a Tarzan movie this weekend that I'm dying to see."

Molly felt a wave of surprise rush through her. *Was Jimmy asking her out on a date?* And, even if he was, did she want to go? She made herself smile. "Uh, I don't think so, Jimmy. There's so much going on these days. So much that keeps me busy. I mean, naturally, I've got school. And then working here to help out. Plus I try to help out at home. And I'm going to plant a victory garden soon. That's what they've been doing in England to help with the war effort." She knew she was blathering on and on, but she couldn't seem to stop herself.

"You see, we have this little plot of land out behind our house. It's really tiny, but I've got it all planned out. And I've already gotten seeds, and I've been reading up on when to plant what—and March is the best planting month. And I write weekly letters to Bridget and some of our other friends who are serving overseas." She paused to catch her breath, knowing she was making herself seem much busier than she really was—but she just didn't want to hurt his feelings.

"I'm going to enlist too," he said eagerly. "As soon as I turn eighteen I'm going into the army."

"Really?" She stared at him in wonder. "When will that be?"

"Oh, not for a whole year yet. And my mom says I have to graduate high school first too. But as soon as I do, I'll enlist."

She pointed to the box. "In the meantime, you better get this delivered because I just took an order for another one. I'm about to get it ready."

He picked up the box. "I'm on my way."

As Molly went back into the store to pack the second order, she couldn't help but giggle. Even though Jimmy's invitation had made her uncomfortable, it was kind of flattering.

"What's so funny?" Colleen asked as she wrapped up a pound of pork chops for the order.

"Jimmy asked me on a date," Molly whispered as a customer walked past.

"What?" Colleen's blue eyes grew wide.

"To a Tarzan movie."

Colleen laughed heartily. "He obviously doesn't know your feelings about Tarzan the ape man."

Molly wrinkled her nose. "Even if it was a fantastic movie, I wouldn't go out with him, Colleen. *Really.*"

"Poor Jimmy."

"But I was nice about it," she said quietly. "I didn't hurt his feelings."

Colleen smiled. "I'm sure you didn't."

Shortly before six o'clock, Margaret began dimming the lights in the store, announcing to the pair of elderly customers that it was nearly closing time. Then with Colleen and Molly helping, they rang up their groceries, bagged up their purchases, and escorted them out. "Thanks for shopping at Mulligans'," Colleen called out cheerfully as she shut and locked the door. "Let's get out of here, girls!"

They were soon in the car where, to Molly's surprise, Colleen got behind the wheel as Margaret climbed into the backseat. "Are you okay?" Molly asked with concern, leaning over to peer at Margaret, who was partially reclined and looked what Mam would call "peaked."

"I, uh, don't feel too well."

"That's why I'm driving," Colleen told her.

"Just drive safely," Margaret pleaded in a weak voice. "Please."

Colleen did drive safely, cautiously slowing down at intersections, coming to complete stops at lights and stop signs, and looking both ways before proceeding through. Molly was impressed. But she was also worried. "Uh, Colleen," she began quietly. "Did you tell Margaret about what I said last night?"

"About the TB test?" Colleen asked.

"Yes," Molly said eagerly.

"Just tell her," Margaret said weakly from the backseat.

"Tell me what?" Molly felt a wave of fear. Did Margaret know she had TB?

"Margaret has some news." Colleen slowed down for the traffic. "Some good news."

"Good news?"

275

"Margaret is going to have a baby."

"A baby?" Molly turned around to stare at her sister. "Really?"

Margaret barely nodded, closing her eyes.

"That's why she's been sickish. It's part of the pregnancy."

"Oh, Margaret, that's the best news ever. A baby! Does Mam know?"

"That's the thing, Molly," Colleen said firmly. "You can't tell Mam. Understand?"

"Why not? Mam will be so happy. She'll be—"

"No!" Margaret said sharply then groaned.

"Margaret needs to go to the doctor first," Colleen explained. "She's got an appointment in two weeks. So you have to keep it under your hat. Just until Margaret knows for sure. Then she'll tell Mam."

"And Brian? Does he know yet?"

"No one knows," Colleen said. "Just you and me and Margaret. And you are not to write about it in your letters either. Not until Margaret gives you the green light."

"Okay." Molly nodded. "I can do that."

"Thank you," Margaret muttered from the backseat.

"Wow." Molly was still letting the news sink in. "That is such great news. A baby will be such fun. Does Margaret know when it will arrive?" she asked Colleen.

"She thinks it'll be in October."

Molly tried to imagine a baby in their house. "I'll help you with it," she told Margaret. "I love babies. Remember how I baby-sat for Mrs. Clayton's twins last summer. That was two babies at the same time, and I managed okay. I'll even change diapers if you want. It'll be so much fun, Margaret. I wonder what it'll be a boy or a girl. Oh, I hope it's a boy. Don't you?" She turned around to see that Margaret was fast asleep.

"She's sleeping," Molly whispered to Colleen.

"Good. I think she's worn out." Colleen lowered her voice. "To be honest, I'm a little worried about going to work at the airplane factory next week. But she insists it'll be okay. Still, I'm not sure. We don't want her to overdo it."

"I'll keep coming to help after school," Molly promised. "I won't let her lift things. And my Easter vacation is coming up soon. I can work full time that whole week."

"That'll help. And Mam promised to start working again when I go to my new job next week. Margaret posted a help-wanted ad this morning. Hopefully she'll get some good prospects and hire someone soon."

"Just think—a baby." Molly sighed as she leaned back in the seat. It was a relief to have some happy news for a change. The only fly in the ointment was she had to keep this happy news to herself! It would be so fun to see Mam's face light up. And what fun it would be to write to Patrick and Bridget about it. Molly was good at keeping secrets—but two whole weeks?

Twenty-seven

Fortunately, Molly did not have to keep Margaret's news under her hat for long. In fact, it was Margaret herself who spilled the beans. Right over chicken and dumplings with Mr. and Mrs. Hammond present. Mam had invited them to join in Molly's "birthday eve" celebration. But when Margaret had to excuse herself, her mother-in-law grew concerned.

"I'm sorry, I have no appetite." Margaret stood, holding on to the back of her chair to steady herself. "Please, enjoy your meal."

"Margaret." Mrs. Hammond's brow creased. "You do not look well at all." She turned to Mam. "See how pale she is."

"Now that you mention it...yes." Mam got to her feet, placing a hand on Margaret's forehead. "Are you ill?"

"No...no, I—I just need to rest."

"But no appetite?" Mam's blue eyes grew wider. "That happened to Riley...when he began to get sick." Her hand flew to her mouth.

"Is it tuberculosis?" Mrs. Hammond asked somberly.

"I'd been worried about the same thing," Molly answered quickly. "But Bridget gave me some material to read up on. Just in case—you know, because we'd been around Dad. And I know, based on what I read, that Margaret probably doesn't have TB."

"How can you know that for certain?" Mr. Hammond demanded.

278

"The girl looks sick to me. She should see the doctor."

"She's made an appointment," Colleen said.

"When?" Mam asked.

"Not for two weeks," Margaret murmured.

"That's not soon enough," Mam insisted. "If you have TB, you must go in immediately. And then we'll all need to get retested and we'll have to—"

"I do *not* have TB." Margaret swayed slightly.

Molly leaped to her feet. "That's right," she said firmly. "She doesn't. She just needs to rest. Come on, Margaret, I'll help you to your—"

"Molly Irene! You cannot possibly know whether or not Margaret has tuberculosis!" Mam looked on the verge of tears. "Only the doctor can assure us—"

"Molly is right," Margaret declared quietly. "I don't have TB. If you really must know, my problem is—oh, it's not really a problem. But...I, uh, I think I'm going to, uh, I'm going to have a baby!"

Everyone in the dining room got quiet for a moment—and then the air rang with joyful congratulations and questions and maternal advice and everyone talking at once. Finally it settled down, but Molly could see that Margaret was still feeling sick. "I'm going to walk her to her room," Molly said.

"No," Mam insisted. "I'll do that. You sit down, Molly. This is your celebration supper. Let me tend to Margaret."

Molly felt relieved as she returned to her chair. It was good to see Mam stepping back into a motherly mode. It was as if she'd been absent these past few months. Perhaps this meant she was coming back.

With Mam and Margaret gone, Molly and Colleen filled the Hammonds in on all the details—well, as much as they knew anyway. "She thinks the baby will be born in early October," Colleen explained.

"And I hope it'll be a boy," Molly added.

"We're going to be grandparents," Mrs. Hammond said to her husband. "I can hardly believe it."

He nodded happily. "Riley will be so pleased."

"I hope we can tell him soon," Molly said.

"I don't see why not," Colleen declared. "It's not as if he can tell much of anyone about it while he's in isolation."

"How is he doing these days?" Mr. Hammond asked.

"I just got a letter from him on Monday," Molly said. "He seemed in good spirits and it sounded like he was getting stronger."

"I'm so glad Margaret decided to tell her news," Colleen said. "I was worried I'd spill the beans and make her mad."

"I wonder if that means I can write the news to Patrick and Bridget now," Molly said.

"Perhaps let Margaret inform Brian first," Mrs. Hammond suggested.

"Yes, of course." Molly nodded. "You're absolutely right."

When Mam returned, there was a new lightness in her voice. And as she carried in the lemon cream birthday cake she'd made for Molly, her whole face was glowing—and not just from the sixteen flickering candles. For the first time in three months, Mam looked happy. And it gave Molly hope. She looked around the table as they sang the happy birthday song to her, trying not to compare this to the way it used to be. She knew that growing up meant that *things changed.* Things had certainly changed for their family these past few months. And she knew they would continue to change throughout her lifetime.

Mr. and Mrs. Hammond didn't stay too late, and when Mam went to check on Margaret, Molly started to do the dishes. Lately, she'd been doing the supper dishes by herself. She knew that Colleen and Margaret were worn out from their long days of work at the store. And Mam, well, she'd just been worn out from life.

"Oh, Molly." Colleen reached for an apron. "I guess I can't let you clean up your own birthday dinner dishes by yourself."

Molly smiled. "It's okay."

"*Please.*" She dramatically rolled her eyes as she turned on the radio, tuning it to a music show. "Don't be a martyr."

"Wasn't it nice to see Mam happy tonight?" Molly started to fill the sink.

"I'll say. I'm so glad Margaret let the cat out of the bag."

"The Hammonds were so happy too. It's about time people started to get happy again."

Colleen grabbed Molly by the hand, giving her a swing as she danced her around the kitchen to a lively jazz song. Colleen was really a great dancer, and Molly had a hard time keeping up with her. But it was fun.

"Wow," Molly said when the song ended. "I bet you'd be good in a dance contest." She started putting the glasses into the hot, sudsy water.

"You got that right." Colleen reached for a dishtowel. "As for you, little sister, you could use a little practice on some of your dance moves."

"Why?" Molly scrubbed a plate.

"Did you forget we're going out for your birthday tomorrow night?"

"You mean we're going dancing?" Molly peered curiously at Colleen. "You and me and Margaret?"

"We planned to celebrate your sixteenth in a great big way. At the USO dance."

"The USO?" Molly frowned in disappointment. "Why?"

"Because it's fun. And you need to go have some fun."

"But I don't—"

"You said you'd go out with Margaret and me, Molly. Are you chickening out now? Maybe you're not really turning sixteen after all."

"But Margaret's been feeling sickish. What if she—"

"Margaret already agreed to go. But if she doesn't feel like it, well, I guess we can do something else." Colleen looked truly dismayed now. "Or we could just sit around home and do nothing."

Molly felt bad now. She didn't like being such a wet blanket. But at the same time, she didn't really approve of Colleen spending so much time at the USO. Something about the whole thing just felt wrong.

"I know what you're thinking." Colleen rinsed a plate.

"How can you possibly know what I'm thinking?"

"It's written all over your face, Molly. Really, you should never play poker."

Molly handed her a soapy glass. "Okay, then what am I thinking?"

"That I'm a bad girl for running around so much and that I shouldn't be a junior hostess at the USO club. I shouldn't go to their dances. I should stay home every night, writing letters to Geoff. And after I've finished my nightly letter, I should spend the rest of my time knitting him nice wooly socks."

Molly couldn't help but smile to imagine this. "You don't even know how to knit," she reminded Colleen.

"Still, I'm right—aren't I?"

"Maybe." Molly turned to look at her. "Colleen, it just seems wrong to me. You're engaged to a really sweet guy. You *shouldn't* be out running around—going to the USO club and dancing with strangers so much. I'm sorry, but it does seem wrong to me."

"That's because you don't even know what you're talking about."

"What do you mean?" Molly scowled.

"For starters, you've never been to the USO club, Molly. And yet you judge it."

"I'm probably not even old enough to—"

"There are junior hostesses your age, Molly."

"Even so. It just seems wrong. You're engaged, Colleen. You should—"

"I'm engaged. Yes, I know," she said hotly. "Does that mean life should stop for me? I'm not even nineteen yet, Molly. Besides that, Geoff understands. He likes going out and having a good time too. He's probably out with his pilot friends drinking beer right now."

"That's another thing." Molly shook a finger at her. "You drink sometimes. And you smoke cigarettes too."

"Yeah, yeah." Colleen rolled her eyes as she dried a plate. "Tell me something I don't know, Molly. Tell me I'm a flibbertigibbet or that I'm the black sheep of the family—and if it makes you feel better, I'll pretend to be so surprised."

Molly locked eyes with her. "Well, I worry about you, Colleen. I'm sorry, but I do. And I pray for you too. I hope and I pray you don't ruin your life."

"Ruin my life?" Colleen just shook her head. "That seems a bit melodramatic."

"Do you remember that Lana Turner movie we saw not so long ago? *The Zigfield Girl?*"

"Oh, yeah. Now that was a *good* movie. Well, except for the ending. Poor Lana Turner—I mean the character she played—she shouldn't have died in the end. In fact, Barbara still claims that the Zigfield girl didn't really die, but I'm not so—"

"That is exactly my point, Colleen!" Molly shook the drippy dishcloth in her sister's face. "Sometimes you remind me of Lana Turner. Not the real Lana Turner. Oh, I mean you do sort of look like her. But I mean the Zigfield girl she played in that movie—the way she was drinking and smoking and carrying on. She was such a party girl that she completely ruined her life. And she came from a nice Irish family too. *Remember?* But she just threw it all away. And then she died."

Colleen's brow creased as if she was actually considering Molly's words.

"I love you, Colleen," Molly said gently. "I would feel so terrible if your life ended up like that. And poor Geoff... Remember how James Stewart was so broken up? Geoff would be even worse. Because it would be real life, not a Hollywood movie."

Colleen placed a hand on Molly's shoulder. "I appreciate that you care about me. But you really don't know everything about me. In fact, I think the only way you'll really understand why I like to go to the USO is if you come with me." Colleen clasped her hands together in a pleading way. "Please, say you'll come with me tomorrow night. And if you hate it, we'll just leave. But I want you to at least see it for yourself. Okay?"

Molly shrugged. "Okay...but what about Margaret? What if she's not up for—"

"You two talking about me?" Margaret said in a teasing tone as she entered the kitchen.

As Margaret helped herself to a piece of birthday cake, Molly explained Colleen's plan to take them to the USO tomorrow. "But you may not be up to it."

Margaret shrugged as she sat down at the kitchen table. "I don't know. I may."

"Feeling better?" Colleen asked her.

"Yeah, I am." She took a big bite of cake. "I'm actually hungry."

"Want some chicken and dumplings?" Molly offered. "I can warm some up."

"No, just cake for now. Maybe some tea, if there's hot water."

"Coming right up," Mam said as she came into the kitchen. "I'd like a cup too."

"Me too," Colleen said.

"So would I," Molly added.

Soon all four of them were sitting around the table, eating more birthday cake and drinking tea—and talking about Margaret's baby and Molly's plans to make a victory garden and all sorts of things.

"This has been the best birthday eve ever," Molly said when they were finishing up. "Thanks so much!"

On Saturday morning, after Colleen and Margaret and Mam all went to work at the store—insisting that Molly should have the day off since it was her birthday—Molly sat down at the kitchen table to write Dad a cheery letter. And because she'd gotten Margaret's permission, she told him the good news—that sometime next fall he would become a grandfather. As she sealed the letter, she could just imagine his eyes lighting up to read those words.

After that, she went out on the front porch stoop, soaking up the sunshine as she worked on the service flag she'd been sewing lately. Her goal was to have it all finished and hanging in the front bay window by the time her family came home this evening.

She'd become interested in service flags a couple of weeks ago, after seeing one displayed in the window of a fancy home near the high school. Her friend Pricilla knew the people who owned the house and explained that the banner represented the family's son who was a general in the army. "But anyone with a family member in military service can have a service flag," Pricilla told her. "You could probably have one too."

And so Molly had done some research and, convinced that the Mulligans needed their own service flag, she started gathering scraps of red, white, and blue fabric, as well as a small piece of sparkling gold lamé. In the evenings, she'd worked on making a service flag for the Mulligan family. She'd started with a field of white that she'd stitched a wide red border around. And then she'd made a cardboard star pattern and cut out five stars—four in blue and one in the gold lamé. Next, she had meticulously stitched them onto the flag in a straight row with the gold star on top. And finally, she'd added shiny gold fringe at the bottom of the banner, running a wooden dowel through the top and tying a piece of gold cord on both ends to hang it with. It was actually quite elegant looking—in a patriotic sort of way.

By late afternoon, finally satisfied with her handiwork, Molly took it inside and hung it in the center of the bay window that overlooked the street. Then, excited to see how it looked, she hurried outside, bounding so quickly down the front steps that she nearly knocked over an old lady walking down the sidewalk.

"Excuse me!" Molly grabbed the woman by the arm to keep her from tottering over. "I was so eager to see something—I wasn't really looking where I was going. I'm sorry."

"What is it you're in such a confounded hurry to see?" the elderly woman demanded. Molly suddenly recognized their elderly neighbor—Widow Bartley from next door. She lived alone with her old housekeeper and, for the most part, kept to herself.

Molly nervously pointed at the bay window. "I just made a service flag for our family." She didn't know Mrs. Bartley very well since the old recluse had never been overly fond of the noisy neighborhood children. Most of the interaction between their two households had consisted of cranky complaints from Mrs. Bartley (over crushed flowerbeds or the occasional broken window), which was always followed by profuse apologies from Mam, and an occasional home-baked goodwill offering. But not so much in recent years as the Mulligan children had outgrown most of their more rambunctious and somewhat destructive childhood activities.

"I'm not blind, child. I can *see* it's a service flag," she said in an irate tone. "But *five* stars? *Really?*" Mrs. Bartley peered suspiciously at Molly. "I thought it was mostly girls in your family."

"We, uh, we had a brother...Peter. He was the oldest."

"Oh, dear." She frowned. "I do remember something now. I was on the East Coast all of December. But did I hear that your brother had been...was *he* in Pearl Harbor?"

Molly nodded sadly. "Yes. He was on the *Arizona*. He died for his country. That gold star is for him." Her eyes watered slightly as she stared at the top star, glistening in the sunshine.

"Oh, my. I'm so very sorry." Mrs. Bartley slowly shook her head and then, blinking in the bright light, pointed up at the banner. "But what about those four other stars? I thought the rest of you Mulligans were girls."

Molly smiled sadly at her elderly neighbor, realizing how little she knew about the Mulligan family. "Well, you're right, Mrs. Bartley. That next star, the blue one beneath the gold one, that's for my oldest sister, Bridget. She's in the ANC—that's the Army Nurse Corps. She got her registered nurse degree in January, and now she's stationed somewhere in the Pacific. The star beneath that one is for my second oldest sister's husband. Margaret married Brian

Hammond in late December. He's a lieutenant in the army, serving on the European front."

"Oh, yes, I do remember hearing that one of you girls got married. I didn't realize it was to a serviceman."

"The next star is for Colleen's fiancé, Geoff Conrad. She almost married Geoff before he left for active duty, but they decided to wait until summer. Geoff is a navy pilot, and he's somewhere in the South Pacific."

Mrs. Bartley nodded with a creased brow. "And that last star?"

"Well, I wasn't quite sure if it was okay to put *that* star on the banner. It's for our dear friend Patrick, but he's not actually a relative," Molly explained hesitantly. "Although he was Peter's best friend, and he's a like a brother. I read that it's okay to include an adopted relative on a service flag—and it's kind of like he's adopted by us. I write to him every week, and I just couldn't bear to leave him off our flag. Besides, we all think he'll want to marry Bridget someday. And that would make him a brother."

Mrs. Bartley smiled at Molly. "Well, thank you for explaining it all to me."

"Do you think it's okay that I included Patrick?" she asked with uncertainty.

"I think it's very nice. I'm sure your young man appreciates being part of your family." Mrs. Bartley sighed. "I lost my only boy in the previous war. Early on too, like with your brother. But I never put up a service flag. Although I did notice a few of them around back in the day. Maybe I should have made one for Henry. Maybe that would've made it less painful." Her voice cracked with emotion.

Molly reached over, clasping the old woman's hand in her own. "I know you don't know me, Mrs. Bartley. But I'm the youngest Mulligan. My name is Molly." She shook her hand. "And I'm so sorry for your loss. I never even knew that you had a son. But I do know how it feels to lose someone you love. We can share in that. And at least we know that they both died for their country. That is honorable, don't you think?"

"Yes, yes, it is." Mrs. Bartley nodded with misty eyes, squeezing her hand. "Thank you, dear." She smiled at her. "You're a very sweet girl."

Molly returned the smile. "And do you know what today is?"

"What?"

"Today is my sixteenth birthday."

"Oh, my!" Mrs. Bartley put her hand over her mouth. "Well, then happy birthday, Miss Molly Mulligan."

"And we have leftover birthday cake. It's lemon cream cake," Molly said with enthusiasm. "I'd love to share a piece with you."

Mrs. Bartley was speechless.

"I'll just run and get it now." And not giving Mrs. Bartley a chance to object, Molly dashed into the house, placed the last piece of cake on a china dessert plate, and took it outside. "Here you go," she told her. "I hope you enjoy it."

"Oh, my." Mrs. Bartley looked shocked but pleased. "This looks delicious. I'll return the plate after I'm done. Thank you very much, Molly."

Molly knew that some of her school friends might think she was perfectly silly to make such an effort with her elderly neighbor, but she couldn't think of anything she would've enjoyed more than befriending this old woman—and on her birthday too.

Twenty-eight

To Molly's delight, Margaret, Colleen, and Mam came home early on Saturday evening. And since the sun hadn't gone down, Molly rushed them all outside to see the service flag she'd hung in the window. They admired it as Molly explained how she'd made it and which stars represented which loved ones, finally confessing how she'd even had a "run-in" with Mrs. Bartley. "But I gave her the last piece of birthday cake," she said as they went inside. "And now we are fast friends."

"Well, now...that would be something," Mam sounded doubtful.

Colleen laughed. "I didn't think it was possible to be friends with the old sourpuss."

"I felt sorry for her when her husband passed on," Mam told them as she let down the blackout curtain. "That was more than ten years ago. I tried to reach out, but she wanted nothing to do with me."

Molly explained about Mrs. Bartley's son.

"I didn't know that," Mam admitted. "He must've been around your father's age."

"Maybe she's just lonely," Margaret suggested.

"Enough about Mrs. Bartley," Colleen declared. "Molly, you need to get ready for our big night. Go take a bath and wash your hair then meet me in your bedroom."

Molly glanced at Margaret. "Are you feeling like going with us tonight?"

"Yes. Thanks to Mam's remedy." Margaret smiled.

"What's that?"

"Potato chips and ginger ale," Mam told Molly. "It always worked for me."

"That sounds good." Molly chuckled. "You're making me hungry."

"The sooner you get cleaned up, the sooner we'll go to dinner." Colleen nudged her toward the bathroom. "And get those fingernails clean too."

"What about Mam?" Molly whispered to Colleen. "She's in such good spirits, maybe she should come with us to—"

"I already called Mrs. Hammond. They're coming over to play cards with Mam tonight." Colleen opened the bathroom door. "Get busy, birthday girl."

Molly knew better than to argue with Colleen, but she still wished there was some excuse not to go to the USO dance. It just felt wrong. But perhaps she and Margaret would be able to make Colleen understand their concerns tonight.

After getting cleaned up, Molly went into the bedroom that she and Colleen used to share—before Colleen moved into Bridget's vacated room. But Colleen wasn't there, and Molly wasn't sure what to do. Still wearing her bathrobe, she began to look through her closet, wondering what she had that would be suitable for a USO dance. She was just pulling out a plaid taffeta dress when she heard her bedroom door squeak.

"Put that back."

Molly turned to see Colleen standing like a sentry in her doorway. Already dressed in her blue satin gown, she looked just as glamorous as ever. "Your presence is required in the front room,"

Colleen commanded. "*Now.*"

"In my robe?"

She smiled. "It's just us girls. Come on." She led Molly out to where Mam and Margaret were waiting. Like Colleen, Margaret was already dressed too. And there on the coffee table were several prettily wrapped gifts as well as a plate of doughnuts, a bowl of potato chips, and some bottles of ginger ale.

Molly's eyes lit up. "A party?"

Once again they sang to her and then, while snacking on their party food, they insisted Molly open her presents. The first one was a Bakelite hair dryer kit from Mam. "Colleen thought you could use it," Mam told her.

"I've always wanted one myself," Colleen confessed.

"It's wonderful." Molly thanked Mam and then turned to Colleen. "And I'll let you all borrow it anytime you want."

"Here." Colleen handed Molly the next present, which turned out to be a small cosmetic case complete with some makeup basics. "Just for special occasions." Colleen glanced uneasily at Mam. "We don't want you going around like a painted lady." They all laughed.

The next package, from Margaret, contained a sweet pair of black suede platform pumps with a dainty ankle strap. "They're beautiful," Molly told her. "I love them."

"I hope they fit."

Molly was already trying them on. "They're perfect," she told her as she modeled the shoes, holding her robe up so they could see them better.

"Very pretty." Colleen winked at Mam and Margaret as she picked up the biggest box. "This is from all of us."

Molly removed the pink bow, opened the lid, and peeled back the tissue paper to see a pale blue satin gown. "Oh, it's so beautiful." She lifted it up, holding it in front of her. With its fitted bodice, sweetheart neckline, and long full skirt, it was sophisticated yet not too old for a sixteen-year-old. "I love it."

"Well, let me do your hair and then you can put it on," Colleen told her. "It should fit perfectly. I already tried it on, and the bust-line was a little tight, which means it will be just right for you."

Before long, with every hair in place and just a touch of makeup, Colleen slid the pretty gown over Molly's head, helping her with the side zipper and hooks and eyes. "There." Colleen smiled with satisfaction. "You look gorgeous." She turned her toward the mirror on the door.

"It's so beautiful." Molly nodded. "I think this is the most beautiful dress ever."

"I told Mam you can wear it to the junior prom. I assume some guy will want to take you."

Before Molly could respond, Mam came into the room. "Oh, Molly, you look so pretty." Mam was holding a china dessert plate with a small flat box on top of a small white envelope. "This just came for you."

"What?" Molly stared at the black velvet box.

"Mrs. Bartley's housekeeper brought it over just now. She said it's a birthday present from Mrs. Bartley—*for you.*"

"What is it?" Margaret asked eagerly from behind Mam.

"Open it," Colleen insisted.

Molly removed the small white note card from the envelope, looking at the spidery handwriting. *Happy Birthday, Molly. From your friend, Mrs. Bartley.*

"Hurry," Colleen urged. "We're all dying of curiosity."

Molly opened the box to see a delicate necklace with a teardrop-shaped pale blue stone in a silver-colored setting.

"My goodness." Colleen came closer to examine it closely. "That is an expensive piece of jewelry."

"How do you know?" Mam asked.

"It looks like a platinum setting and, unless I'm mistaken, that stone is Molly's birthstone. And aquamarine stones—real ones—cost more than diamonds."

"And that's a big stone," Margaret said in wonder. "It must be valuable."

"You really won the old lady over," Colleen declared.

"You need give it back to her," Mam said quietly.

"*Why?*" both Margaret and Colleen demanded.

"Because it's too nice," Molly told them.

"It's probably a family heirloom." Mam shook her head. "What was the old woman thinking? Giving away something that valuable to a girl? Is she senile?"

"She seemed perfectly sane to me," Molly told her.

"She obviously likes Molly a lot." Colleen sounded defensive. "Why shouldn't Molly keep it?"

"It goes so perfectly with your dress," Margaret said sadly.

"Can't she just wear it tonight?" Colleen asked Mam. "For her birthday?"

"I suppose that's okay." Mam shrugged. "Just don't lose it."

"Let me help you with it." Colleen slipped it around Molly's neck, securing the clasp, then stepped back. "Oh, my!"

"It looks beautiful on you," Margaret told her.

"But it's too fine a gift," Mam said. "It just doesn't sit right with me."

"Well, Molly can sort it out tomorrow," Colleen declared. "We need to get going if we're going to make our dinner reservation."

"But first we need to take pictures," Molly insisted. "To send to

Dad and Bridget and everyone."

They took several photos, and finally the three Mulligan sisters—dressed to the nines, as Colleen proclaimed—were getting into the car. "Just think," Molly said as Margaret drove toward town. "I'm old enough to get my license now."

"Well, if you're a safer driver than Colleen, I may even let you drive by yourself occasionally," Margaret told her. "It would be nice to have someone else able to run errands."

"Thanks a lot," Colleen said with sarcasm. "But if I really wanted a car, I could go get Geoff's. He already offered it to me, and I may take him up on it one of these days."

Before long they were seated in the elegant Fairmont Hotel restaurant. Molly had already questioned if they could really afford this, but Colleen had told her that with her new job at the airplane factory starting next week, she could afford to be generous. And Margaret assured her that she'd just gotten her monthly stipend from the army. And so, feeling a bit like Cinderella, Molly decided to simply enjoy this magical night.

As they were eating their desserts of cherries jubilee, Colleen explained a bit about the workings of the USO club. "We want to get there a bit early so that you can both register as junior hostesses. Because I'm a junior hostess, I can recommend you, and I already got you both a reference from Father McMurphey as well as a note from Mam."

"Father McMurphey knows about this?" Molly asked in surprise.

"Yes. You need two references and—"

"But Father McMurphey knows I'm married." Margaret was clearly distressed.

"That's fine, Margaret. Junior hostesses are allowed to be married."

"I don't understand." Margaret still looked uneasy.

"The USO is *not* a dating club," Colleen told her. "In fact, they discourage any romantic interaction with servicemen. You'll even have to sign an agreement. The USO is simply a social club to help our boys to have a good time while they're on leave or getting ready to ship out. We're performing a service, Margaret. Sort of like the Red Cross."

"I, uh, I didn't realize that." Margaret frowned.

"Of course, you didn't," Colleen told her. "You both assumed that it was something bad. And you're about to find out it's something quite nice. You'll see."

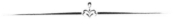

After Margaret and Molly were both approved as junior hostesses, it was clear to see that they had both been wrong about the USO club. Molly was relieved to discover that it was actually a very nice place with well-mannered young men and women. The band was talented, but there was more to do than simply dance. There were games and refreshments and all sorts of fun things. But it was a young soldier sitting on the sidelines that caught Molly's eye. His expression seemed so glum that she decided to see if she might be able to encourage him.

"Hello," she said brightly. "My name is Molly Mulligan. Would you like to talk?"

His eyes lit up as he stood. "Yeah, I mean, *yes.* Sure. My name is Tom Foster. Have a seat."

She sat down next to him and began to tell him about herself, explaining about her family and finally telling him that today was her birthday.

"You came here on your birthday?" He looked impressed.

"I'm only sixteen."

"I'm eighteen," he shyly told her.

"I don't plan to come here a lot. I mean, until I'm older." She explained about Colleen's insisting she come tonight. "You see, I'd been worried that the USO wasn't such a nice place. But I was wrong. And now I'm glad Colleen talked me into coming." She smiled. "Do you like to dance?"

"I'm not very good at it."

"I'm not either," she confessed. "But I know enough steps that I could teach you a few...if you like."

"I'd like that." He stood and, reaching for her hand, led her to the dance floor.

To Molly's relief, despite some missteps, he did not manage to trample her new platform shoes. And after a couple of dances, he asked her to get refreshments with him. Then they sat down at a table together.

"Can I tell you something?" he asked as he forked a piece of chocolate cake.

"Of course."

"I'm feeling a little, uh, a little scared."

She simply nodded.

"I mean, it's embarrassing to admit that. Especially to a girl."

"Well, it seems very normal to be a little scared. I think anyone going into active duty should feel a bit uneasy." She suddenly remembered her brother's bravado, acting as if he was invincible. "Perhaps if you go into this war knowing that it's dangerous—and that people will get hurt—you will be more careful and thoughtful. I don't know much about it, but it seems that it could be wise to be cautious. It seems it could only help you to succeed as a soldier. Don't you think?"

He seemed to consider this. "I think you could be right." He smiled.

"How did your family feel about you enlisting?"

He shrugged and looked down at his dessert.

"Were they opposed?"

Tom looked back up with sad eyes. "I grew up in a children's home," he confessed. "Until I finished school last year. Since then I've been on my own. I thought maybe if I enlisted, well, I'd feel like part of something. Like being in a family. You know?" He frowned.

"I'm sure it will be like that," she said eagerly. "Once you get to know people."

"Except that I'm just not very good at that—I mean, getting to know people."

She looked him up and down. "I don't see why, Tom. You're a good looking guy. You seem bright. And you're certainly nice enough. I should think that anyone would be glad to get to know you."

"You really think so?"

"I most certainly do," she proclaimed. "I'm glad to get to know you."

He brightened. "And you're a very pretty girl. And smart too. I can tell."

She nodded. "So if I'm glad to know you, shouldn't everyone else be too? And if they're not, well, you're better off not knowing them anyway. But I'm sure you will make some very dear friends before this war is over." She thought of something. "Do you have anyone to write to? I mean, from the home front?"

He just shook his head.

"Well, I'm a pretty good letter writer, Tom. If you like, I'd be glad to stay in touch with you."

His brown eyes grew large. "You'd do that?"

"I'd be proud to." She grinned. "I'll even send you photos, if you like."

"Photos of you?" His eyes got even bigger now.

"Sure, if you want." She laughed. "You could even show them to your buddies if you like."

He made a sheepish grin. "That'd sure be nice. And I wouldn't claim you were my girl or anything like that. But I'm sure they'd think I was lucky to know such a pretty girl—and to get letters from her."

And so it was agreed, and before the Mulligan sisters left the USO club, Molly had Private Thomas Foster's address tucked in the little black velvet evening bag that Colleen had loaned to her.

As the three of them walked to the car, Molly told them about Tom. And Margaret told them about several of the men she'd spent time with. "But I had to straighten out one of the officers." She giggled. "It was my second dance with him, which should've been a warning. I'd already shown him my ring and explained that I was married, but he was obviously flirting with me. So as the dance ended, I looked him directly in the eyes and said: 'Not only am I happily married to a man I've loved for most of my life, *I am expecting his baby.*" She burst into loud giggles. "Well, he dropped me like a hot potato."

They all laughed over this. "I must admit it's a little strange," Colleen confessed as they came to the car. "Me, being engaged to the most wonderful man alive—and yet I'm dancing with these guys I never would've agreed to have coffee with before. With or without Geoff in the picture." She elbowed Margaret. "And then there's you, newly married—and a little bun in the oven." And now she pointed to Molly. "And we bring our baby sister who's only sixteen. My goodness, what a trio. The Mulligan sisters do the USO in style." They all laughed even harder now.

Molly noticed the moon now, full and round and brightly shining overhead. "Look at that," she said. "Remember the last song the band played tonight?"

"That's right," Margaret said with enthusiasm. "They played 'I'll Be Seeing You.'"

"Yes." Colleen started humming the tune, and soon all three of them were singing some of the hauntingly beautiful lyrics about seeing one's love in old, familiar places.

"I do see places around town sometimes," Molly said dreamily. "Places that remind me of our loved ones who are gone. I go past the nursing school, and I imagine I see Bridget there."

"I know what you mean. I feel like I see Brian in so many places," Margaret said wistfully. "Just ordinary places like our favorite coffee shop, our neighborhood, even Old Saint Mary's. Sometimes I imagine he's there with me."

"I felt like I could see Geoff at the Fairmont tonight," Colleen admitted. "I was remembering when he proposed over dessert there. I miss him so much."

Molly sighed. "And I doubt I'll ever be able to go to Golden Gate Park without seeing Peter there. But I think that's a nice thing. I like seeing Peter."

"Yes," Colleen said eagerly. "I have places that remind me of Peter too."

"I imagined him in the store just last week while I was arranging the tomatoes—you know, the way he taught us to do it," Margaret said. "And, really, it felt like he was right there with me."

"He is with us," Molly declared. "We'll never lose our memories of Peter."

"And I've decided," Margaret said slowly, "if I have a boy—and if Brian agrees—he will be called Peter."

Molly reached for her sisters' hands and started to sing "I'll Be Seeing You" again. Standing out in the parking lot, the three of them sang in sisterly harmony until they reached the final stanza—and then they all looked upward, sweetly singing, "I'll be looking at the moon...but I'll be seeing you."

Over the years, MELODY CARLSON has worn many hats, from pre-school teacher to political activist to senior editor. But most of all, *she loves to write!* In the past few years, she has published over 200 books for children, teens, and adults—with total sales of over six million copies. Several of her books have been finalists for, and winners of, various writing awards. Melody is the recipient of a Romance Writers of America Lifetime Achievement Award. She and her husband have two grown sons and live in Sisters, Oregon with their lovely Labrador retriever, Audrey. They enjoy skiing, hiking and biking in the beautiful Cascade Mountains.

Book 2 ~ April 2017

AS
Time
GOES BY

Book 3 ~ October 2017

STRING OF
Pearls

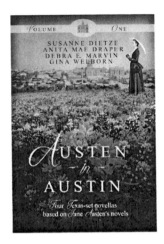 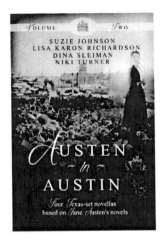
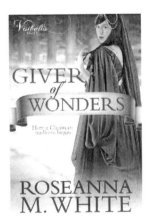

CPSIA information can be obtained
at www.ICGtesting.com
Printed in the USA
LVOW08s1743151116
513059LV00005B/841/P